THE HAWKS OF DELAMERE

Also by Edward Marston

In the Domesday Book Series

The Wolves of Savernake
The Ravens of Blackwater
The Dragons of Archenfield
The Lions of the North
The Serpents of Harbledown
The Stallions of Woodstock

In the Nicholas Bracewell Series

The Queen's Head
The Merry Devils
The Trip to Jerusalem
The Nine Giants
The Mad Courtesan
The Silent Woman
The Roaring Boy
The Laughing Hangman
The Fair Maid of Bohemia
The Wanton Angel

THE HAWKS
OF DELAMERE

Volume VII of the Domesday Books

Edward Marston

ST. MARTIN'S MINOTAUR
NEW YORK

ISBN 0-312-20948-7

First published in Great Britain by Headline Book Publishing,
a division of Hodder Headline PLC

First U.S. Edition: February 2000

10 9 8 7 6 5 4 3 2 1

To SLB
A saintly guide to the mysteries of Cheshire.

This man, with the help of many cruel barons, shed much Welsh blood. He was not so much lavish as prodigal. His retinue was more like an army than a household, and in giving and receiving he kept no account. Each day he devastated his own land and preferred falconers and huntsmen to the cultivators of the soil and ministers of heaven.

ORDERIC VITALIS

Domesday Cheshire and North Wales

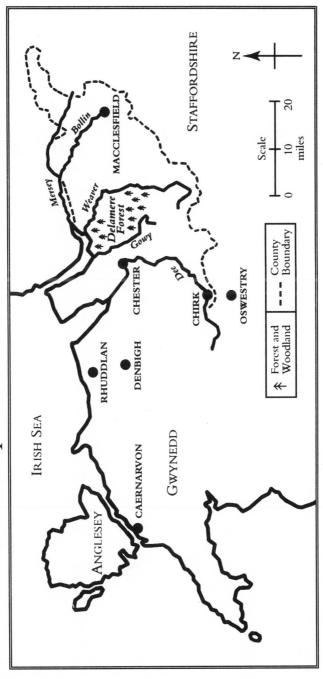

Prologue

It took three strong men to help him into the saddle. Hugh d'Avranches, Earl of Chester and master of all he surveyed, was now so fat and cumbersome that he could barely waddle along. When he came lumbering into the courtyard, he supported himself on the sturdy shoulder of Dickon the Falconer. The rest of the hunting party were already mounted and they waited patiently until the three servants hoisted their master on to his horse, a mighty destrier specially chosen to bear the excessive weight of its noble rider.

Hugh gazed around the assembly with a twinkling eye. 'Are you in the mood for sport, my friends?' he asked.

'We are, my lord!' came the unanimous reply.

'Sport by day and more sport by night, eh?' said their host with a lecherous grin. 'Hawking in one forest then hunting in the dark in another!'

Crude sniggers greeted the ribald comment but Hugh's own laughter rose above it. Like the man himself, it was vast and overwhelming, beginning somewhere deep in the cave of his lungs before spreading quickly through the crevices and valleys of his mountainous frame until he shook uncontrollably with mirth. The sound reverberated throughout Chester Castle.

Earl Hugh was amused. It was a good omen.

They were all there. Robert Cook, Richard Vernon, Hamo of Mascy, Gilbert Venables, Ranulph Mainwaring, William Malbank, Reginald Balliol, Bigot of Loges and Hugo of Delamere were leading barons in the shire, holding their land directly from the earl and regular members of his court.

1

Dozens of other important guests had come from far and wide to enjoy the fabled hospitality of Chester Castle and to share in the pursuits and appetites of its notorious master.

'Are we ready?' boomed Hugh.

'Ready and waiting, my lord,' said William Malbank, acting as spokesman for all. 'We will lead where you follow.'

'You will have to catch me first!'

Pulling sharply on the reins to turn his horse's head towards the castle gate, Hugh jabbed his heels into its flanks and set off at a canter. Taking up the challenge, the rest of the party went after him amid a cacophony of yells, giggles and hoofbeats. They were soon scattering the crowd uncaringly in the streets of a city which had long ago been taught never to complain at the antics of the earl and his retinue.

By the time they reached their destination, the cavalcade had slowed to a trot. The Delamere Forest was a wide stretch of woodland which ran all the way from the River Mersey in the north to the southernmost fringes of the county. Bounded on the east by the River Weaver and on the west by the River Gowy, the forest was a series of woods, coppices, clearings and open land where several hamlets or small villages had taken root. Delamere was the favoured hunting ground of Earl Hugh. Those who dwelt in the forest feared his visits and always took care to keep well out of his way.

Riding beside Hugh at the head of the long procession was William Malbank, a tall, thin, wiry man in his thirties, wearing the distinctive helm and hauberk of a Norman baron. Malbank was in a boastful mood.

'You have met your match at last, my lord,' he said.

'Never!' replied the earl with chuckling confidence.

'My gerfalcon is a magical creature.'

'No bird can compete with my hawk.'

'This one can,' argued Malbank. 'I have not met a creature who can take partridge, snipe and rabbit with such speed. She comes out of the sky like an avenging angel.'

'There is nothing angelic about my hawk,' said Hugh, glancing over his shoulder at the bird carried on its perch by his falconer. 'She is the devil incarnate and leaves havoc in her wake. No other bird is safe in the air when she is on the wing. Hares, squirrels and badgers are no match for her and I would even back her against a wild cat.'

'Do not wager against my gerfalcon,' warned the other.

'She is a mere sparrow beside my hawk.'

'We shall see, my lord.'

They plunged into the forest and followed a winding path through the undergrowth until they emerged into a heath. Earl Hugh raised an imperious hand and the raucous banter which had marked their journey ceased at once. Hawking was a serious business. It demanded quiet and concentration. The noise of their approach had already frightened most of the game away. A watchful silence was now needed so that prey might be lured back to the area.

They waited for him to begin the day's sport. Nobody dared to unleash his hawk before Hugh d'Avranches. In everything he did, the earl had to be first and foremost. A stillness eventually fell on the Delamere Forest, broken only by the song of invisible birds and the occasional jingle of a tiny bell as one of the hawks shifted its feet on its perch. Hugh remained alert, his piggy eyes scanning the heath in all directions, his ears pricked for telltale sounds.

When he was ready, he gave the signal and Dickon the Falconer untied the hawk, coaxed it on to his arm, then passed the bird to his master. Its claws sank into the thick leather gauntlet as it settled on its new perch but it did not stay there for long. A crane went flapping across the sky in search of marshland and Hugh responded swiftly. Slipping the hood from his hawk, he flicked his arm to send it soaring up into the heavens after the larger bird.

The crane saw the danger in time and altered its course to dip and weave but the hawk did not go in pursuit. It had spotted a more enticing prey in the long grass and it hovered above its target for a full minute before descending with stunning speed. The hare had no chance. The impact knocked it senseless and the talons squeezed the life out

3

of it. One more hapless victim had been claimed by the earl's hawk.

'Did you ever see such a strike?' he asked proudly.

'Let my gerfalcon have a turn,' said Malbank.

'What will it hunt – mice?'

'Do not mock, my lord. My bird has been trained to kill almost any prey. She is the equal of your hawk.'

'Impossible, William!'

'Do you wish to place a wager?'

'It would be an act of cruelty against a friend.'

'Can it be that you are afeared?' teased the other.

'I fear nothing!' retorted Hugh, his voice darkening to an angry snarl. 'Are you accusing the Earl of Chester of being frightened, William?'

'Only in jest, my lord.'

'Then I will throw that jest back in your teeth. If you invite a wager, you shall have it. Pit your gerfalcon against my hawk, if you must, but offer a stake worthy of the contest.'

'Whatever you suggest,' said Malbank with an appeasing smile. 'Name it, my lord, and it is agreed.'

'Very well,' decided Hugh, stroking his flabby chin. 'If your bird proves to be the finer of the two, you can have the best horse in my stables.'

'That is a worthy prize indeed!'

'I will take something of like merit from you.'

'My own best horse?'

'No, William,' said Hugh, slapping him on the back. 'Your best mistress. Every time I ride her, I will reflect on your folly in parting with such a sublime creature.'

Malbank writhed in discomfort and wished that he had never been so bold as to offer the challenge, but the wager had been set and it was sealed by the general hilarity of the company. It would grieve him to lose his mistress and she would never forgive him if she were subjected to the merciless attentions of the man who was nicknamed Hugh the Gross for reasons not entirely related to his sheer physical bulk. There was no turning back now. Malbank was trapped.

Earl Hugh made the trap more deadly. After taking advice from Dickon, his shrewd falconer, he insisted that they ride on to another part of the forest. Malbank's bird was a high-bred Norwegian gerfalcon. In open country, it would be seen at its most effective. In more wooded locations, however, its long wings would put it at a severe disadvantage. Hugh's short-winged hawk would be able to manoeuvre much more easily among the trees.

So it proved. The gerfalcon was a fine bird of prey but it had been principally trained to hunt waterfowl on a lake. The hawk, by contrast, was in its element and showed the greater speed and accuracy throughout. Regretting his rash wager, Malbank soon conceded defeat and shuddered as he imagined how tearfully his mistress would react when he told her that her favours had been surrendered to Hugh the Gross.

The earl was delighted at the outcome and sent his hawk up into the sky for one last celebratory kill. It rose, searched with a ruthless eye, observed its prey and hovered menacingly. Hugh looked up at it with the beaming delight of a father watching a child at play, but that delight soon changed to gaping horror. Before the hawk could make one more murderous descent, an arrow suddenly came hurtling up through a gap in the trees and knocked it out of the sky. One feathered weapon of destruction was itself summarily destroyed by another.

Hugh d'Avranches watched in disbelief as his beloved hawk came spinning downwards with the arrow embedded in its breast. He let out a roar of fury which mingled with the shouts of dismay and indignation from his companions. Recovering quickly, he issued a curt command.

'Silence!'

The tumult ceased at once. There was no sign of the archer but Hugh hoped that sound might betray his position. It was a long wait but it finally yielded bounty. Dickon the Falconer was the first to detect them. He had the keen ears that were vital to his trade and had learned to sleep lightly so that he would pick up the faintest sound of a falcon's bells in the night. What he heard this time was the muted crackling of bracken under foot.

5

'Over there!' he hissed, pointing to some wild hedgerow. 'There are two of them. Trying to creep away.'

'Catch them!' ordered Hugh.

Four of his knights kicked their horses into life. Pursuit was short and arrest was brutal. Terrified that they had been discovered, the two figures who had been sneaking away in the ditch behind the hedgerow now took to their heels in a mad but doomed dash for freedom. Before they had gone more than thirty yards, they were kicked violently to the ground and swiftly overpowered. Stripped of their weapons and dazed by the assault, they were dragged unceremoniously through the undergrowth.

Both were Saxon peasants in the rough garb of men who tilled the soil. The older of the two was in his forties, a solid, broad-shouldered man with a thick beard covering most of his face. His companion, barely half his age, bore such a close resemblance to him that he had to be his son. They were lifted upright to face the ire of the Earl of Chester.

'You killed my hawk!' he thundered.

The father recovered enough to shake his head and gabble his innocence, but his Saxon tongue was incomprehensible to Norman ears. Earl Hugh was, in any case, not in the mood to listen. Sentence was passed without the refinement of a trial. The quiver of arrows slung across the older man's back was all the evidence that the judge needed. After giving himself the pleasure of buffeting each of them viciously to the ground, Hugh indicated a tall tree with an overhanging bough.

'Hang the rogues from that!'

'My lord!' bleated the younger man piteously.

But they were the last words he ever spoke. Snatching a lance from one of his knights, Hugh used the end of it to knock him unconscious. Rope was brought, the men were pinioned, then both were hauled up high by the neck to the derisive cheers of the huntsmen. The victims turned and twitched helplessly in the wind as the rope slowly choked them to death. The father tried to plead their innocence to the last but no words came out of his parched mouth.

6

Even that grim punishment was not enough to satisfy the bloodlust of the Earl of Chester. He drew his sword and lashed at both men indiscriminately until they were dripping carcasses. When his anger had run its course and the mutilation was complete, his voice was cold and peremptory.

'Cut them down and throw them in the ditch!' he decreed. 'Let them rot among the vermin where they belong. Leave them unburied so that their offence can stink to heaven.'

Chapter One

Ralph Delchard was in an unusually tetchy mood.

'What are we *doing* here?' he said with irritation. 'Why did we have to come to this God-forsaken part of the country?'

'To serve the King,' Gervase Bret reminded him.

'The King! He's had more than enough service out of me. Twenty years of it, Gervase. Loyal and unquestioning devotion. It's high time the King started serving *me* for a change. Why am I always given the most boring assignments?'

'Try to see it as an honour, Ralph.'

'Honour!' snorted the other.

'You were chosen because you are trusted.'

'It is completely unjust.'

'Nothing could be more just,' said Gervase reasonably. 'Ralph Delchard was appointed as a royal commissioner yet again for one solitary reason.'

'Nobody else was fool enough to take on the work.'

'You were the best man for the task in hand. Doesn't that make you feel proud? Are you not pleased that the King has shown such confidence in you?'

'No, Gervase.'

'Why not?'

'Because I have had my fill of riding the length and breadth of England on royal business. I am weary of travel – and so are my buttocks. They are smarting like raw wounds. I need a rest. I yearn for the pleasures of retirement.'

Gervase Bret smiled indulgently. What his friend really yearned for was the company of his wife, Golde, but she

9

was visiting her sister in Hereford and would not be joining the party until later in the week. Ralph missed her. Genial and buoyant when she was beside him, he became moody and irascible whenever they were apart. The further north they rode, the greater distance they put between man and wife.

Ralph lapsed into a brooding silence. The two commissioners were at the head of the cavalcade as it followed a meandering track through woodland. They were eighteen in total. To ensure safe travel on the long journey, fourteen knights from Ralph's own retinue acted as escort and their presence in Chester would emphasise the importance of the embassy. In helm and hauberk, they were fretful after hours in the saddle.

At the rear of the column, ambling reluctantly along on their mounts behind the sumpter horses, were the portly Canon Hubert and Brother Simon, the spectral scribe. They were even more unhappy about their latest assignment than Ralph Delchard. It was stretching their duty of obedience to the absolute limit.

Simon shivered so violently that his bones rattled. 'Are the stories about Earl Hugh all true?' he asked.

'Alas, they are!' sighed Hubert.

'Is he really such a monster of depravity?'

'Yes, Brother Simon.'

'But I understood that he was married.'

'The state of holy matrimony has not, I fear, imposed any restraint on his carnal appetite,' said Hubert sonorously. 'It is common knowledge that the Earl of Chester has numerous mistresses and a large brood of illegitimate offspring.'

Simon shivered afresh. 'And this vile creature is to be our host in the city?'

'Happily, no. We will be the guests of Bishop Robert.'

'But we are bound to come into contact with Earl Hugh.'

'Unhappily, yes.'

'I will feel contaminated to be in the same room as him.'

'I feel appalled to be in the same county. Yet,' added Hubert with a wheezing practicality, 'we must respect his position.

10

Hugh d'Avranches is more than merely an earl. Cheshire is a county palatine. King William has no land under his direct control here. To all intents and purposes, Earl Hugh is king. He is a law unto himself.'

'Will he accept the authority of royal commissioners?'

'He must, Brother Simon.'

'And if he does not?'

Canon Hubert displayed his most ecclesiastical scowl.

'Then we have all made a very long journey in vain!'

The riders ahead of them came to a sudden halt and Hubert had to tug on the reins to prevent his donkey from colliding with the rump of a bay destrier. Simon brought his straggly mare to a standstill and feared the worst.

'Is there trouble up ahead?' he wondered nervously.

'We are well protected, Brother Simon.'

'The countryside is crawling with outlaws.'

'That's why we brought such a sizeable escort with us. I am sure there is an explanation for this pause.'

Gervase Bret's horse came trotting back towards them.

'We have decided to break the journey here,' he said. 'It will give everyone a chance to stretch their legs before the last few miles to Chester.'

Most of the riders were already dismounting. Tethering their horses, they took advantage of the stop to satisfy the wants of nature among the trees. Canon Hubert rolled off his braying donkey and tied the animal to a bush.

'Brother Simon and I are deeply disturbed,' he confided.

'About what?' asked Gervase.

'The character of Hugh d'Avranches, Earl of Chester.'

Gervase shrugged. 'He is no saint, certainly, but he has served the King exceedingly well. North Wales has been quiescent since Earl Hugh inherited the earldom. He rules the border with a strong hand.'

'We have no complaint about his military exploits,' said Hubert with a sniff. 'It is to the other activities to which he puts that strong hand that we take exception.'

'The earl's private life is his own.'

11

'Even when it spills so outrageously into the public arena? Come, Gervase, you must have heard the gossip.'

'Heard it and disregarded it, Canon Hubert.'

'How can one disregard such villainy?'

'We are not here to make moral judgements about Earl Hugh,' observed Gervase quietly. 'Our task is simply to determine who owns what land in this county and how much tax they should pay on it.'

'It is not as straightforward as that,' said Simon, as he dropped from the saddle with astonishing nimbleness. 'We are not able to separate Earl Hugh from his actions.'

'Indeed, we are not,' boomed his companion. 'Actions, may I remind you, Gervase, have consequences. In the case of the Earl of Chester, those consequences are all too apparent. He has populated the whole county with his illicit progeny. I was expecting to see their faces peep out from behind every hedge.' He raised a homiletic finger. 'More to the point, he has misappropriated land on a vast scale and the major victim has been Bishop Robert.'

'Earl Hugh is not directly concerned in any of the cases that will come before us,' noted Gervase. 'If he were, then we would not be able to accept his hospitality at the castle. Show me where his name appears in our documentation.'

'It does not,' confirmed Simon.

'Exactly!'

'I have been through every inch of those documents.'

'Earl Hugh is far too cunning to be caught working his wickedness directly,' said Hubert with vehemence. 'He uses others as the instruments of his evil will. They bear the blame while he pockets the benefits.'

'That is only your supposition, Canon Hubert.'

'I feel it in my bones, Gervase.'

'We need a more reliable test than that.'

'My instincts are never wrong.'

'Until now,' said Gervase, gently, 'your instincts led you unswervingly along the path of justice and truth. In the past, you would neither prejudge someone you had not met nor reach hasty decisions about a case without sifting all the evidence very carefully.'

'The evidence here is overwhelming, Gervase.'

'Everyone deserves a fair hearing.'

Canon Hubert bit back a reply and nodded soulfully.

'I am properly rebuked,' he admitted. 'You are correct. I should not condemn a man solely on the basis of common report. Reputation can often distort the truth. Look at King William.'

'Yes,' agreed Simon, 'he has a fearful reputation.'

'Those of us privileged enough to get close to him have been able to appreciate his finer qualities. Earl Hugh may yet turn out to have some redeeming features.' His voice hardened. 'Though I harbour grave doubts on that score.'

'Suspend your judgement,' suggested Gervase.

'I will try.'

'We must be strictly impartial.'

'You will not find me wanting.'

'I am sure we will not,' said Gervase. 'You understand the implications of our work better than any of us.'

'That is so true!' chimed in Simon with an admiring glance at his colleague. 'Canon Hubert is an exemplary arbiter.'

'He is, Brother Simon. And his even-handedness was never more in demand. Almost every case which comes before us sets Church against State. We must show favour to neither side.'

'It would never cross my mind to do so,' asserted Hubert.

'Quite so,' said Gervase.

'I judge every dispute on its individual merits.'

'So do we all.'

'This assignment will be no different from any other.'

'No different, Canon Hubert.'

'My integrity speaks for itself.'

'Loud and clear!' declared Simon.

Hubert basked in the unquestioning reverence of the scribe for a full minute before a tiny crack appeared in the façade of his impartiality. His eyes rolled and his cheeks inflated.

'I am prejudiced against no man,' he remarked with an

upward tilt of his chin, 'but I will not be seen to approve of
drunkenness and debauchery. It is a mockery of all Christian
precept. I condemn the earl's behaviour.'

'Robert de Limesey is not entirely without fault,' said
Gervase softly. 'Even bishops go astray at times.'

'Bishop Robert is above reproach. His name has no place
in this discussion, Gervase, and I am disappointed that you
strive to bring it in. All things are relative,' continued Hubert
as if addressing a larger congregation than two people from
his woodland pulpit. 'Place the two men side by side and you
see what so dramatically divides them.'

'What?' asked an open-mouthed Simon.

'Self-respect. Earl Hugh is sadly deficient. He lacks even
a vestige of self-respect or he would not indulge so openly
in licentious behaviour.' The finger came into play again.
'Compared with him – whatever minor indiscretions the bishop
may have committed in the past – Robert de Limesey is an
archangel.'

Robert de Limesey, Bishop of Chester, was a tall, thin, stately
man of middle years with an odour of sanctity about him that
was intermingled with a whiff of distant scandal. As he sat at
the table with his Bible open before him, he wore the saturnine
expression of someone who was not entirely content with his
lot yet was unable substantially to improve it. There was an
air of resignation in the sag of his shoulders. He stared at Holy
Writ through lacklustre eyes. For once in his life, the Revealed
Word failed to restore his spirits and provide sure guidance.

There was a polite tap on the door, then it swung back
on its hinges. The bishop did not even look up when a
short, stout, red-faced man in his thirties padded in to stand
before him. Archdeacon Frodo waited in patient silence until
Robert deigned to notice him. An obedient little smile lit up
the archdeacon's chubby countenance.

'Well?' said the bishop.

'You asked to hear news of their approach, your grace.'

'And?'

'They will enter the city within the hour.'

'Much good will that do us!'

'Have more faith in the commissioners.'

'I wish that I could, Frodo,' said the other, clicking his tongue and shaking his head. 'But they will probably get no further than their predecessors. Earl Hugh will tie them up in knots as he did the first commissioners.'

'They were shrewder than you give them credit for,' said the archdeacon. 'They took the measure of Earl Hugh. He did not fool them for one moment. These second visitors have come to call him to account.'

'Nobody has ever done that with any success.'

'It has to happen one day, your grace.'

'Yes, Frodo – at the Last Judgement.'

'That is effectively what this survey is,' reminded the other with outspread palms. 'It is no mere inventory. Its inquiries have been so thorough and its scope so wide that it is a veritable Domesday Book. All our earthly deeds are entered neatly in its abbreviated Latin.' He clasped his hands across his paunch. 'Our deeds – and our misdeeds.'

The bishop grimaced. 'They will need a separate volume to record the misdeeds of our noble earl in their gruesome entirety. Each day brings fresh horrors from the castle. I pray continually for divine intervention but the Lord sees fit to allow Earl Hugh to continue unchecked and unchastised.'

'Until now.'

'Do you really believe that these newcomers will be able to exert some influence over him?'

'They are royal commissioners.'

'The only royalty in Cheshire is the earl himself.'

'He is still a subject of King William.'

'He has never behaved like one.' Rising to his feet, he made an effort to shake off his pessimism. 'I am sorry, Frodo. I must not despair of Ralph Delchard and his colleagues before they have even arrived. Who knows? Perhaps they *can* achieve the impossible. Perhaps they can muzzle that wild bear who holds sway over us. At the very least, they deserve our full support.'

15

'I will ensure that they are given it.'

'You must be my intermediary here, Frodo.'

'Gladly, your grace.'

'I will work zealously in the background but you must represent me in public. It would not be politic for me to be seen to be in direct opposition to the earl. Neither politic nor healthy. I must haunt the shadows. Speak on my behalf.'

'With full voice.'

'I trust you implicitly.'

Frodo allowed himself a complacent smile. Trained by the bishop himself, he was a skilful negotiator and a tactful diplomat. Robert de Limesey might have greater experience but his archdeacon had a tenacity and resourcefulness which made him, in some ways, even more formidable in debate. In the forthcoming dispute, the Church would indeed have a cunning advocate. The bishop felt partially reassured.

'What do we know of these commissioners?' he asked.

'They have built an excellent reputation.'

'For what?'

'Honesty, independence and firm action.'

'Where else have they been?'

'Hereford and York are the only places that have come to my ears,' said Frodo. 'I have friends in both cathedral chapters and their letters were full of praise for this Ralph Delchard and Gervase Bret. In Hereford, it is reported, they helped to stop an uprising on the Welsh border.'

'Men of action, clearly.'

'And considerable guile, I suspect.'

'Is Canon Hubert held in the same high regard?'

'Not exactly, but he is reckoned to be an upright judge and a man of great moral certitude.'

'Such a person is much needed in Chester.'

'We already have one, your grace.'

'Thank you, Frodo,' said the bishop, responding to the flattery with a weary nod. 'But the sad truth is that my moral certitude is slightly frayed at the edges. Living cheek by jowl with Earl Hugh is enough to make any man question his beliefs.' He drew himself up to his full height. 'Canon Hubert must be given a cordial welcome. I had mention of him in a letter from Bishop Walkelin of Winchester. He commended the good canon to me.'

'There is approval from an even higher source.'

'Higher than a bishop?'

'Yes,' explained Frodo. 'No less a person than Archbishop Lanfranc. Hubert was sub-prior at Bec when Lanfranc was the prior there. Canon Hubert's history is impeccable.'

'Not too impeccable, I trust, Frodo.'

'Your grace?'

'I like at least a hint of human fallibility.'

'We all bear that defect.'

'Indeed, we do. Indeed, we do.'

Bishop Robert crossed to the window to gaze out of it as he reflected on his own occasional wandering from the strait path of righteousness. An imperfect Christian, he had learned to accept his imperfections and to be highly suspicious of those whose lives seemed to be impelled by greater piety and purity. A man with an impeccable history was a disturbing phenomenon. He began to wonder if he was going to like Canon Hubert as much as he had first thought. More important, he feared that he might not be able to influence such a person in the way that he hoped.

Frodo seemed to read his companion's mind. 'Leave him to me, your grace,' he whispered.

Seen from a distance, Chester was a handsome city, surrounded by a high stone wall and cradled in a loop of the River Dee. Its dominant feature was the castle, built by the Conqueror over fifteen years earlier as the key fortress on the troublesome road to North Wales. Conforming to the motte and bailey design that was so characteristic of Norman military architecture, it rose high above the wall in the south-west corner of the city where it could command both the port area and the bridge across the river. Like the castle, the bridge was constructed of solid timber hewn from the extensive forests in the county.

Ralph Delchard brought his party to a halt in order to take stock of the place that was to be their home for at least a couple of weeks. Reactions to the prospect varied. Gervase Bret was fascinated, running a keen eye over every detail that was visible from their standpoint. Canon Hubert found nothing in the scene to enlist his interest. To him, Chester was no more than the lair of a wild animal who had assumed unlimited power. Brother Simon was plainly terrified at the thought of having to meet the dangerous creature who bore the title of earl, and wished that they could abandon their task and ride straight back to the safety of Winchester.

To the knights who made up the escort, Chester had no special significance. They were simply grateful that they had at last reached their destination and could look forward to rest and refreshment. Ralph took a wholly different attitude. He had been there once before. His second visit to the city was marred by uncomfortable memories of the first, when he had been part of a conquering army that crushed all before it. Chester might have a stark beauty when viewed from afar but closer acquaintance would reveal a grim legacy.

With the exception of Yorkshire, no county in England was as badly devastated by the Normans as Cheshire. Signs of that devastation had been seen everywhere on their journey but they would be most marked inside the city itself, where no fewer than two hundred houses had been destroyed. Ralph was not proud of his small part in the hostilities which had killed many citizens and made over a thousand others homeless. His guilt stirred.

Marriage to a Saxon wife had profoundly altered his view of his military career. Golde had made him feel sympathy for an indigenous population whom they had subdued with ruthless efficiency. Ralph could no longer dismiss what happened as the inevitable result of the fortunes of war. When an earlier assignment took the commissioners to York, he had been tormented by memories of his role in the Harrying of the North, the most brutal and merciless operation ever mounted by the King. Something of the same grief afflicted

Ralph now. He would be riding into the city with blood on his hands.

Gervase nudged his horse alongside his friend. 'What are we waiting for?' he asked.

'Nothing,' said Ralph curtly. 'Follow me!'

With severe misgivings, he led the column on.

Gervase was under no illusions as to what they would find in the city. He had seen all the Domesday returns for the county in the Exchequer at Winchester and knew that Chester was described in more detail than almost any other city in England. What was omitted from the account was almost as eloquent as what was included. When they finally reached the bridge and clattered across it, Gervase was not surprised by what they saw on the other side.

The narrow winding street had a number of empty or dilapidated houses and other wounds of war were on display. Though the market was busy and the crowd thick, the atmosphere was curiously sombre. A resentful hush fell as the newcomers rode in through the gate. People pushed quickly to the side of the street and watched in sullen silence as the cavalcade passed. Citizens accustomed to the furious and uncaring canter of the earl and his cronies were taken aback by the civilised trot of the visitors. Murmuring their gratitude, they went back to their haggling at the market stalls.

Ralph Delchard, meanwhile, took his company in through the main gate of the castle and reined in his horse. The rest of the party followed suit. The courtyard was alive with soldiers and there was an impressive air of order, but the person who caught their attention was standing no more than a dozen yards away. He was a massive man in the cowl of a Benedictine monk and he turned to greet them with a gesture of welcome that had a strong resemblance to a papal blessing.

Canon Hubert and Brother Simon were relieved to see a fellow member of the order in such a godless place and they smiled back at him. They would have at least one friend inside the castle. But their optimism was premature. As the monk rolled slowly towards them on sandalled feet, they noticed how much deference the castle guards seemed to be according him. There was something extremely odd about the imposing figure in the black cowl.

Ralph introduced them in a clear, ringing voice. 'We have come from Winchester on royal business,' he announced, 'and we are to lodge here at the castle as guests of the Earl of Chester.'

The monk pushed back his hood and beamed up at them. 'Welcome, friends!' he said benevolently. 'I am your host.'

Earl Hugh's raucous laugh was distinctly unmonastic.

Chapter Two

The visitors were completely dumbfounded. Expecting to meet a notorious reprobate, they were instead confronted by this hulking individual in a Benedictine habit. Ralph Delchard's jaw dropped, Gervase Bret blinked in amazement and Canon Hubert's eyebrows shot up to a precarious altitude. Brother Simon all but fainted and he had to hold tight to the pommel of his saddle to prevent himself from keeling over.

A second shock was in store for the newcomers. Earl Hugh was not alone. His sheer physical bulk obscured the man who had stood behind him and now came into view as if emerging from the capacious folds of his master's cowl. Short, slim and wearing his own cowl as if he had never known any other garment, Gerold was the earl's chaplain and spiritual mentor. Though still in his thirties, his wizened face, greying wisps of hair and scholarly hunch made him seem much older. Earl Hugh might be a bogus monk but there was nothing false about the ascetic Gerold. He positively exuded religiosity.

With his chaplain beside him, the earl's manner changed at once. The roaring extrovert disappeared, to be replaced by a subdued figure with a penitential expression. His voice took on an almost sepulchral note.

'You catch me at my devotions,' he explained. 'Permit me to introduce Brother Gerold. You will see a great deal of him during your time here at the castle.'

'Welcome to Chester!' said Gerold with a meek smile. 'We have been looking forward to your arrival and hope that your stay with us will be a pleasant one.'

'Thank you,' said Ralph. 'We are glad to have reached you at last. I am Ralph Delchard. And these,' he added, indicating each person as he was named, 'are my colleagues. Master Gervase Bret, Canon Hubert of Winchester and our faithful scribe, Brother Simon.'

'Your reputation has come before you,' said Hugh. 'The King holds you in high esteem and has entrusted you with important business in my county. Call on me to assist you in any way that I can.'

'We appreciate that offer, my lord,' said Ralph.

'It is given in all seriousness.'

'Thank you.'

'Now,' continued the other, rubbing his palms gleefully and shedding his monkish restraint, 'there is something else that you will appreciate. A banquet has been laid on in your honour this evening. All of you are cordially invited.'

Ralph was pleased. 'That is very kind of you, my lord.'

'We are most grateful,' said Gervase.

'Yes,' agreed Hubert, 'though in our case, alas, that gratitude is tinged with regret. Brother Simon and I are the guests of Bishop Robert and we are bidden to his table this evening. We must decline your generous invitation.'

Earl Hugh stiffened and his beetle brows converged. 'I am not used to refusals,' he warned.

'It is unavoidable, my lord,' said Hubert.

'And I am not used to yielding position to Bishop Robert. It is not right. It is not natural. I am sure that he could excuse you for this evening. Tell him that I have issued an express request and the worthy bishop will understand,' he said meaningfully. 'Places will be set at my table for you and for Brother Simon.'

The very notion made Simon gasp in dismay.

'We would not wish to offend the bishop,' said Hubert.

'Would you prefer to offend *me*?'

'No, my lord. Offence is not intended, I assure you. We are deeply grateful for your kind invitation but the long journey has sapped our strength and left us weary. We would be poor companions at a banquet.'

'Yet you are prepared to eat with Bishop Robert.'

'A frugal meal, perhaps. Nothing more.'

'I am displeased by this rejection, Canon Hubert.'

'It is not a rejection, my lord.'

'Then what else is it?' demanded Hugh, glowering at him.

Hubert blustered until Brother Gerold came to his rescue.

'It is a perfectly reasonable explanation, my lord.'

'I am not interested in explanations.'

'You should be,' the other reminded him softly. 'Have you so soon forgotten the subject of my instruction today? We talked about the importance of understanding the needs and wishes of others. Tolerance is a virtue, my lord.' He gave the earl a few moments to digest his words before pressing on. 'Besides,' he said, indicating the other monks, 'Canon Hubert and Brother Simon have ridden here all the way from Winchester. I would wager anything that they carry letters of greeting from Bishop Walkelin to our own Bishop Robert.'

'That is true,' confirmed Hubert.

'You should let them deliver those missives, my lord.'

Hugh sulked. 'Should I?'

'Undoubtedly.'

'Why?'

'Because it is what I would advise.'

The earl gave him a truculent stare but made no verbal protest. Brother Gerold had subdued him in a way that made the others look on with admiration.

'Release them from any obligation, my lord.'

Hugh scowled but eventually managed an affirmative nod. 'I will expect them both another night.'

'We can discuss that in private.'

'I was looking forward to a theological discussion with Canon Hubert. News of his scholarship has preceded him.'

Hubert beamed at the unexpected praise but Simon was even more outraged. Was the devil planning to quote scripture at them? It was unthinkable. Simon reflected inwardly that he would rather debate the value of the gospels with his horse.

'Very well,' said the earl at length. 'I will not enforce your attendance at the banquet. Go to Bishop Robert, if you must. But I remain disappointed.'

'Our profound apologies, my lord,' said Hubert soothingly.

'You may leave.'

It sounded more like an order given than a permission granted. Hubert and Simon reacted with speed. After a flurry of farewells, they rode swiftly out of the castle they abhorred and headed for the sanctuary of the cathedral.

Earl Hugh brought the niceties abruptly to an end. 'You will be shown to your apartments,' he said curtly, clapping his hands to bring servants running. 'Your men will be bestowed in their lodging. Everything is in readiness. When you have unloaded your baggage, I would be happy to take you round my castle. If that offer appeals to you.'

'Very much, my lord,' said Ralph.

'So be it.'

Their host turned on his heel and strode off briskly across the courtyard. After offering them a placatory smile, Gerold went trotting after him. Ralph watched the pair of them until they vanished into the chapel.

'What did you make of that, Gervase?' he asked.

'Earl Hugh does not like to be crossed.'

'There is no love lost between him and Bishop Robert.'

'That is clear from the disputes we are here to settle,' agreed Gervase. 'A trial of strength is obviously going on here between Church and State.'

'Real power in Chester lies with the State.'

'Yet the Church has a powerful ally.'

'Bishop Robert?'

'No, Ralph,' said the other. 'Brother Gerold. Unless I am much mistaken, he is the only man with any appreciable influence over the earl. We can learn from him.'

The search was entirely fruitless. For several long and anxious hours they combed the Delamere Forest, but without success. Gytha began to despair. Still only eighteen, she had been worn down by family responsibilities and her pretty face was beginning to lose its youthful bloom. Fear etched new lines around her eyes and mouth. She used the edge of her hood to wipe away the beads of perspiration on her forehead.

She turned to the boy who trudged reluctantly beside her. 'Was this the clearing?' she said.

'I do not know, Gytha.'

'You must remember.'

'I'm trying to.'

'Try harder, Beollan.'

He looked around and shrugged. 'I can't be sure.'

'Is there nothing that you recognise?'

'Not really.'

'But you know every inch of the forest.'

The boy turned away so that she would not see the guilt which flooded into his face. Beollan was barely ten, a tousle-haired lad in rough attire with cross-gartered stockings. He and his sister were the children of a Saxon cotarius, a cottager without any land. Beollan carried a stick to aid him in his search but he had used it without conviction to poke among the bushes. It was almost as if he did not really wish to find what they were seeking.

Gytha finally lost patience with him. 'What are you hiding?' she challenged.

'Nothing!' he retorted.

'I know you too well, Beollan. You've been behaving strangely since we left the house. I think that you're keeping something back from me. Are you?'

'No!'

'Is that the truth?'

'Yes. I've told you all I can.'

'Have you?' she said, taking him by the shoulder to spin him round. 'When you came back home, you were in a terrible state. You could hardly get the words out. What really happened out here in the forest?'

'I told you,' he bleated. 'I lost them.'

'You would never do that.'

'I did, Gytha. I swear it.'

25

'You're lying.'

'I'm not, I tell you.'

'Why?' she said, grabbing him by the arms to shake him.

'Let go of me.'

'*Why*, Beollan?'

'You're hurting me.'

'Tell me the truth.'

'I already have.'

'We must find them.'

'Stop shaking me.'

She released her hold and he rubbed his arms to ease the pain inflicted by her strong grip. Head down, Beollan avoided his sister's blazing eyes. Gytha's interrogation continued.

'Where did you last see them?' she pressed.

'Somewhere in this part of the forest.'

'Be more exact.'

'I wish I could.'

'Why did you lose touch with them?'

'I wandered off.'

'They would never let you do that.'

'It was an accident.'

'Stop deceiving me,' she said. 'I am sick with worry. I need all the help that I can get. Not lies and deception.'

'There's nothing else I can tell you.'

'Are you quite certain?'

'Yes, Gytha.'

She looked around with heightened anxiety. 'You have places where you hide any game you kill. Take me to the nearest one.' He shook his head vigorously. 'Take me, Beollan.'

'No.'

'It's important.'

'I want to go home.'

'Take me,' she demanded. 'We might find some clues.'

'I don't know where the nearest hiding place is.'

'Yes, you do.'

'I've forgotten.'

'You've forgotten far too much.'

'What do you mean?'

'You know full well what I mean,' she said, confronting him again. 'You've been holding something back ever since we started to search for them. And I want to know what it is. Now,' she added, hands on hips, 'are you going to tell me or do I have to beat it out of you?'

Torn between guilt and apprehension, the boy began to tremble visibly. Then he burst into tears. Before she could stop him, he turned tail and scampered off wildly into the undergrowth. Gytha raced after him but he was far too quick and elusive for her. His knowledge of the forest gave him a thousand places in which to hide. She would never find him until he was ready to come out of his own accord. Gasping for breath, she abandoned the chase and rested against an elm. When she had recovered, she retraced her steps to the clearing.

Then she resumed the feverish search on her own.

Ralph Delchard and Gervase Bret were conducted to their respective apartments high up in the keep of Chester Castle. Both had a clear view of the city itself, a sizeable place with a population of some fifteen hundred or so. Winchester was considerably larger, as befitted the nation's capital, but Chester was easily the biggest community in the north-west. Like the former, it had its castle, cathedral, churches, civic buildings and higgledy-piggledy arrangement of houses. Each also had a resident king. All that Earl Hugh's authority lacked was a formal coronation.

As Ralph and Gervase gazed down from their windows, the market clamour rose up from below and the pungent smells of town life drifted up to their nostrils. Beyond the city, they could see the long road which twisted its way towards Wales before disappearing among some foothills. The winding track had been trampled flat by the feet of warriors over many centuries. It was only a matter of time before it would echo once more to the march of armies.

Hugh d'Avranches was justifiably proud of his fortress. As

soon as he had changed out of his Benedictine cowl, he sent for his guests and escorted them on a tour of his home. Ralph was duly impressed with the fortifications. The battlements were high, solid and patrolled by alert guards. On the southern and western sides, the River Dee was itself an additional defence and the earl explained how the wooden bridge across it could be closed – or even destroyed – to hamper any attack.

'Yes,' he growled. 'Sooner than let an enemy use it to cross the river, I'd burn it to the ground.'

'Are you ever likely to be in that situation?' said Ralph.

'Never.'

'How can you be so confident?'

'I have taken steps to keep everything under strict control here on the border. Anyone who has dared to raise a sword against me has been savagely dealt with, Ralph. I am a great believer in the value of scapegoats. Brutality is the only language that the Welsh understand.'

'That is not true, my lord,' averred Gervase.

Hugh bristled. 'What do you mean?'

'We had some dealings with the Welsh during our stay in Hereford. They proved amenable to reason in the end.'

'I do not waste my breath on reasoning,' said the other dismissively. 'Actions speak louder than words. Violent action has the most persuasive voice of all.'

'That is a matter of opinion, my lord.'

'I can see that you are no soldier, Gervase.'

'I am eternally grateful for that.'

'Someone has to keep those Welsh devils at bay.'

'That can often be achieved by diplomacy, my lord.'

'Not on this troublesome border,' said Hugh. 'I long ago found that sharp weapons are the best diplomats. They achieve results in the most effective way.'

Gervase was tenacious. 'But they also leave a legacy of resentment which can work against you in the long term,' he said. 'Peace which grows out of mutual interest is far more lasting and valuable than a truce which is imposed by indiscriminate force.'

Teeth bared in a snarl, the earl rounded on him. 'Do you dare to question my methods?' he snapped.

'Of course not, my lord.'

'How much experience have you had of subduing the Welsh?'

'None whatsoever.'

'I have had over fifteen years at it,' boomed Hugh, inflating his chest. 'Fifteen years of keeping the peace and protecting the citizens of Chester. To save the lives of the people under my care, I have had to take the lives of others. But that is in the nature of conquest.'

'Indeed, it is, my lord,' said Ralph, keen to appease him before he lost his temper completely. 'Gervase was not criticising you in any way. He was merely pointing out that our dealings with the Welsh during our stay in Herefordshire were on a very different footing.' He shot his friend a warning glance. 'Is that not so, Gervase?'

'Yes.'

'I have special memories of that visit to Hereford.'

'Why so?' asked Hugh.

'Because that is where I met my wife.'

'A Welsh girl?'

'A Saxon lady, my lord.'

The earl chuckled. 'I endorse your choice, Ralph. I can speak up for Saxon ladies. Their men may be uncouth and hairy but their womenfolk are sometimes very beautiful.' His chuckle became a lecherous snigger. 'And very amenable.'

'Golde will be joining us in a day or two.'

'I look forward to meeting her.'

They continued their tour of the fortifications, then descended into the courtyard. Stables, storerooms and lodging for the garrison were arranged neatly round the perimeter. Everything was scrupulously in order. Soldiers were practising with their weaponry. Horses were being groomed. The clang of hammers could be heard from the armoury. There was an air of readiness about the whole place.

Ralph showed an immediate interest but something else

aroused Gervase's curiosity. He pointed to the chapel on the other side of the bailey. It was a large stone structure with a bell in its tower.

'I am glad to see that religion has a place inside your stronghold,' he remarked.

'A crucial place,' agreed Hugh piously. 'A castle without a chapel is like a body without a soul. My soldiers are not callous murderers who kill for pleasure. Brother Gerold blesses all their enterprises. They ride out under the banner of God. Like crusaders.'

'May I visit the chapel, my lord?' asked Gervase.

'Please do.'

'Ralph?'

'I would rather see the rest of the defences, Gervase.'

'Then I will leave you to it.' He gave a nod of farewell to his host. 'My lord.'

'Gerold will show you all that you wish to see.'

'Thank you.'

As Gervase walked away, Hugh kept one glaucous eye on him. 'Your young friend is contentious, Ralph.'

'Ignore him, my lord,' said Ralph with a grin. 'Gervase is a lawyer. He loves to argue.'

'I do not tolerate argument.'

'Not even from your wife?'

'She does not argue,' returned the other with a laugh. 'She simply complains. Like every other wife. What is marriage but an endless series of moans and reproaches?'

'That has not been my experience, my lord.'

'Then your wife has no tongue in her head.'

'She does,' Ralph assured him, 'but I manage to stay on the right side of her anger. Life is much happier that way.'

'Is Gervase married?'

'Not yet.'

'Betrothed?'

'Yes, my lord. To a gorgeous creature called Alys.'

'That might explain it.'

'What?'

30

'His restless urge for debate,' said Hugh. 'If he had a woman in his bed, she would take him between her thighs and squeeze it out of him.' He turned to Ralph. 'He is a handsome enough lad. There are ladies aplenty in Chester who would willingly do the office for him. Should I provide one or two?'

'Gervase would not even look at them, my lord.'

'Is he too shy?'

'Too faithful to Alys.'

'Fidelity is the enemy of true happiness.'

'I am not sure that I agree with that.'

'Gervase will learn.'

'Perhaps.'

Their conversation was interrupted by the arrival of a newcomer. Flanked by four armed soldiers, a big, bearded, sturdy man came into view and marched round the edge of the courtyard. Even with his hands tied behind his back, the man had an undeniable dignity about him. There was real pride in the upward tilt of his chin. The dark hair, swarthy skin and telltale attire helped Ralph to identify him.

'A Welsh prisoner, I think.'

'Yes, Ralph.'

'A member of their nobility.'

'Of higher rank than that.'

'Who is he?'

'Gruffydd ap Cynan.'

Ralph was surprised. 'The Prince of Gwynedd?'

'No less.'

'And you have him under lock and key?'

'Yes, Ralph. He is let out for exercise twice a day.'

'I thought that Gruffydd ap Cynan collaborated with us.'

'He did at first. Then he was gripped by the folly that he could unite his people and put us to flight. I thought it safer to let him cool his heels in my dungeon. He will not cause any problems in there.'

'Will they not try to rescue him?'

'Nobody can escape from Chester Castle.'

'They are bound to seek the release of their prince.'

31

'Yes, Ralph,' said Hugh grandly, 'but I will hear none of their entreaties. They have offered me money, land or both in return for their beloved prince but he is far more valuable to me in a dungeon.'

'Why?'

'Release him and he might start a Welsh uprising.'

'He is a doughty soldier, I know that.'

'And an inspiring leader. Locking him up is the only sensible course of action. We have had uninterrupted peace on the border since Gruffydd became my guest.'

The Welshman walked past and shot them a glare of hatred.

'He is not entirely happy with his lodging,' said Ralph.

'Who cares?' replied Hugh. 'At one stroke, I have crippled the Welsh army. They cannot operate without Gruffydd ap Cynan at their head. As long as he is my prisoner, there is no danger whatsoever of a Welsh uprising.'

Chapter Three

The cathedral church of St John stood outside the city walls.
It was at once an integral part of Chester and a detached
appendage and the bishop sometimes felt that its ambiguous
situation accurately reflected his own relationship with the
city. He was both accepted and limited, recognised as a key
feature in the community yet held back from exercising his full
episcopal power and influence. Earl Hugh cast a long shadow.
Bishop Robert had not yet found the way to escape it.

The church of St John Baptist was a seventh-century foundation
which had been refounded in 1057 as a collegiate establishment by
Leofric of Mercia, one of the three great earls of the day among
whom the government of the kingdom had been divided. At the
time of the Conquest, the county of Cheshire was in the diocese of
Lichfield, but that city became so impoverished and its cathedral so
poorly maintained that Archbishop Lanfranc eventually moved the
bishop's seat to Chester. It had been a cathedral city now for over
ten years and that decade had seen some extensive rebuilding as the
collegiate church was extended and improved in accordance with
its new status.

When Canon Hubert and Brother Simon entered the pre-
cincts through the high round-headed arch, they were met by
the soaring stone of the eastern end of the nave. They paused
to appraise the building before moving slowly round it to study
its salient features on all sides. Wooden scaffolding was still
in place around the chancel and stonemasons swarmed busily
over it, but the visitors were able to see more than enough of
the edifice to make a sound judgement.

They were deeply impressed. It might lack the grandeur of Canterbury cathedral and the breathtaking scale of York minster – both of which they had visited in the course of their official duties – but Chester cathedral had a dignity and character all of its own. Bishop Robert, they decided, was to be congratulated on transforming a humble collegiate church into such an inspiring structure. After their bruising confrontation with the earl at the castle, both men were relieved to be on consecrated ground once more.

Brother Simon crossed himself and emitted a long sigh. 'We are safe,' he said.

'We are always safe in the hands of the Lord,' corrected Hubert pedantically. 'He is there to help us at all times and in all places.'

'I did not feel His comforting touch at the castle.'

'I did, Brother Simon. It sustained me.'

'I went weak at the knees,' confessed the other.

'Put on the whole armour of God.'

'Yes, Canon Hubert. It will be necessary apparel.'

'It will protect you against that fiend in human shape.'

'Earl Hugh terrified me. Wearing that cowl was a calculated insult to the Benedictine order.'

'He will be made to pay for it in time.'

The plump figure of Archdeacon Frodo bore down on them. His face was wreathed in a smile and his podgy hands were gesturing a welcome. Introductions were made and friendship instantly established. Hubert recognised at a glance that the archdeacon was a man after his own heart, and Simon was profoundly reassured by the warmth of their reception. Chester was not, after all, an antechamber of Hell.

'How was your journey?' inquired Frodo.

'Long and tedious,' said Hubert.

'Then you will want to rest.'

'Not until we have seen Bishop Robert. We would like to pay our respects and deliver some letters from Bishop Walkelin of Winchester.'

'Bishop Robert will be delighted to see you,' said Frodo,

'but he is engaged at present with another visitor. Let me show you to your lodgings so that you may deposit your baggage and shake some of the dust of travel from your feet.'

'Teach us the way, Archdeacon Frodo.'

'We are so grateful to be here,' confided Simon. 'We met with a dispiriting welcome at the castle.'

'From whom?'

'Earl Hugh.'

'Yes,' said Frodo tactfully. 'He is a creature of moods. Catch the earl at the wrong time and it can be a distressing experience. But,' he continued, trying to redress the balance of his implied criticism, 'he has many good qualities.'

Simon gaped. 'Has he?'

'Earl Hugh has done an immense amount for this city.'

'In the name of self-aggrandisement,' opined Hubert.

'That is not for me to say.'

'We have eyes and ears, Archdeacon Frodo.'

'Do not underrate Earl Hugh's contribution to the safety of this community,' warned the archdeacon. 'Chester has been a far more secure place to live under his aegis.'

'How much freedom do you enjoy within that security?'

'We have no complaints, Canon Hubert.'

'Indeed?'

'None at all.'

'I find that astonishing.'

'The holy church must adapt itself to the conditions in which it finds itself,' said Frodo evenly. 'And that is what Bishop Robert has done.'

Hubert's jowls shook in disagreement. 'I have always held that the holy church should lead rather than follow,' he said with a glance up at the heavens. 'It is for man to adapt to God and not the other way round.'

'I have great sympathy with that point of view as well,' consoled the archdeacon. 'Here in Chester, I think you will find, we have achieved a workable compromise.'

'Between what?'

'You will see.'

Frodo led them off to their lodgings and waited while each of them settled into the small cell which had been set aside for him. Brother Simon was pleased by the monastic simplicity of his accommodation, but the four bare walls and rude mattress held less appeal for Canon Hubert. Back in Winchester, he was accustomed to a far more comfortable chamber and to food of a higher quality and quantity than he expected to find here. While Simon offered up a prayer of thanks for his return to his natural habitat, Hubert's limbs ached in anticipation and his stomach began to rumble mutinously. He was even prey to envious thoughts about the banquet at the castle.

When the guests were ready, Frodo took them away. They made an incongruous trio. Beside the emaciated scribe the fleshy archdeacon looked truly corpulent, but he himself appeared slim when viewed against the adipose canon. A master of the middle way, Frodo was glad that he occupied an intermediate position between the two newcomers, physically and theologically. It would enable him to communicate easily with both.

'Where was your last assignment?' he asked.

'Oxford,' said Hubert. 'Ill health prevented me from joining the commission at first, but they could not manage without my services and I was summoned from my sickbed to help my colleagues out of the pit into which they had fallen in my absence.'

'Canon Hubert was their salvation,' said Simon.

'I am not surprised,' said Frodo, without irony.

'Several complicated disputes came before us,' explained Hubert, 'but we managed to settle all of them satisfactorily. We certainly left Oxford a far healthier and more just place than we found it.'

'I hope that you do the same with Chester.'

'We will, Archdeacon Frodo. We will.'

The three men strode on in companionable silence until they came to Bishop Robert's chamber. In the short time he had known them, Frodo felt that he had learned a great deal about the visitors, all of it encouraging news, while, for their part,

Canon Hubert and Brother Simon were convinced that they would be far happier as the guests of an obliging bishop than of an egregious earl.

That conviction was summarily shattered. The door of the room swung open to reveal another visitor to the cathedral. Hubert and Simon recoiled in horror. A small, wiry, wild-eyed and sprightly man in his late thirties stood before them, wearing a ragged lambskin cloak that was spattered with mud and reeking with decay. Indeed, since the cloak hid most of his diminutive body, he looked and smelled more like a dead sheep than a live churchman. Hubert and Simon were frankly appalled.

Here was the last man in the world they wished to meet again. What added to their distress was the patent enthusiasm with which he greeted them. The wild eyes intensified, the animated body went into a spasm of joy and the inimitable face became one large grinning rictus. He let out a cackle of pleasure which chilled them to the bone.

'This is Archdeacon Idwal,' said Frodo.

Hubert and Simon gave their response in perfect unison. 'We know,' they groaned. 'We *know*!'

Gervase Bret knelt at the altar rail for several minutes in private communion with his Maker. The chapel was dark and dank but its atmosphere had a spirituality which he found conducive to prayer and meditation. It was only when he rose to leave that he realised he was not alone.

Brother Gerold slipped out of the shadows at the rear of the little nave and greeted him with a smile of approval. 'That was a long grace before a meal,' he commented.

'I was giving thanks for our safe arrival.'

'God watched over your journey.'

'Indeed,' said Gervase. 'It remains to be seen if He will be equally vigilant on our behalf during our stay here.'

'Do you feel in need of divine assistance?'

'It is always welcome. Will you show me round the chapel?'

'With pleasure.'

Their inspection completed, the two men came out into the bailey and headed towards the keep. Gerold was an easy companion, quiet, unassuming and friendly. His questions were searching and yet remarkably inoffensive.

'I believe that you were once destined for the cowl.'

'Who told you that?'

'The lord Ralph.'

'It's true,' conceded Gervase. 'I was a novice at Eltham Abbey but drew back at the last moment.'

'Fear or lack of faith?'

'Human frailty, Brother Gerold.'

'A young woman?'

'Her name is Alys. We are betrothed.'

'I congratulate you, Gervase.'

'Thank you.'

'I am pleased to see that her presence in your life has not distracted you from your devotions.'

'Quite the opposite,' admitted Gervase. 'Not a day passes but I thank God for bringing me Alys in the first place. My work as a commissioner means that we are perforce apart a great deal, and that causes much heartache. Prayer is not merely a way of dulling the pain. God is indulgent. I find that through Him I can keep in touch with Alys.'

'And she with you, no doubt.'

'Yes, Brother Gerold. She is a devout Christian.'

'I expected no less.'

They began to ascend the steps set into the huge mound on which the keep was set. Gerold probed gently away.

'Have you never had regrets about leaving the abbey?'

'Frequently.'

'What do you miss most?'

'The comforting ritual of the Benedictine order.'

'It is supposed to tax as well as comfort.'

'I found it reassuring,' said Gervase. 'When I was at Eltham, my whole day was shaped in the service of God. I lived and worked alongside holy men and that is always instructive.'

'I can see that you were an apt pupil.'

'My modest gifts are employed elsewhere now.'

'There is nothing modest about your talents, Gervase.'

'I have been fortunate.'

'Eltham Abbey was the loser when you departed.'

'They would have gained nothing from having a discontented monk in their midst. I chose the right path.'

'I am glad that it has crossed mine.'

Gervase was touched by the obvious sincerity of the remark. Having heard so much about the excesses of the Earl of Chester, it was refreshing to discover that there was someone like Brother Gerold at his side to impose a degree of control over his master.

As they approached the hall, further conversation became impossible because the sound which came through the closed doors was deafening. Evidently, the banquet was already in full swing. When the doors swung open to admit the newcomers, the noise surged out like a tidal wave. A combination of music, clapping, singing, shouting and cheering washed over them. They plunged into the maelstrom with misgivings.

Long oak tables were set out in a horseshoe pattern. They were laden with every conceivable variety of rich food, and pitchers of wine stood everywhere. Almost a hundred guests were packed into the hall, laughing, joking and generally swelling the cacophony. In the flickering candlelight, it looked like a scene of wild abandon.

'Over here, Gervase!' called Ralph, waving to him. 'I have been keeping a place for you beside me.'

'Thank you,' said Gervase, making his way towards him.

When he turned to bid farewell to Gerold, he saw that the chaplain had already been swallowed up in the crowd. Gervase dedicated all his energies to pushing past the jiggling bodies of the other guests to the table at the very centre of the horseshoe. Ralph Delchard was in a chair beside the earl who was in turn seated beside his wife, Ermintrude, a woman of great poise and beauty who seemed out of place in such a gathering.

'Where have you been?' said Ralph as Gervase sat down.

'In the chapel.'

'You missed the start of the banquet.'

'It looks as if it started days ago,' observed Gervase, gazing around at the drunken guests. 'How long can they keep this pandemonium up?'

'They know how to enjoy themselves, that is all.'

'Bear in mind that we have work to do in the morning.'

Ralph was peeved. 'I can hold my wine.'

'It looks as if you will have ample opportunity to prove it,' said Gervase as a servant arrived to pour him some wine and to refill Ralph's cup. 'The King himself does not dine in such style as this.'

'It is all in our honour!'

'Is it?'

'Yes,' said Ralph. 'That is why we must not hold back.'

Gervase grinned. 'Nobody could accuse you of doing that.'

Ralph chuckled and slapped him on the back. Servants came to load Gervase's plate with some spiced rabbit and he sampled the delicacy. When his ears became used to the din, he slowly began to enjoy the meal. It was superb, comprising ten courses, each of which was paraded round the room on huge pewter plates before it was served to the guests. Minstrels played but nobody listened. Dancers whirled but few watched. There was so much revelry at the tables themselves that everything else was merely a garnishing.

Though his wife was beside him, Earl Hugh paid her little attention and let his eye rove libidinously over the many gorgeous young ladies whom he had invited to decorate his banquet. From the compliant smiles which they gave him, it was clear that most of them were more than casual acquaintances. Hugh was not possessive about his womenfolk.

'Take your pick,' he offered.

'Not me, my lord,' said Ralph.

'Would you prefer me to choose for you?'

'No, thank you.'

'Do you like a buxom wench with plenty to squeeze or some wild and willowy creature who will flail around beneath you like a giant eel? We have plenty of both here.'

'I will take your word for it.'

'What is wrong with you, man?'

'Simple fatigue.'

'One of these ladies will soon revive you.'

'I am married, my lord.'

'So?'

'My wife will arrive in a day or two.'

'Will you deny yourself pleasure in the meantime?'

'I will honour my vows.'

'More fool you!' He leaned across Ralph. 'Gervase?'

'My lord?'

'Will you go off to an empty bed tonight as well?'

'I hope so.'

'The ladies will be disappointed.'

'They have entertainment enough without me, my lord.'

'I like my guests to have *everything*.'

'We do.'

'We do, indeed,' echoed Ralph. 'I have never seen such a magnificent feast. Lavish banquets were held in our honour both in York and in Oxford but they pale beside this one.'

'I never stint,' boasted Hugh.

'That is very plain, my lord.'

Dishes of quail were brought in from the kitchens and taken round the tables to tempt the appetites of the guests. Before anyone was served, however, a fresh plate was set before the earl and one of the quails placed upon it. Out of the fireplace where he had been lurking came a strange, misshapen, dwarfish creature with a bulbous nose and massive ears. Taking the food from the earl's plate, he sniffed it like a dog then took a tentative bite, chewing it slowly until he was satisfied that it was edible. He nodded to his master then withdrew to his position in the fireplace.

'Who is that?' asked Gervase.

'Durand,' said Earl Hugh. 'My taster.'

'Is such a position necessary?'

'I fear that it is, Gervase. Power makes for unpopularity. Those who cannot kill me with their swords may try to poison

41

me instead. I put nothing into my mouth until Durand has tasted it first. It is a sensible precaution.'

'Has he ever detected any poison?' wondered Ralph.

'Twice.'

'What did you do?'

'Killed the chef responsible for cooking that food.'

'Was Durand not affected by the poison?'

'He spat it out. His tongue is infallible.'

Gervase glanced across at the dwarf, who had now curled up beside one of the mastiffs in front of the fire. He seemed to have far more kinship with the dogs in the room than with the humans. Durand had reverted to nature.

The Lady Ermintrude rose and excused herself from the table. She was patently out of place in the gathering and wished to leave before the revelry overflowed into true licentiousness. Ralph gallantly escorted her to the door before bidding her farewell and returning to his place, wondering how his host came to have such a beautiful and gracious wife. He and the earl then fell into a discussion of the Battle of Hastings in which they had both fought with distinction.

Since he could take no part in military reminiscences, Gervase let his gaze drift around the room until it finally located Brother Gerold. He was sitting at the extreme end of one of the tables, eating quietly and washing down the food with a cup of ale. Gerold might have been alone in the privacy of his lodging. He was quite impervious to the tumult all around him. When the behaviour of his immediate neighbours became still rowdier, he did not even look up from his repast. Why was the chaplain present at such an occasion? Vices which he would surely condemn were exhibited on all sides of him. Was he inured to such antics or did he attend in order to prevent the banquet from spilling over into a complete riot?

Gervase was intrigued. A grotesque dwarf, a high-minded monk and an indifferent wife. Hugh d'Avranches kept peculiar company at his table.

The soldiers won the Battle of Hastings all over again.

'Golden memories!' sighed the earl.

'A day that changed our lives,' said Ralph nostalgically.
'And that of every man, woman and child in this country.'
'No question but that it did, my lord.'
'I miss the excitement of battle.'
'It is something I have happily put behind me.'
'You are getting old, Ralph,' teased the other.
'Old but wise.'
'Where is the wisdom in denying your true instincts?'
'Instincts?'
'Once a soldier, always a soldier,' insisted Hugh, clapping
him between the shoulder blades. 'Join us tomorrow on a stag
hunt and revive those memories of warfare.'
'It is a tempting offer, my lord.'
'Then take it.'
'I may not and will not,' said Ralph, turning to Gervase.
'Our work begins in earnest tomorrow and Gervase will not
spare me. While you pursue stags, we will be hunting game
of another kind.'
'Wild boar? Hares? Rabbits?'
'Human game, my lord.'
'Cheats and liars,' explained Gervase.
'Show them no mercy,' urged Hugh, banging the table with
a fist. 'Summary justice. Be firm, be brutal. Nothing is served
by temporising. I was judge, jury and executioner myself only
this morning and it gave me a feeling of exhilaration. It also
assuaged my desire for revenge.'
'Revenge?' repeated Ralph.
'Against the men who killed my favourite hawk.'
'Why did they do that?'
'I did not bother to ask them, Ralph. When someone shoots
an arrow at your prize bird, you do not allow him to deliver
a sermon on his reasons for doing so. We hanged the rogues
from the nearest tree. You should do the same.'
'We do not have the power to execute,' said Gervase. 'We
can only report malefactors to the King.'
'That is too slow a process for me. I will not wait upon
the King's word. I crave instant retribution.' He pulled out

his dagger to emphasise his point. 'If someone dares to cross the Earl of Chester, he will not live to boast about it.'

The dagger was embedded in the table with force.

It was no idle gesture. Ralph and Gervase knew they had received a grim warning from their host. He would be watching them.

Chapter Four

Archdeacon Idwal was in a typically combative vein that evening. His whole body was pulsing with vitality.

'I blame the Synod of Whitby!' he said accusingly, chewing a mouthful of capon. 'It reached a foolish decision and set the Christian Church on the wrong path.'

'It is rather late in the day to say that,' observed Frodo drily. 'Your censure is over four hundred years behind the times, archdeacon.'

'It is still relevant.'

'Hardly.'

'I say that it is,' asserted Idwal pugnaciously. 'What was the main reason for calling the Synod of Whitby?'

'To resolve the paschal controversy.'

'Exactly, my friend. To remove once and for all disputes about how to decide on the date for Easter. The Celtic Church, which, may I remind you, was in existence for centuries before St Augustine began his Christian mission in Kent, had its own method of identifying Easter in the calendar.'

'But the Synod was in favour of the Roman practice.'

'That is where the hideous mistake was made,' argued the little Welshman before gulping down a generous measure of ale and belching melodiously. 'Celtic custom and practice should have been respected. In Wales and elsewhere, we had come willingly to God at a time when the English counties were still worshipping false idols. If it were left to me, we would revert at once to Celtic tradition.'

'Fortunately,' said Canon Hubert tartly, 'that decision has

not been left in your hands, Archdeacon Idwal, experienced and manipulative as they are. In my view, the Synod of Whitby made the correct election and the English Church has been the beneficiary ever since.'

'The English Church – yes! But what about the *Welsh*?'

'They are effectively the same thing.'

'Nonsense!'

'Please!' said Bishop Robert. 'Moderate your language.'

'Then get Hubert to moderate his idiocy.'

'You are subservient to Canterbury,' reminded Hubert.

'More's the pity!'

'Archbishop Lanfranc is your primate.'

'Only at the moment.'

While Idwal ranted on, the others suffered in silence. He was a bellicose companion. The four men were sharing a meal at the bishop's palace within the city. Brother Simon had been invited but the mere thought of eating with Idwal had played havoc with his digestion and he declined. Hubert was beginning to wish that he had done likewise. The privilege of dining with the bishop was vitiated by the ordeal of listening to the patriotic Welshman. Since their last meeting, Idwal had not mellowed in even the slightest way with the passage of time. In Hubert's opinion, he had become still more intemperate.

Robert de Limesey sought to move the conversation to a more neutral topic. He dislodged a chicken bone from between his teeth then bestowed an episcopal smile upon them.

'Our cathedral is still a relatively new phenomenon in Chester,' he said, 'but it is a foundation stone on which we hope to build. My predecessor, Bishop Peter, began his work at the cathedral church of St Chad's in Lichfield.'

'St Chad!' sneered Idwal contemptuously.

'When the see was translated to Chester,' continued the bishop, sailing over the interruption, 'Peter was eager to develop the scope and the physical presence of the Church here. Sadly, he died before that work could be brought to its culmination. I see it as my duty to carry on where he left off. The establishment of the cathedral was the first major undertaking, but it may soon be possible to move on to the next project.'

'And what is that?' inquired Hubert.

'Frodo will explain.'

'Gladly,' said the archdeacon, seasoned by the bishop's habit of delegation and therefore always ready to step in when called upon. 'Bishop Robert is turning his attention towards the founding of an abbey in the city.'

'A worthy initiative!' praised Hubert.

'Where will it be?' asked Idwal.

'We are still at the early stages of discussion,' said Frodo smoothly, 'and there are many crucial issues still to be settled, but Bishop Robert is confident that an abbey will be established here in Chester in due course.'

'I congratulate you, Bishop Robert,' said Hubert.

'Thank you,' replied the bishop, 'but, as Frodo has just indicated, there are still several difficulties to surmount.'

'With regard to finance?'

'That is only one area of contention.'

'What are the others?' asked Idwal bluntly.

'Problems of personality are involved,' said Frodo discreetly. 'We have yet to win over the hearts and minds of significant people in the community.'

Idwal snorted. 'That means Earl Hugh. You would need a battering ram to get through to his heart and mind. And then you will find that his heart is made of stone and his mind of even harder substance. Is he against the notion of an abbey?'

'Far from it,' explained Frodo. 'The earl has given the idea his blessing in principle. It is when we address the practical details that dissension arises. But I am sure that all our differences can be reconciled in time. Who knows? When either of you visits us again, the Benedictine Abbey of St Werburga may well be playing an active part in the Christian life of this community.'

Hubert frowned. 'Werburga?' he said. 'I am not familiar with the name or provenance of this saint.'

'A Saxon nun,' said Idwal disapprovingly.

'Already commemorated in this city,' said Frodo, 'when her bones were brought here for safety over two hundred years ago. The abbey will be a refoundation of the church of secular canons dedicated to St Werburga.'

Hubert was curious. 'Who was the lady?'

'The daughter of Wulfhere, King of the Mercians. She first entered the nunnery of Ely before becoming the superintendent of all the nunneries in Mercia. Werburga was duly canonised,' said Frodo knowledgeably 'because her life was a shining example of Christian virtue and self-denial.'

'That is not true,' countered Idwal.

'I believe you will find that it is,' returned Frodo.

'Werburga is unsuited to this honour.'

'Why do you say that, archdeacon?'

'Because I know her history better than you, Frodo.'

'I doubt that.'

'You only mentioned her father, King Wulfhere,' noted the Welshman. 'What you omitted was the name of her grandfather, King Penda, a notorious heathen who was responsible for the murder of St Oswald of Northumbria. Is the granddaughter of a repellent pagan fit to be enshrined in an abbey?'

'Yes,' said Frodo.

'Without question,' added Bishop Robert.

'Werberga is a saint. She cannot be held responsible for the shortcomings of her grandfather. She is the natural choice here. Besides,' said Frodo, raising an eyebrow, 'if the abbey is not founded in her name, to whom else can it be dedicated?'

'St Deiniol,' urged Idwal.

'Who?'

'St Deiniol.'

'The name means nothing to me,' said Hubert with a sniff.

'And little enough to me,' added the bishop.

'Shame on you both!' chided Idwal. 'Your ignorance appals me though, I have to admit, it does not entirely surprise me. Even here on the border, you prefer to look over your shoulder to England rather than straight ahead into Wales.' He took a deep breath before continuing. 'St Deiniol was a Celtic monk and bishop.'

Hubert grimaced. 'I had a feeling that he might be.'

'He founded the two monasteries of Bangor Fawr, on the Menai Straits, and Bangor Iscoed, which – you may read in the pages of the Venerable Bede – was once the most famous monastery in these islands with no less than two thousand monks under its roof.' His eyes twinkled mischievously. 'Will the Abbey of St Werburga attract that number?'

'No,' conceded Frodo honestly, 'but times, alas, have changed since the days of St Deiniol.'

'That is why his name should be preserved,' argued the other, rising to his feet and striking a pose. 'To remind us of an age when monastic life was held in such high regard. Those two thousand monks, incidentally, were routed at the Battle of Chester so there is a direct connection with this city. St Deiniol has another claim to our attention.' He looked round the upturned faces of his companions. 'Do you know what it is?'

'No,' sighed the bishop.

'Not yet,' said Frodo.

'But we suspect that you are about to tell us,' said Hubert with heavy sarcasm. 'Whether we wish to hear the information or not.'

'Be grateful, Hubert. I am educating you.'

'That is not the word I would have chosen.'

'Tell us about St Deiniol,' encouraged Frodo.

'It was he and St Dyfrig who persuaded St David to take part in the Synod of Brefi,' announced their self-appointed teacher. 'In other words, Deiniol was considered to be of comparable status with the blessed Dyfrig and the revered David. Those three bishops were nothing less than the triple pillars of the Welsh Church.' He sat down again with a triumphant grin. 'What do you think of that, Bishop Robert?'

'We will hold fast to St Werburga,' said the other.

'St Deiniol has prior claims.'

'St Werburga.'

49

'Deiniol!'

'Werburga!'

'The Welsh bishop!'

'The Saxon nun!'

'Think again, Bishop Robert.'

'The matter is decided.'

'It is an act of madness.'

'Then it is one with which we will have to live,' said Frodo calmly, ending the argument with a benign smile. 'We must agree to differ here, Archdeacon Idwal. You are entitled to your opinion, eccentric as it may be, but you can hardly expect to thrust your preferences upon us. How would it be if we were to cross the Welsh border and insist that your next monastic foundation be dedicated to St Werburga?'

'There would be an armed uprising.'

'Let the matter rest there.'

'But I can save you from a catastrophic error.'

'The catastrophic error was in inviting you here,' said Hubert under his breath.

'What was that?' demanded Idwal, sensing hostility.

'I was just wondering what brought you here,' replied the canon through clenched teeth. 'Since you espouse the cause of your nation with such vigour – not to say fanaticism – I am surprised that the Bishop of Llandaff allows you out of his diocese. Does he not have need of you there?'

'I am no longer attached to Llandaff.'

'Yet you are still an archdeacon.'

'Yes, Hubert,' said Idwal with pride, 'but of an even nobler diocese. I was called by Bishop Wilfrid to work with him in St David's.'

'Then what are you doing in Chester?'

'Fulfilling his wishes. Bishop Wilfrid enjoined me to visit all the English dioceses along the border with Wales in order to forge closer links with them. That is why I am here, my friends,' he said, getting to his feet again and releasing his ear-splitting cackle of pleasure. 'I have come to build bridges between the two nations.'

'Bridges?' gasped Bishop Robert.

'Build them or burn them?' muttered Hubert.

Idwal beamed. 'See me as a peacemaker.'

It was a feat of perception beyond all three of them.

Ralph Delchard had to make a concerted effort simply to open one eye. It was several minutes before he could raise the second lid even a fraction. Both eyes throbbed in time with the pounding of his head. His stomach felt as if a herd of horses was stabled inside its inadequate space and his mouth was parched. In such a fragile state, he found that his memory was uncertain. All he knew was that he had drunk far too much, far too fast, at the banquet on the previous night. How he had got to his apartment he did not know, but one thing was clear. He needed to sleep for at least a week if he was to recover.

Duty called with a harsh, insistent voice. It simply had to be heeded. Cursing his misfortune, Ralph dragged himself upright then almost collapsed from the exertion. His stomach now turned to a whirlpool and his brain seemed to be on fire. He reached clumsily for the pitcher of water on the table and poured it over himself, plastering his hair to his forehead and momentarily blinding himself. Relief slowly came. By the time he had dried his face, he was feeling marginally more like a human being and even managed to stagger to the window without falling over.

What he saw below jerked him into a semblance of life. Gervase Bret, looking as bright and alert as ever, was talking to Canon Hubert and pointing up at the keep. The two of them strolled towards the mound and ascended the steps. Within a minute, they would be banging on his door and Ralph could not let either of them see him in such a wounded state. Sheer pride forced him fully awake. As he struggled manfully into his attire, he fought off pain and discomfort.

When his colleagues arrived outside, he was almost ready.

'It is time for breakfast, Ralph,' called Gervase.

'I have already eaten,' he lied, vowing inwardly never to let

51

food or drink pass his lips ever again. 'Go ahead without me.
I will join you shortly.'
  'Did you sleep well, my lord?' said Hubert.
  'Too well, Hubert. And you?'
  'A restless night, I fear.'
  'Why?'
  'I will tell you when you come out.'
Half an hour later, Gervase had eaten his breakfast, Ralph
had shaken off the worst of the banquet's legacy and Hubert
was telling them about the unexpected guest from Wales.
Attended by Ralph's men, they left the castle and followed
the directions they had been given to the shire hall. Hubert
was still shaken by his exchange with Idwal.
  'It was like meeting a ghost,' he recalled.
  'Thank heaven he is not staying at the castle,' said Ralph.
'I would be more than happy never to set eyes on that ragged
pestilence again. Archdeacon Idwal is a menace.'
  'But a helpful one,' Gervase remembered.
  'Helpful!'
  'Yes, Ralph. He came to our assistance in Hereford.'
  'He was a thorn in our flesh from start to finish.'
  'A *Welsh* thorn,' said Hubert. 'The sharpest kind.'
  'What is he doing in Chester?' asked Ralph.
  'Haunting us.'
  They arrived at the shire hall to find Brother Simon awaiting
them. Satchels of documents were slung from his shoulders.
There was such an expression of anguish on his face that they
thought he was suffering from some malady, but the real cause
of his grief was standing a few yards away. A young woman in
the garb of a Saxon peasant was loitering hopefully with a boy
at her side. Her proximity to Simon was enough to transform
him into a furnace of embarrassment. Females were anathema
to him. No monk had more willingly taken the vow of celibacy.
When he saw Canon Hubert approaching, he scuttled hastily
across to him.
  The young woman, meanwhile, accosted Ralph and Gervase.
'May I have a word with you, good sirs?' she pleaded.

Ralph had learned enough of the Saxon tongue from his wife to be able to understand her entreaty, but he left the reply to Gervase. With a Saxon mother and a Breton father, Gervase was conversant with both languages.

'What is the trouble?' he asked her.

'My name is Gytha and this is my brother, Beollan,' she said. 'We are in great distress and need your help.'

'In what way?'

'Our father and brother have disappeared.'

'Where?'

'In the Forest of Delamere.'

'Perhaps they merely went astray.'

'There is no chance of that,' she explained. 'Our home is within the bounds of the forest. We know its paths by heart. Our father and brother have been missing since yesterday and we fear that something dreadful has happened to them.'

'Why come to us?' wondered Gervase. 'We are strangers to the city. Take this inquiry to the castle.'

'We already have and we were turned away.'

'Then seek out the sheriff.'

'He, too, spurned us,' she complained. 'We were told that royal commissioners would be coming to the shire hall this morning so we appeal to you as a last resort.'

'This is none of our business,' decided Ralph, grasping the gist of what she was saying. 'We came to sit in judgement on claimants to property, not to search for missing persons.'

'*Please*, my lord!' she begged.

'Stand aside,' he advised.

'We implore your help.'

'There is nothing that we can do.'

Ralph pushed gently past her and went into the shire hall with Hubert and Simon at his heels, but Gervase lingered. Gytha's plight concerned him and her brother's attitude puzzled him. While she was on the verge of tears, the boy had an air of quiet resignation. It was almost as if he had given up hope of ever seeing his father and brother again.

53

Gytha clutched at the sleeve of Gervase's black gown. 'We fear for their lives!' she wailed.

'When did you last see them?'

'Early yesterday morning. When they left the cottage.'

'Where did they go?'

'Into the forest. All three of them.'

'Three?'

'Beollan went with them.'

Gervase turned to him. 'What happened to them?'

'I . . . lost sight of them,' stuttered the boy.

'Where?'

'I . . . can't remember.'

'What were the three of you doing in the forest?'

When the boy shifted his feet and studied the ground guiltily, Gervase had his answer. They were poaching. He thought of the two men whom Earl Hugh had hanged in the forest when his hawk was brought down with an arrow. Could they be the missing father and brother? He hoped not and he certainly did not wish to alarm Gytha and Beollan unnecessarily by mentioning the possibility. He needed more facts before he could help them.

'Leave this matter with me,' he suggested.

'You'll find out the truth?' she said anxiously.

'I will do what I can.'

'Thank you, sir. Thank you, thank you!'

Tears of gratitude streamed down her face and Gervase felt a surge of sympathy. Beollan, by contrast, was watching him with a mixture of dislike and distrust. Gervase sensed that the boy was hiding something, but this was not the place to try to wrest his secrets from him. A degree of reassurance was all that he could offer at this stage.

'I will make inquiries,' promised Gervase.

'Shall I wait for you here?' she said.

'No, Gytha. My colleagues and I have work to do in the shire hall. I may not be able to look into this matter until much later on. Tell me where you live and I will get a message to you somehow.'

54

She was touched. 'You would do that for me?'

'If it will ease your mind, I will do it with pleasure.'

'You are so kind, sir.'

'I cannot guarantee that I will find out what you want.'

'But you will try. That is all I ask.'

'I will try, Gytha. Very hard.'

She explained where she lived and gave him precise instructions about the route he should take. Gervase listened intently. Struck by her pale beauty, he was also startled by her resemblance to Alys. She had the same blue eyes, the same curve of chin and the same complexion. When he thought how distraught Alys would be if he ever went missing, he had some insight into Gytha's misery. It made him resolve to help her.

'We will go back home directly and wait,' she said.

'Do that,' he counselled. 'God willing, you may even find that your father and brother are there ahead of you.'

There was hope in his voice but none in his heart. Gervase felt certain that she would never see them again.

The excesses of the banquet left no mark on Hugh d'Avranches. He was up at the crack of dawn and riding out with his guests for a morning in the forest. Deer were plentiful. While his huntsmen stalked their quarry with leashed dogs, Hugh and his friends waited in a clearing.

When the deer were sighted, word was sent to the hunting party and they mounted their horses at once. The dogs were taken in a circle to intercept the herd's line of retreat. All three breeds, the lyme, the brachet and the greyhound, were kept on their leashes until the right moment.

Earl Hugh was impatient for action. Holding a lance aloft, he threw out a challenge to his companions.

'I will kill the largest stag of all,' he boasted.

'Only if you get to it first, my lord,' said William Malbank. 'My lance is just as deadly as yours.'

'You could not kill a mouse, let alone a stag.'

'Watch me, my lord.'

55

'Are you so sure of yourself, William?'

'I am, indeed.'

'I admire a man with confidence.'

'Nobody has more than William Malbank.'

'Then you will risk another wager?'

'No,' said the other, checked by the memory of his severe loss on the previous morning. 'There is no need for a wager.'

'Do you have no more mistresses to spare?'

Malbank blenched and the others ridiculed him but the earl stopped the laughter at once with a wave of his lance. Stag-hunting required stealth. He did not want the herd to be frightened away before he had made his first kill.

In the middle distance, one of the huntsmen advanced on foot with a pair of lyme-hounds to drive the deer towards the hunting party. The horn was soon raised and a loud blast echoed through the greenwood. It was the signal they had been waiting for and they did not hesitate. The deer fled, the hounds were released and the chase was on.

For all his bulk, Hugh kept his horse at the front of the pack, slashing at overhanging foliage with his lance and urging his mount into reckless pursuit. The whole forest reverberated with the clamour. Frightened deer darted wildly and baying dogs slowly closed in. Hot blood coursed through the veins of the hunting party. For many of them, the thrill of the chase was enough in itself, but not for Earl Hugh.

He needed a kill to satisfy his bloodlust and no slender deer would content him. Only a stag would suffice. He charged on through the forest with increasing speed until the hounds finally cornered their quarry in a clearing. It was a full-grown stag with huge antlers which it used to jab at the snarling dogs, catching the first to attack and tossing it yards across the grass. But there was no defence against Hugh the Gross. Reining in his horse in front of the beast, he raised his arm and needed only one vicious thrust of the lance to pierce the stag's breast and drain the life out of it.

By the time that William Malbank arrived, the earl had dismounted to stand beside the fallen animal. Huntsmen swiftly leashed the dogs again to prevent them from eating the stag.

'What did I tell you, William?' said Hugh.

'I was a fool even to accept your challenge, my lord.'

'No hunter can ever get the better of me.'

He gave a laugh of celebration but it died in his throat as an arrow suddenly came whistling through the air to miss him by a matter of inches. It buried itself instead in the chest of one of the huntsmen and knocked him off his feet.

The man was killed instantly.

Chapter Five

It was a productive day at the shire hall. The town reeve had everything in readiness for the commissioners and they were able to examine a steady stream of witnesses without delay or interruption. Several minor disputes were settled and they were left with the feeling of having made substantial progress in a relatively short time. More complex cases still awaited them but they seemed less daunting now that such a promising start had been made.

The shire hall itself was very similar in design and construction to the many other places in which they had deliberated. Long, low and airless, its small windows admitted poor light and its sunken floor had undulations which could trip the unwary, but efforts had been made to introduce some elements of comfort for the distinguished visitors. The four chairs behind their long table each had a cushion and a second table bore refreshment in the form of wine, beer and a liberal supply of girdle breads and honey cakes. Candles stood in holders should more illumination be required.

Benches were set out in front of the commissioners for use by the many disputants and witnesses who would be called during their stay in the city. Six of Ralph's men remained on guard at the back of the hall while the remainder took it in turns to provide sentry duty outside the building. Their presence was far more than merely decorative. Past experience had shown that armed soldiers were often needed to subdue an unruly gathering or to separate angry disputants who traded blows. At that first session, however, they were not called upon to provide either service to the commissioners.

Ralph Delchard called an end to the day's judicial work. His headache had finally subsided and his stomach was no longer in rebellion, but he still resisted the temptation to touch any of the refreshment which had been supplied for them. Canon Hubert needed no encouragement to consume all of Ralph's share and most of Brother Simon's as well as his own.

The four of them gathered up their documents and rose to leave the table. Ralph gave a nod of congratulation.

'We have done well,' he announced. 'Let us hope that every day is as painless as this one.'

'It is highly unlikely,' said Hubert.

'Yes,' agreed Gervase. 'When we deal with major disputes where far more is at stake, we are bound to encounter greater difficulties.'

'Nothing that is beyond our capacity to handle,' said Ralph complacently. 'I foresee no real problems.'

'Then you have not studied the cases carefully enough,' Hubert reproved him, slipping the last honey cake into his mouth. 'We will soon be dealing with disputants who have the backing of Earl Hugh and it is an open question whether they accept our authority without protest or simply ignore our judgements and appeal to their master.'

'We speak for the King,' said Ralph firmly. 'Our decisions must be accepted without complaint or resistance.'

'Nobody will surrender land without complaint, my lord.'

'Or pay taxes without resistance,' said Gervase.

'The status of royal commissioners must be respected,' resumed Ralph. 'So far, it has been. Most importantly, by Earl Hugh himself. We must never forget that he is the King's nephew and trusted vassal. Even our headstrong host will surely do nothing to offend his uncle.'

'I would question that presumption,' said Hubert.

'You question everything.'

'I have learned to take nothing for granted, my lord.'

'We have noticed.'

'Someone has to safeguard our interests.'

'That is my task,' said Ralph, stung by the criticism, 'and I perform it with diligence. But I do not make a fetish of suspicion. You spy danger on every side, Hubert. You see peril where none exists. I know how to distinguish petty inconvenience from real threat.'

'We will have our share of both before we are done.'

'Let us not rush to meet adversity,' suggested Gervase, trying to terminate the latest argument between two men whose relationship was uneasy at the best of times. 'Today has seen definite progress. We should be heartened by that.'

'I am, Gervase,' said Brother Simon. 'We have had a most effective and profitable session. I am deeply sorry that we have suspended our work for the day.'

'Why?'

'Because it means that Canon Hubert and I must return to the cathedral to face further torment.'

'Torment?'

'From that turbulent archdeacon from Wales.'

'Do not remind me!' groaned Hubert.

'You could always stay at the castle,' taunted Ralph.

Simon shuddered. 'That would be even worse!'

'Yes,' said Hubert gloomily. 'We are caught between a tyrant and a torturer. Archdeacon Idwal is the lesser of two evils. His oppression is only verbal.'

'And spiritual,' corrected Simon. 'Whenever that madman is near me, my soul shrinks into oblivion.'

'I have the urge to reach for my sword,' said Ralph.

'And I to flee on my donkey,' said Hubert.

Gervase Bret was the only apostate among them. 'Strange!' he remarked. 'Why do you shun him so? I have always rather enjoyed Idwal's company. I like the man.'

Ralph was aghast. 'You *like* him?'

'Incredible!' said Simon.

'Unnatural!' boomed Hubert. 'That voluble Welshman is the human equivalent of the seven plagues of Egypt. How can anyone welcome such suffering?'

61

'You wrong him,' said Gervase stoutly. 'Idwal has many fine qualities and I saw them on display in Herefordshire. He is a true Christian with a profound knowledge of the scriptures. You must not condemn a man because he has a lively mind.'

'It is the lively tongue that we fear,' said Simon. 'It never stops, does it, Canon Hubert?'

'No, Brother Simon. It ripples like the River Dee.'

He led the way through the door and out into the street. It was still afternoon and the bright sunlight made them squint. After a day in the musty shire hall, they found the fresh air bracing. Taking their leave, Hubert and Simon trudged off in the direction of the cathedral, discussing ways in which to avoid the Welsh threat which loomed over them. Ralph dismissed his men then strolled amiably with Gervase towards the castle.

They did not get far. Commotion erupted behind them and they turned to see Earl Hugh, bristling with fury, riding at a canter through the crowd with the hunting party at his back. When he recognised the commissioners, he brought his horse to a halt beside them. They could see the black rage in his eyes.

'What is amiss, my lord?' asked Ralph.

'I was attacked in the forest.'

'By whom?'

'We do not yet know. The assassin eluded us.'

'Assassin?'

'Yes, Ralph,' said the earl, lifting up the arrow that he held in his grasp. 'He aimed this at me. By the grace of God, it missed its target and struck another instead.'

He moved aside to reveal the dead body of the huntsman, slumped across the saddle of the horse behind him and tied into position. Accustomed to return from the Delamere Forest with a plentiful supply of venison, Earl Hugh was livid that all he brought back this time was the corpse of a friend.

'Did you find no trace of the assassin?' said Ralph.

'None. We have searched for the best part of the day.'

'He cannot have vanished into thin air.'

'That is exactly what he did, Ralph,' said Hugh ruefully. 'We hunted high and low. The only signs of life we found were at a cottage some distance away. Two women were weaving baskets. They could not help us. They had seen nothing.'

'Do you have any clues at all, my lord?'

'Only this.' He held up the arrow again. 'It came from a Welsh bow and matches the one that killed my hawk yesterday.'

'Then you hanged the wrong men,' Gervase pointed out.

'What do you mean?'

'If the archer is still at liberty, neither of the men you captured yesterday could have fired the arrow which killed your hawk. They were innocent of the crime.'

'So it appears,' said Ralph.

'Both men carried bows,' argued Hugh.

'Were their quivers full of arrows like that?'

'No,' he grunted. 'But that makes no difference.'

'It does, my lord. They must have paid for a crime they did not actually commit,' concluded Gervase. 'While you were arresting them, the true culprit was making his escape.'

'They deserved to die,' said Hugh angrily. 'What were they doing in Tarvin Hollow, if not poaching my game? Forest law is rigidly enforced. I was right to hang them without wasting time on a trial.'

'Were they Saxon or Welsh?' pressed Gervase.

'Does it matter?'

'A great deal, my lord.'

'In what way?'

'Saxon poachers would not use Welsh arrows in their bows.'

'And honest men would not need to run away as they did,' retorted Hugh, annoyed at being cross-examined in the street. 'Their flight was an admission of guilt and they were rightly hanged. They were lucky. I was lenient.'

'Lenient?'

'Yes, Gervase. Death was mercifully swift. That will not be the case for this Welsh assassin when we finally catch him. As we will,' he vowed. 'He will suffer all the rigours of torture before we burn him alive. Stand back.'

Ralph and Gervase moved aside as Earl Hugh kicked his horse into a trot. The column moved off after him, the dead man hanging limp across his mount, which was towed along by a lead rein. Ralph turned to grin at his companion.

'I think you upset him, Gervase.'

'There was no other choice.'

'What do you mean?'

'I wanted information about those two men he hanged.'

'Why? What is your interest in them?'

Gervase remembered the tears running down Gytha's face. 'I believe I know who they might be.'

Brother Gerold was alone in the chapel, standing before the lectern and reading in silence a passage from the Gospel according to St Matthew. He meditated for a long time on what he had read, searching for a new meaning in words which had become comfortingly familiar over the years but whose depths he had never yet fully plumbed. Gerold was so completely submerged in his study that he did not hear the latch being lifted on the door or see the figure who stepped quietly into the chapel.

Gervase Bret waited until the chaplain closed the Bible and walked back down the nave before moving out to intercept him.

'May I trouble you for advice, Brother Gerold?' he said.

'Well met, Gervase!'

'I need your help.'

'It is yours before you even ask for it.'

'Thank you.'

'Do you seek spiritual guidance, my son?'

'Not exactly,' said Gervase, 'but guidance is involved.'

'Speak on.'

'How far away is Tarvin Hollow?'

'Not far. With a sound horse, a man could probably ride there in under an hour.'

64

'Then that is what I will do,' decided the other. 'Could you give me precise directions? Which road should I take?'

'Hold on a moment,' counselled Gerold. 'Why this rush?'

'I have to honour a promise.'

'To whom?'

'A young woman and her brother. They were waiting at the shire hall this morning and begged our help to find their missing father and brother.'

'Are you in a position to offer that help?'

'I think so, Brother Gerold.'

He explained the circumstances and the monk reached the same conclusion. The two men who were hanged on the pevious day might well be the missing family members. Clearly, neither of them could be the Welsh archer who had apparently fired an arrow at the Earl of Chester. At the worst, the men were poaching and that was normally punishable by blinding or mutilation. It did not merit the violent death forced upon them. Brother Gerold was not simply overcome with compassion. He was ready to give practical assistance.

'I will take you there, Gervase.'

'All the way to Tarvin Hollow?'

'It is heavy news to bear. You might appreciate another pair of hands to share the load.'

'Indeed, I would.'

'Besides,' said Gerold, 'you might easily get lost on your own. Tarvin Hollow is an appreciable distance from the village of Tarvin itself.'

'Gytha lives close to somewhere called Willington.'

'That would be even more difficult to find.'

'Then I need a pathfinder.'

'I am at your disposal, Gervase.'

'Your kindness is overwhelming.'

'The thought of these young people troubles me,' said Gerold. 'They may have suffered a grievous loss. I am used to imparting dread tidings in a way which can lessen the blow. And until their parish priest can be found, Gytha and Beollan may welcome the consolation that I am able to provide.'

65

'Assuredly.'

'Then let us repair to the stables at once, Gervase, and collect our horses. This embassy brooks no delay. You can furnish me with more detail on the journey.'

'I will.'

They left the chapel together. Gervase was delighted. He would not only have someone to lead him through the forest; he would have the opportunity to get to know Brother Gerold better.

Gytha filled the wooden pail with water then began the long trudge from the stream back to the cottage. It was tiring work but it had to be done. Since her mother's death, the chore had fallen to Gytha and she did not complain. As she struggled back through the undergrowth, she tried to convince herself that her father and brother would soon return with a plausible explanation for their long and worrying absence. They may have gone hunting further afield, or been detained at the home of friends, or one of them might have been injured and forced to rest overnight before coming back. It was foolish to fear the worst when all might be well.

They never told her where they were going. Gytha was not supposed to know because they feared that she would fret. When they brought home food for the pot, she realised they had been poaching even though they invented tales of having found a dead rabbit or hare or game bird lying in their path. Gytha was aware of the risks that her father and brother were taking but they had evaded the foresters and verderers for so long that she assumed they would never be caught. They were too wily and skilful at their trade.

Their hovel was a mean dwelling. It was a small, squat building made of rough timber and roofed with thatch. Its single room was divided into two tiny bays by a wooden screen. Five of them had lived in its cramped interior until her mother's untimely death from fever. It was not a home that allowed either privacy or secrets. They were a close family.

When she finally reached the cottage and rested the heavy

pail on the ground, she found Beollan sitting on the grass, absent-mindedly whittling a piece of wood with the knife his father had made for him. The boy was sullen and withdrawn. Since the disappearance of the others, he had hardly spoken a word. Beollan was no longer the noisy younger brother whom Gytha had to control with a mixture of firmness and affection.

'Where have you been?' she asked.

He took a long time to answer and did not look up. 'Nowhere,' he grunted.

'You wandered off earlier.'

'Did I?'

'There are chores, Beollan. I cannot do them all.'

'Why not?'

'Because it's unfair.'

'What am I supposed to do?'

'Help.'

He gave a dismissive shrug. 'Later.'

'We must pull together.'

'Must we?'

'How else will we get through?'

'Get through?'

'We *need* each other.'

The second shrug was a gesture of hopelessness. Gytha softened and went across to give him an involuntary hug. Beollan seemed embarrassed. He looked down at the piece of wood in his hand then tossed it away into the bushes. Rising to his feet, he walked to the door of the cottage but paused when he heard hoofbeats approaching. The knife was now a weapon of defence and he gripped it tightly. Gytha moved to stand beside him and waited for the riders to emerge.

Gervase Bret and Brother Gerold came round the angle of a beech tree on their horses, pleased that they had found their way to the cottage. Beollan remained on the defensive but Gytha ran impulsively towards Gervase.

'Well?' she said. 'Do you have any tidings?'

'All in good time,' he promised, dismounting.

67

'You would not have come otherwise.'

'That is true, Gytha. But first let me introduce Brother Gerold. He has been my guide through the Delamere Forest.'

Gervase made no mention of his companion's position as chaplain at the castle lest she be frightened by his intimate association with Earl Hugh. As it was, she took a step backward and regarded the monk gravely. He was a Norman and that imposed the utmost caution upon Gytha. Notwithstanding his cowl, she viewed him as a natural enemy.

Brother Gerold promptly disarmed her with a soft smile and proof of the ease with which he had mastered her language. His voice was friendly and persuasive.

'Do not be afraid, my child,' he said gently. 'I have come to help you and Beollan. Gervase has told me about your predicament and my heart reaches out to you.'

'Thank you,' she said, moved by his concern.

'We have come to aid the search for your father and brother, Gytha.'

'We have some idea where they may be,' explained Gervase.

'Where?'

'Tarvin Hollow.' Out of the corner of his eye he saw Beollan start. 'Do you know where that is?'

'Of course,' she said.

'Have you searched there already?'

'Close by, but not in the hollow itself.'

'Will you come there with us now, Gytha?'

'What are we going to find?' she said warily.

'Clues,' replied Gervase. 'Clues as to the wherabouts of your father and brother. That is where the trail begins.'

'How do you know?'

'I kept my word. I made inquiries for you.'

Gytha needed only a second to make up her mind. 'We will both come,' she decided. 'Beollan will lead the way because he knows the forest paths even better than me.'

The boy was a reluctant guide but his sister scolded him until he agreed to help. Expecting to walk all the way, Gytha was astonished when Gervase took her by the waist and hoisted her up on to the saddle of his mount, clambering back up behind her to hold the reins. She had never been on a horse before, still less had such courtesy shown to her by a royal agent. Her nervousness was matched by a strange feeling of privilege.

Beollan spurned the offer of riding with Brother Gerold and instead set off at a steady trot. It was like following a young dog. The boy went scampering off through the forest and took them through its labyrinthine interior with sure-footed confidence. Without him they would never have been able to find such a complicated route through the undergrowth.

Gytha said nothing but Gervase could feel the warmth of her body and sense her excitement. The ride on the horse might somehow help to distract her a little from the bad news which he suspected might lie ahead for her. Beollan, too, anticipated grim tidings. Fifty yards or so short of Tarvin Hollow, he came to a halt and refused to go any further.

'Take us all the way,' she ordered.

'No, Gytha.'

'What is wrong with you?'

'I will stay here,' he said.

'Why? What are you afraid of?'

'Leave this to us,' advised Gervase.

He and Brother Gerold dismounted and went forward on foot. They came to a large clearing, beyond which was the deep hollow which gave the place its name. But it was not the depression in the ground which caught their attention. Both noticed the marks on an overhanging bough where something had chafed the bark. They exchanged a glance and moved in closer.

Dried blood covered the ground beneath the bough and there were signs of something being dragged off in the direction of a nearby ditch. The two men followed the trail with tentative steps. They soon found what they sought and feared.

'Dear God in heaven!' said Gerold, crossing himself.

'May the Lord have mercy on their souls!'

The bodies were lying in the ditch at unnatural angles. Both were covered with ugly wounds and sodden with blood. The faces were hideous masks, distorted by the manner of their deaths then attacked by forest vermin. One man's eyes had been pecked out, the other's nose had been nibbled off. They were less like human faces than pieces of raw meat.

Gervase's first thought was for the orphans. 'I'll cover them up,' he said. 'Gytha and Beollan must not be allowed to see them in this state. It would be cruel.'

Chapter Six

Hugh d'Avranches rolled the jewelled cup between his palms and gazed down at his wine as if searching for something in its liquid heart. He was seated alone in the hall at the castle, reflecting on the events of the day and considering what response he should make to them. Anger had now hardened into bitter recrimination. Though he accepted that he was a natural target for assassination, whether from motives of envy, hatred or political expediency, he was highly indignant that an attempt had actually been made on his life. Years of unchallenged power on the Welsh border had given him the feeling that he was utterly invulnerable. One arrow had destroyed that illusion.

The Earl of Chester was human, after all.

When their master was in such a black mood, his servants knew better than to disturb him, but one had the courage to knock on the door and let himself in. He conducted Ralph Delchard into the hall and coughed discreetly to attract Earl Hugh's attention.

'My lord,' he said, keeping just out of reach. There was no reply. He raised his voice a little. 'Forgive this interruption, my lord.'

His words still went unheard. Earl Hugh was far too preoccupied. Ralph dismissed the servant with a wave and the man scurried away gratefully, closing the door behind him with a bang which echoed through the hall. Hugh did not even look up. Ralph walked round the table to stand in front of his host and waited until his presence was finally registered.

71

Earl Hugh was not at his most sociable. 'Well?' he growled.

'I came to offer you my sympathy, my lord,' said Ralph.

'Sympathy?'

'And support. I know what it is to lose a good man in a cowardly attack. If there is anything I may do to help, you have only to call on me.'

'Thank you.'

'My knights are at your command, should you need them.'

'I have no shortage of soldiers, Ralph,' said the other. 'Hundreds will come running to my call. But I cannot deploy them against an invisible enemy. That archer disappeared as if he had never existed.'

'His escape must have been planned in advance.'

'How did he know I would be in that part of the forest? That is what baffles me. I was pursuing a stag. It was pure chance that I finished up where I did.'

'But you would have been easy to track, my lord.'

'Easy?'

'The noise of the chase must have been heard a mile away.'

'True.'

'Someone stalked you. Yet he could not have done so on foot. Only a horse could have kept up with the speed of the hunt. Did your men see any sign of a stray animal when they searched?'

'They neither saw nor heard another horse.'

'Then how did the assassin come and go so quickly?'

'Sorcery!'

'There is no such thing, my lord.'

'What other explanation is there?' Earl Hugh drained the wine at a gulp then reached for the flagon to replenish his cup. He indicated the chair opposite and Ralph sat down. It was time to examine the outrage with cold objectivity. Lust for revenge needed to be muffled.

'Has such an attack been made on you before?' asked Ralph.

'Never.'

'And you had no warning?'

'None.'

'How often do you hunt in the Delamere Forest?'

'Almost every day.'

'Without incident?'

'Invariably,' said Hugh. 'Whether I go hawking or hunting, I always bring back plenty of game. Nobody dares to interfere with my sport. The forest is mine to play in all day.'

'How many of you rode out today?'

'Forty or fifty.'

'You were well protected, then.'

'I am my own best protection.'

'What happened yesterday?'

'Yesterday?'

'Your hawk was killed by an arrow,' Ralph reminded him. 'The same archer may have stalked you today. Take me through the events of yesterday. How many of you were in the party on that occasion? Where exactly did the archer strike? What was his avowed purpose?'

'To ruin a day's hawking.'

'But why kill your hawk when he could just as easily have aimed his arrow at you? And how did he escape, as he must have done if he was back today with his deadly bow? I need more detail, my lord.'

Hugh regarded him through narrowed lids for a long while. 'Then you will have it,' he decided eventually.

Ralph leaned forward in his chair and listened with the utmost concentration as his host recounted in copious detail what had transpired on the previous day. Hugh moved on to describe the foul murder which had disturbed that morning's stag hunt. The parallels were clear.

'You are right,' concluded Ralph. 'The same archer was almost certainly involved on both occasions.'

'There will not be a third,' said Hugh grimly.

'I hope not, my lord.'

'We will track down this Welsh assassin.'

'Perhaps,' said Ralph thoughtfully, 'but I am not entirely convinced that he hails from across the border.'

'You saw the arrow. It came from a Welsh bow.'

'But the weapon could just as easily have been held by a Saxon,' argued Ralph. 'Or a Dane. Or even a Norman. What better way to throw suspicion on to someone else?'

'What are you saying?'

'That there is one simple reason why you were unable to find this phantom Welshman. He does not exist. The man who fired those arrows was not lying in wait in the forest, my lord. You may have taken him with you.'

'In the hunting party?'

'Yes,' reasoned the other. 'In a group as large as that, it would not have been difficult for one man to detach himself and shoot an arrow from a concealed position.'

'That never crossed my mind.'

'Give it due consideration now, my lord.'

'One of my own friends?' said Hugh, trying to adjust his mind to the possibility. 'No, you are mistaken, Ralph. I know them all. They are loyal to a man. That assassin was Welsh.'

'Or a Norman in the pay of the Welsh.'

'I refuse to believe it.'

'Look to your entourage,' advised Ralph. 'It may yet contain the cunning archer. When your men began their search, they would not have looked for one of their own. No sorcery was involved here, my lord. The assassin simply made you all look in the wrong direction.'

Earl Hugh pondered for several minutes before reaffirming his view with a shake of his head. None of his men betrayed him. He would not even entertain the possibility.

'Who was the murder victim?' asked Ralph.

'Raoul Lambert, my finest huntsman.'

'I know that name. Does he hold land in the forest?'

'He did,' said Hugh. 'Raoul was one of my tenants with substantial holdings within the bounds of Delamere and beyond. He gave sterling service and I always reward that generously.'

'Some of his property was in dispute.'

'Raoul had a legal right to every acre in his possession.'

'The Church claims otherwise.'

'It would.'

'If memory serves me,' said Ralph, scratching his head, 'this same Raoul Lambert was due to be called before us tomorrow to dispute the matter with Archdeacon Frodo. It seems an odd coincidence that he should be the man who was killed.'

'Are you suggesting that Frodo fired the arrow?'

'Of course not, my lord. But the death of Raoul Lambert may well advantage the Church. Where is the body now?'

'In the mortuary.'

'Has it been examined by a physician?'

'Yes,' said Hugh, 'but he has told us nothing that we did not know already. The arrow pierced Raoul's heart. Death was almost instantaneous.'

'What reason would someone have to kill him?'

'None whatsoever, Ralph. He was a popular man, liked and respected by all. But, then, he was not the intended victim. His death was purely accidental.'

'Was it?'

'The arrow was aimed at me.'

'Are you certain?'

'It passed within inches.'

'Only because you stood so close to Raoul Lambert.'

'Someone tried to assassinate me,' insisted Hugh.

'That may be so,' said Ralph, 'but there are two questions that still need to be answered. The first is this. If Raoul Lambert was an accidental victim, why was the arrow aimed so accurately at his heart?'

Hugh was jolted. Hauling himself to his feet, he glowered across the table at his guest. Ralph was telling him things which he did not wish to hear. His pride was wounded by the suggestion that he might not, after all, have been the target for an assassin's arrow. It was a species of insult.

'What is the second question?' he demanded.

75

'Only a skilful archer could pick off a hawk in mid-air in the way that you have described. Do you agree?'

'Yes.'

'Then ask yourself this, my lord,' said Ralph, running an eye over Hugh's massive frame. 'When he can shoot an arrow with such unerring accuracy at a small bird, why does he miss the much larger and easier target which you present?'

As soon as they saw Brother Gerold walking towards them, they knew that some terrible discovery had been made. Each reacted in a quite different way. Gytha immediately lunged forward and tried to run past the monk, but he caught her by the wrist to detain her. Beollan, by contrast, slunk back to the bushes where the horses had been tethered. His sister's urge to see what they had found was offset by his unwillingness to confront a hideous truth. The boy was smouldering with guilt.

Gytha tried to break away from Brother Gerold's grasp.

'Let me go,' she pleaded.

'In a moment, my child.'

'Have you found them?'

'We believe so.'

'Where are they?'

'You will see them in a moment.'

'I have a right,' she argued. 'Leave go of me. They are my father and my brother.'

'You may not recognise them as such.'

His words were gentle but they had the force of a blow. Gytha stopped struggling and backed away. He released her wrist. She brought both hands to her face in horror then steeled herself to know the worst.

'Dead?' she whispered.

'I fear so.'

'*Both* of them?'

'Unhappily, yes.'

'Why?'

'They were in the wrong place at the wrong time.'

'How were they killed?'

'Unkindly.'

He glanced over his shoulder to see Gervase beckoning him forward. Taking the girl by the arm, he led her slowly into the clearing and across to the ditch. Gytha mustered what little composure she could. Beollan shadowed them cautiously.

Gervase had worked quickly. Ferns had been used to cover the faces and chests of the two corpses, obscuring the worst of the mutilation. A fallen branch had been placed across the right leg of the older man to hide the fact that the limb had all but been hacked off. Gervase stood in the ditch between the two supine figures as Gytha and Beollan approached.

She forced herself to look down at the scene below. It was definitely her father and brother. Enough of their bloodied attire was still visible to make identification certain. Gervase held up a knife with a long blade.

'I found this on one of them. Do you recognise it?'

'My father's,' she whispered.

'I feared that it might be.'

'Who did this to them?' she wailed.

'I believe that they were caught poaching, Gytha.'

'We can look into that at a later stage,' said Gerold, taking charge and putting a consoling arm around the girl. 'We have found them, that is the main thing, and we can now arrange for them to have a Christian burial instead of being left out here in the forest. Come, my child,' he said, turning her away from the ditch. 'You have seen enough. Be brave. You are the head of the family now. Be strong for your brother.'

Gytha nodded and wept silently in his arms. With words of comfort, Gerold escorted her in the direction of the horses. Gervase was glad that he had brought the chaplain with him. His help was invaluable in every way. Gerold was schooled in the arts of consolation.

Beollan ventured close enough to take one glance at the dead bodies then moved hastily away. Gervase went after him. The boy's behaviour aroused his curiosity. There was no real surprise in Beollan's face when he viewed the corpses.

He seemed to be getting visual confirmation of something he already knew.

Gervase caught up with him and put a hand on his arm. 'One moment, Beollan.'

The boy spun round and stared at him with suspicion. 'What do you want?' he mumbled.

'Information.'

'I know nothing.'

'I think you do,' said Gervase quietly. 'And it may help us to understand what actually happened here.'

A frightened look came into the boy's eye. After a glance at the ditch where the bodies lay, he turned on his heel and tried to run away, but Gervase was far too quick for him. Grabbing him firmly by the shoulders, he eased Beollan behind the trunk of an oak tree so that their conversation was neither seen nor overheard and forced the boy to face him.

'Now,' he said, 'let us have the truth, Beollan.'

'I can't help you.'

'You can and we both know it.'

'No,' Beollan protested. 'No, no, no!'

'Do not be afraid of me. Whatever you tell me, you will not be in any danger. I have no wish to report you or see you punished. Your family has suffered enough. For Gytha's sake, the truth must come out.' He released the boy. 'Have you told her yet?'

'No.'

'Why not?'

Beollan studied the ground and shifted his feet.

'Why not?' pressed Gervase. There was a long pause. 'In that case, I will tell you. I think that you were with them yesterday. With your father and brother when they went out poaching.'

'They were not poaching,' protested Beollan. 'Nor was I.'

'Then what were the three of you doing?'

'Going for a walk.'

'Do not lie to me, Beollan.'

'I'm not.'

'And look at me when you speak.'

'I don't have to say anything.'

'No,' agreed Gervase. 'You can hold your tongue as you've done so far and what will that achieve? Nothing. You'll be eaten up with shame and guilt. And your sister will suffer the terrible pain of not knowing how and why your father and brother met their deaths.' He knelt down to look up into the boy's face. 'Is that what you want?'

Beollan bit his lips and shook his head slowly.

'Gytha will have to look after you from now on. It would be cruel to keep the truth from her.'

The boy said nothing but his resolve was gradually weakening.

'Let me say what I believe happened,' continued Gervase. 'Your father and brother went out poaching yesterday. Times are hard. The harvest was poor. There is no other way of getting enough food for the family. You went with them.'

'I did not!'

'You went with them to act as their lookout.'

'No!'

'When they were caught, you saw everything.'

The boy issued another stream of denials then burst into tears. Gervase put a soothing arm round him. Beollan's defences began to crumble.

'I told you,' whispered Gervase, 'you're safe. I'm your friend. Whatever you tell me is between the two of us. I will not report you to anyone for taking part in poaching. For that is what you did, Beollan, didn't you?'

His nod was almost imperceptible but Gervase saw it.

'What happened?' he coaxed.

'I was . . . their lookout.'

'And?'

'I let them down.'

'No, Beollan.'

'I did. When the hunting party came, I took fright and fled. I should have stayed with them in their hiding place.'

79

'Thank God you did not,' said Gervase sadly, 'or you might well have ended up in that ditch with them.'

'I ran. I ran away. I feel so *ashamed*.'

'There is no need.'

'My place was beside them.'

'You did the right thing. You saved your life at a time when you could not possibly have rescued them.' He cupped the boy's chin in his hand. 'Now, Beollan. Did one of them shoot an arrow at Earl Hugh's hawk?'

'No. They would never have dared to do that.'

'Are you sure?'

'Quite sure. Quite sure.'

'Then who did kill that hawk?'

'I do not know, but . . .' His voice trailed away and his feet betrayed him again.

'Go on, Beollan.'

'I thought I saw someone else leaving.'

'Someone else?'

'Running off through the trees,' the boy recalled. 'I have no idea who it was. I only caught a glimpse. But I did see a bow. Yes, there was a bow, I remember that.' He gave an involuntary shudder. 'Then my father and brother were captured. When I heard them yelling for mercy, I ran home as fast as I could.' More tears threatened. 'I was weak. I was a coward. I should have stayed to help.'

'They were beyond it,' said Gervase.

'Gytha will blame me.'

'No, Beollan. She will understand.'

Nothing more could be wrested from the boy. Gervase gave him a comforting hug then led him back to the others. Brother Gerold had managed to ease Gytha's grief and she had lapsed into a wistful silence. The chaplain read the message in the boy's face and donated a smile of approval to Gervase. Their journey to the Delamere Forest had not been in vain. Solace had been offered to two orphans.

'Who is your priest?' asked the chaplain.

'Father Ernwin,' murmured Gytha.

80

'A sound man. I know him well. Leave everything to me. When we have escorted you back, I will go to Father Ernwin and tell him what has occurred. He will send a cart to collect the bodies so that they can be buried at your parish church.' He flicked a sad glance back at the ditch. 'Their gruesome death is of no account now. It is past. Put it out of your minds. They deserve a proper funeral and I will ensure that they receive one.'

'Thank you,' said Gytha.

Beollan gave a low murmur of gratitude.

It was time to go home.

Robert de Limesey strolled round the perimeter of the cathedral in the twilight and stopped to inspect the day's progress on the exterior wall of the chancel. The last of the stonemasons was descending the scaffold with his tools and he gave the bishop a respectful wave of farewell. Robert smiled in reply. He was blessed in his craftsmen. They were skilled artisans with a due reverence for the project in which they had been engaged for so long.

Bishop Robert was still appraising their work when he heard footsteps approaching and caught an unpleasant whiff in his nostrils. He turned to see Idwal coming towards him.

'Good evening, Bishop Robert,' said the Welshman.

'I am pleased to see you again,' lied the other. 'Have you had a busy day, Archdeacon Idwal?'

'My days are always busy. The devil makes work for idle hands so mine are never allowed to be idle. I have been finding my way around this beautiful city of yours and speaking to some of its citizens. In vain, alas.'

'In vain?'

'Yes, Bishop Robert,' complained Idwal. 'They did not seem to understand how much better off Chester would be if it were part of Wales, which, by right, of course, it should be.'

'Only in your opinion.'

'It is not a question of opinion but of geography.'

'I believe that it is a question of conquest.'

81

The firm rebuff actually silenced Idwal for once. Robert basked in the respite but it did not last long. Wrapping his disgusting cloak around him, the visitor turned his attention to the cathedral.

'Do you have rich endowments?' he said artlessly.

'Alas, no.'

'Wealthy patrons?'

'Very few.'

'Where, then, does your money come from, Bishop Robert?'

'Rents and the offertory box. I hold over fifty houses in the city and this eastern suburb around the cathedral. It is called the bishop's borough and is part of Redcliff, so named because of the red sandstone cliff on which the cathedral stands. There are other small sources of income,' he said evasively, 'but nobody could describe us as prosperous.'

'What of holy relics?'

'One or two.'

'Any of particular note?'

'Nothing that would interest a Welshman like yourself. If you seek the bones of St Deiniol or the skull of St David, you will have to go back over the border.'

Idwal gave a ripe chuckle. 'I will do that very soon.'

'When?' asked Robert, eager to speed him on his way.

'When I am ready.'

'In a day? Two days? Three?'

'Who knows, Bishop Robert?' said the other with a wicked grin. 'You and Frodo have made me so welcome that it will be an effort to tear myself away. And I can hardly deprive Canon Hubert of our theological contests. He thrives on them.'

'Hubert is in Chester on important business.'

'So am I, believe me. So am I.'

Idwal flung back his cloak and went off towards the main door of the cathedral with an arrogant strut. Bishop Robert found an expletive rising to his lips and clapped a hand over his mouth. The laws of Christian fellowship had to be obeyed.

The Welshman, meanwhile, walked slowly down the nave of the cathedral to make sure that he was quite alone. When he stopped under the chancel arch, he could hear and see nobody. Evening shadows dappled the aisle behind him and darkened the outer corners of the building. Idwal smirked. He was on his own in the house of the Lord.

After genuflecting to the altar, he moved swiftly across to the door of the vestry and lifted the latch. A single candle burned within and cast an inviting glow over a large wooden casket which stood against the wall. Idwal rubbed his hands together and went over to the casket, stroking its weathered lid with an almost paternal affection. There was a key in the lock and he turned it firmly.

Before he could lift the lid, however, someone came out of the gloom behind him to subject him to an accusatory glare.

'What are you looking for, archdeacon?' asked Frodo.

Idwal was unperturbed. He patted the casket gently.

'God,' he said.

Chapter Seven

Brother Gerold was an accomplished horseman. As they rode back to Chester in the fading light, Gervase was highly impressed with the way that his companion handled his mount. Canon Hubert invariably travelled on his donkey, his bulk dwarfing the beast and his feet all but touching the ground. Brother Simon always rode his spindly horse with excessive nervousness as if it was the first time he had ever been near the animal. It was refreshing to find one Benedictine monk who was patently at ease in the saddle.

When they joined the main road to the city, they were riding at a steady canter. The great, dark, sprawling Forest of Delamere slowly receded behind them.

'Thank you for taking me there,' he said.

'It was you who took *me*, Gervase.'

'I would never have found my way without you.'

'I was glad to help,' said the other. 'When two young people are in such distress as Gytha and Beollan, they need all the succour they can get.'

'How will they manage?'

'Who knows? But they will somehow.'

'Will they?'

'Yes, Gervase. They are forest dwellers. Survivors.'

'Their father and brother were forest dwellers as well. They did not survive. They were the victims of misfortune.'

'So it seems.'

'They violated forest law but they did not deserve the treatment which was handed out to them.'

85

'No man deserves to suffer that butchery.'

Gervase forbore to point out that it was the chaplain's master who had been responsible for the summary execution of the two men. Brother Gerold's position at the castle made for a slight awkwardness between them. While he had shown great compassion to two young people in a dire situation, his loyalty was owed to Earl Hugh. In the circumstances, Gervase found it very difficult to express himself as freely as he would have wished. He chafed in silence.

Brother Gerold seemed to read his mind. Glancing across at Gervase, he nodded sadly.

'Earl Hugh can be harsh at times,' he admitted.

'This went beyond the bounds of harshness.'

'He realises that now.'

Gervase was surprised. 'Does he?'

'I believe so.'

'Do you have any proof of that, Brother Gerold.'

'Not in the sense that you would understand it,' replied Brother Gerold. 'But I am closer to the earl than anyone. I will not betray the secrets of the confessional but this I can tell you. Earl Hugh is no stranger to feelings of contrition.'

'Such feelings come rather late in the day.'

'Granted.'

'Two men died because of his anger.'

'He is learning to control it.'

'How many others have been victims of his rage?'

'I am his chaplain and not his keeper, Gervase. There are some areas of his life in which I have no right to interfere. Earl Hugh is a fearless soldier and brutal action is sometimes necessary in combat. He would not have established peace on the frontier if he had not been such a forceful commander.'

'Are you trying to excuse him, Brother Gerold?'

'No,' said the other. 'I merely point out that he has been forced to behave with a degree of savagery by the situation in which he finds himself. The same might be said of the King himself. What you call rage is often no more than a soldier's bold response to danger.'

86

'That was not the case yesterday.'

'Perhaps not.'

'You saw those bodies,' Gervase reminded him. 'Those men were not assassins who threatened his life. They were simple souls whose only concern was to provide food for their family. Hanging them was a barbaric enough punishment. Why did they have to be mutilated in that way?'

'It was reprehensible.'

'Supposing that Gytha or her brother had found the bodies in that state? What effect would it have had on them?'

'A disastrous one.'

'Their lives have been shattered as it is,' said Gervase. 'Think how much worse it would be for them if they had to carry such gruesome memories inside their minds for the rest of their days. It would be unbearable.'

'You were right to cover the bodies, Gervase.'

'I could not disguise the fact that they were dead.'

'Or the cause of that death.'

'Yet you claim that Earl Hugh is contrite?'

'I say that he is not as uncaring as he may appear. Yes,' Brother Gerold added with a wry smile, 'I know I am trying to defend what you consider to be indefensible but there has been marked progress. Earl Hugh is a God-fearing man. That may not always be the face which he offers to the world but it is there.'

It was an extraordinary claim to make. Gervase suppressed the cynical comment which rose to mind and spoke instead in a judiciously neutral tone.

'I will have to take your word for it.'

'You may see direct evidence in time.'

'I am bound to doubt that.'

'In your position, I would feel the same.'

'My position imposes certain limitations on me.'

'Limitations?'

'Earl Hugh is our host,' said Gervase apologetically. 'It is not really my place to accuse him.'

'Those two dead bodies were an accusation in themselves.

87

I sympathise with your feelings and admire your restraint. Do not worry, Gervase,' said the chaplain, turning to look at him. 'I will not carry tales back to the castle.'

'I never thought that you would, Brother Gerold.'

They rode on in silence for a while. When the city finally came in sight, the chaplain was jerked out of his meditations, and fished gently for enlightenment.

'What did he tell you?' he asked.

'Who?'

'Beollan.'

'Very little.'

'I saw you take him behind that tree to talk in private. The boy knew far more than he pretended. Did you contrive to draw any of it out of him?'

'I need more time to win his confidence.'

'I think you did that extremely well, Gervase. Come,' he said in an almost jocular tone. 'There is no need for you to protect the boy. I will not harm him.'

'I never thought that you would.'

'Do you fear that I might betray him to Earl Hugh?'

'No, Brother Gerold.'

'Then why hide from me what I can already guess?'

'And what is that?'

'Beollan was involved,' said the other. 'When his father and brother went poaching, they probably took him along as their lookout. That is what the boy strove to conceal: the fact that he was there yesterday.'

'He *should* have been there,' said Gervase.

'But?'

'He became scared and ran away.'

'Who could blame him for that?'

'He blames himself, Brother Gerold.'

'Did you assuage his guilt?'

'Only partially.'

'What else did he tell you?'

Gervase hesitated for a moment then plunged straight in. 'He saw someone else sneaking away from the scene.'

'An archer?'

'Yes. The one thing he does remember is the bow.'

'Did he describe the man?'

'He barely got a glimpse.'

'But he saw enough to exonerate his father and brother. They would never have been so foolish or audacious as to kill Earl Hugh's favourite hawk. He doted on that bird.'

'He made that clear.'

'Two human lives are not a fair exchange for the death of a hawk. Especially when the two men in question were innocent of the charge. They paid dearly for someone else's crime.' He became brisk. 'I will not divulge this intelligence to Earl Hugh. He would immediately send for Beollan to question him more rigorously and the boy would not withstand such scrutiny. It would be wrong to subject him to it. Beollan is quite safe. Tell him that.'

'Tell him?'

'When you next visit their cottage.'

'I have no plans to do so, Brother Gerold.'

'Oh, I think you have.'

Gervase blushed. The chaplain had read his mind again.

Ralph Delchard left Earl Hugh still brooding in the hall and made his way down to the bailey. Torches had been lit to ward off the dusk and there was a smell of acrid smoke. His men were lodged in some of the huts used by the garrison and Ralph sought out his captain to discuss a number of matters with him. Some of the men were leaving the castle in search of pleasure in one of the city's many inns. Ralph waved them off. In earlier days he might have gone with them, but marriage had mercifully ended that rudderless period of his existence when he was hopelessly adrift. Golde had given him a purpose in life. It was one of the many things for which he was indebted to her.

When he found his captain, they needed only a few minutes to complete their business. The man had overheard the gossip from soldiers who had accompanied the hunting party that morning and Ralph listened to it with keen ears. He was given a slightly different perspective on events from the one which the earl himself had provided, though the central facts did not alter. Everyone believed that the assassin's arrow had been destined for Hugh d'Avranches.

Ralph was making his way back across the courtyard when a strident voice hailed him from behind.

'My lord! My lord!'

Recognising the voice, Ralph quickened his pace at once.

'Wait for me!' howled Idwal. 'My lord!'

Ralph tried to ignore him but the Welshman would not be denied. Breaking into a trot, he overhauled the other and stood directly in front of him with a broad grin.

'Do you remember me, my lord?' he asked.

'Only too well!'

'Idwal, Archdeacon of St David's.'

'You were at Llandaff when we last met.'

'I have been called to a higher authority.'

'Then do not let me hold you up,' said Ralph, trying to push past him and finding his arm seized in a strong grip. 'What are you doing, man? Release me at once.'

'Only when you agree to help me, my lord.'

'Help you?'

'In the name of friendship.' Idwal let go of Ralph's arm and grinned inanely. 'There – I knew that you would agree.'

'I have agreed to nothing.'

'All I ask from you is one little favour.'

'There is one *big* favour I would ask of you, Idwal.'

The archdeacon cackled. 'You still have your sense of humour, I see. *Diu!* It is good to see you again after all this time. I have already met Canon Hubert and Brother Simon. They could not believe their good fortune when I popped up in front of them. Is Gervase with you still?'

'Yes.'

'A studious young man. I admire him tremendously.'

'So do I.'

'As much as a Welshman can admire a foreigner, that is.' A sly smile touched his lips. 'While we are on the topic of admiration, my lord, what happened to that charming lady whom we met in Hereford? What was her name?'

'Golde,' said Ralph.

'That was it. Golde. A woman of independence.' The smile spread itself. 'Though I suspect that she may no longer enjoy quite so much independence.'

'She is now my wife.'

Idwal clapped his hands. 'I knew it! I saw the first stirrings of interest on both sides. I sensed that there was a deep bond between you. I am never wrong about such things. Praise the Lord! These are wonderful tidings! You have my warmest congratulations, my lord.'

'Thank you,' said Ralph uncomfortably.

'I know what it is to enjoy connubial bliss.'

Ralph refused to accept that Idwal's wife would say the same.

'My only regret is that this romance did not burgeon in Hereford itself. Then I could have had the privilege of joining you and Golde in holy matrimony.'

Ralph was appalled at the suggestion. Instead of blessing their union, the garrulous archdeacon would have put a curse upon it. He became brusque.

'You spoke of a favour.'

'Yes, my lord,' said the other conspiratorially. 'It concerns Hugh, Earl of Chester.'

'In what way?'

'He refuses to speak to me.'

'I can understand why,' muttered Ralph.

'He will not even admit me to his presence and it is vital that I see him as soon as possible. I need his permission to speak with the prisoner.'

'Gruffydd ap Cynan?'

'The same, my lord,' said Idwal, suddenly frothing with righteous indignation. 'Apart from anything else, I wish to protest against the irreverent treatment of the Prince of Gwynedd. Royal blood flows in his veins. Yet he is kept in a dungeon like a wild animal in a cage.'

91

'He is held hostage, Idwal.'

'That does not mean he has to be so abused.'

'How do you know that he is?'

'There is little that affects a Welsh prince that I do not learn about sooner or later. Please, my lord. Speak on my behalf to Earl Hugh. Plead our case. All I am asking is an hour alone with Gruffydd ap Cynan.'

'Then you ask in vain.'

'Why?'

'He would never leave you alone with a prisoner,' said Ralph. 'No more would I or anyone else who exercised simple caution. Any visit would be carefully supervised. If you were left alone with Gruffydd ap Cynan, you might supply him with a weapon or plot his escape.'

Idwal was shocked. 'Would *I* do either of those things?'

'Given the opportunity, you would do both.'

'Calumny!'

'Common sense!'

'I am a man of honour.'

'The word has a wholly different meaning in that gibbering nonsense you call the Welsh language.'

'Gibbering nonsense!' Idwal was outraged. 'Welsh is an ancient and beautiful language, my lord. Our word for honour is *anrhydedd* and it carries great significance in my country. It stands for integrity, for allegiance to moral principles. Celts are the most honourable people on earth.'

'That would not stop you trying to rescue the prisoner.'

'It would never cross my mind.'

'Why else go to see him?'

'To talk to him, comfort him, pass on messages of support.'

'And take out orders for members of his army.'

'Never, my lord.'

'You are wasting your time, Idwal.'

'Then you will not act as my ambassador?'

'There is no point,' explained Ralph. 'Earl Hugh does not look favourably upon the Welsh nation at any time but, at this precise moment, he is more prejudiced against it than ever. When he was hunting in the forest this morning, someone fired an arrow which only just missed him. He believes that the would-be assassin was a Welshman.'

Idwal's ears pricked up. 'Was the earl injured?'

'Not physically. But his pride was badly lacerated. He is certainly in no mood to grant favours to anyone from across the border. My advice would be to delay your request until he has calmed down again.'

'Sage counsel. I'll obey it.'

'Then I can be excused.'

'Not so fast, my lord,' said Idwal, plucking at his sleeve. 'Our paths have not crossed for such a long time. I would like to know what has befallen you since we parted in Hereford. Apart from your fortunate marriage, that is. And you, I am sure, are anxious to hear my news.'

'I dream of nothing else,' said Ralph sardonically.

Idwal beamed. 'In that case, I'll begin . . .'

'Another time.'

And Ralph fled the field like the most craven deserter.

Darkness was starting to fall with more conviction by the time they reached the castle and they needed the help of the flaming torches to pick their way across to the stables. Ostlers took charge of their horses. They stretched themselves to ease their aching limbs. As he walked across the bailey with the chaplain, Gervase Bret had to stifle a yawn.

'Thank you again, Brother Gerold,' he said.

'I was glad to be of assistance,' said the other. 'And it was a pleasure to see Father Ernwin again, albeit in such sad circumstances. He will sustain Gytha and Beollan through this desperate period.'

'And the bodies will be buried in consecrated ground.'

'Father Ernwin gave us his word.'

'I was much reassured after speaking with him.'

'He will know what to do.'

93

Gerold came to a halt near a torch and studied his companion's umbered face with shrewd eyes. Gervase became slightly self-conscious.

'What is the matter?' he said.

'You look pale and drawn, my friend.'

'I am fine.'

'This has been a strain for you. Go and rest.'

'I could say the same to you, Brother Gerold.'

'Grief is an almost daily element in my life. It does not oppress me in the way that it did when I was younger. I have learned to withstand its crushing power and to lessen its hold over the minds of others.'

'That is a rare gift.'

'I am always happy when I can use it,' said Gerold.

'Gytha was profoundly grateful to you.'

'She should have been thanking you instead, Gervase.'

'Me?'

'You were the one who listened to her plea.'

'I was moved by their plight.'

'So was I,' said the chaplain, 'but I would have been unable to relieve their minds without Gervase Bret. He was my passport.'

'Passport?'

'To that stricken family. Had they known that I was chaplain at the castle and in the service of Earl Hugh, they would not have let me within a hundred yards of them. It was the earl who caused those two deaths. I would have been tainted with his actions.' He squeezed Gervase's shoulder. 'You enabled me to get close to Gytha and her brother because they trusted you.'

'I hope so.'

This time the yawn would not be denied. Gervase brought a hand up to his mouth but it was far too late. Gerold smiled.

'Let us part. You, to your bed: me, to my duties.'

'At this late hour?'

'The chapel never closes.'

'When do you find time to sleep?'

'When nobody else is watching me.'

He stole quietly away until his black cowl merged with the darkness. Gervase headed for the keep and a well-earned rest. The journey to and from the forest had been taxing and he was still jangled by the discovery they had made in the ditch. But there were consolations to be drawn. The chaplain was turning out to be a valuable friend and Gytha's resemblance to the lovely Alys grew stronger every time that Gervase looked at the girl. Without quite knowing why, he certainly did want to see her again.

Brother Gerold, meanwhile, let himself into the chapel and closed the door gently behind him. A solitary candle burned on the altar, its tiny flame illumining little more than the crucifix beside it and a patch of the white altar cloth. Everything else was shrouded in darkness. Gerold knew at once that he was not alone. He waited beside the door and listened until he heard the sound of breathing. As his eyes gradually became accustomed to the blackness, he moved forward warily down the aisle. His caution was justified. Long before he got anywhere near the pale circle of light on the altar, his toe met an obstruction.

He knelt down until he could pick out the contours of the figure lying prone on the cold floor. The sheer size of the man confirmed his identity. Hugh d'Avranches, Earl of Chester, was stretched out in an attitude of total submission. His breath came in shallow bursts as if he were in some kind of pain. Gerold was not surprised. He said nothing, but remained kneeling patiently beside the huge body until his master finally spoke to him.

'Brother Gerold?'

'Yes, my lord?'

'Where have you been?' hissed Earl Hugh.

'On an errand of mercy.'

'Where?'

'Outside the city.'

'We needed you here.'

'I am back now.'

'My wants are paramount.'

'I am here to see to them, my lord.'

95

'Only you can help me, Brother Gerold.'

'It is God who comes to your aid. Through me.'

'I need Him mightily.'

The massive figure came to life and crawled forward towards the altar rail. The chaplain knew what to do. He moved swiftly to the vestry. A few minutes later, he was standing in front of the single candle and holding a piece of unleavened bread between his fingers.

'*Accipe, frater, Corporis Domini nostri Jesu Christi, qui te custodiat ab hosti maligno, et perducat in vitam aeternam . . .*'

Alone in the dark, Earl Hugh was taking communion.

Chapter Eight

It took Ralph Delchard a long time to shake off Idwal. The Welshman was a tireless bloodhound, sniffing his trail with assurance, bounding along with glee and baying at his heels whenever he got close enough. They seemed to make a circuit of the entire castle. It was an undignified game for a royal commissioner to have to play and Ralph eventually wearied of it. Unequivocal confrontation was needed. When Idwal pursued him into the keep, Ralph held his ground and swung round to face him. It was no time for diplomatic niceties.

'Go away!' he ordered.

'But we have so much news to exchange, my lord.'

'Do not pester me so, man! I have no interest in your news and I will not be chased like some runaway stag.'

Idwal was hurt. 'I thought that we were friends.'

'Friends do not hound each other.'

'I am pleased to see you, that is all.'

'Reflect on that pleasure elsewhere.'

'But we grew close when we were in Hereford together.'

'Too close!'

'We joined forces to avert a Welsh rebellion.'

'You are a Welsh rebellion on your own.'

There was a long pause as Idwal assessed the situation. His frown eventually melted away and his palms opened in a gesture of mild contrition.

'I see the problem,' he said, recovering his good humour with remarkable speed. 'I come to you at an inopportune time. I am sorry, my lord. I should not have ambushed you as I did. Appoint a more fit hour when we may converse at length.'

Ralph was firm. 'We have said all that we need to say to each other. I do not wish to hear any more about Llandaff.'

'St David's.'

'Or St David's.'

'Though I do have news of Llandaff as well.'

'Spare me!'

'And good tidings from Bangor.'

'Bangor?'

'Not to mention Brecon.'

'Convey your tidings to Bishop Robert. They may have some relevance for him. Or to Canon Hubert,' said Ralph, grasping at any straw to rid himself of the persistent Welshman. 'He will argue about the Church for as long as you like. Llandaff, St David's, Bangor, Brecon or Bethlehem. Hubert is your man.'

'We have spoken already.'

'Speak to him again, Idwal.'

'Oh, I will, I will.'

'He relishes a debate with you.'

'I have noticed, my lord.'

Idwal cocked his head to one side and scrutinised Ralph through glinting eyes. He said something in Welsh under his breath then let out a rich chortle.

'Hereford!' he teased. 'That is why you try to elude me, is it not, my lord? Hereford! You have never forgiven me for spying in advance what it took you days even to notice.'

'What are you talking about?'

'Love. Marriage. Happiness. I saw the possibility of all three dancing in your eyes and in those of the dear lady who is now your wife. I can claim some credit for bringing you together, my lord. In some sort, I played the part of Cupid.'

'Heaven forbid!'

'I brought the pair of you turtle doves together.'

'This is intolerable!' groaned Ralph.

'Deny it if you will but I know. I was there.'

'Could I ever forget!'

Idwal took a step backwards. 'I will trouble you no more at this time, my lord,' he said abruptly. 'I bid you farewell.'

'At last!'

'We can resume our conversation in the full light of day. When you are less taxed by your affairs and refreshed by sleep. Both you and Earl Hugh, I trust, may be more amenable tomorrow.'

'Only a madman would wager on it.'

Idwal grinned. 'I have always had a streak of madness.' He became serious. 'One last thing,' he warned. 'You *need* me. I can talk with men of consequence on both sides of the border. Nobody else in this castle can do that. Impress it upon Earl Hugh. I am the key to continued peace in Cheshire. If he grants me permission to see Gruffydd ap Cynan, I will help to prevent more warfare.'

Before Ralph could ask him how, his tormentor flung one side of his evil-smelling cloak over his shoulder and marched away with Messianic certainty in his stride. Ralph was left alone on a cold staircase. It was ironic. Pursued by the effusive archdeacon, his instinct had been to strike out at the man, but now that the chase had been called off he felt a vague sensation of guilt.

Idwal was only trying to show friendship. And he might indeed be able to glean information from the Prince of Gwynedd which could be of benefit to his captors. Idwal was by instinct a man of peace, as he had proved in Herefordshire. He did not really merit the summary rejection which had been meted out to him. Ralph could never warm to the man himself but the fact remained that Golde actually liked him. The Welshman had been the first to discern the strength of feeling between the pair of them. Like it or not, Ralph had to concede that Idwal was part of their private history.

He went up to his apartment in reflective mood. There were times when his military training was a severe handicap. Attack and defence were his only natural options. Both were ineffective against someone like Archdeacon Idwal. The only way to keep such a man at bay was to use methods as cunning and devious as his own. Ralph had to devise a new strategy.

He was still puzzling over what it might be when he opened

the door of his chamber. All thought of Idwal vanished in an instant. Standing before him was the one person who could cleanse his mind of its accumulated worries and fire him with real pleasure. It was Golde. She was wearing a pale blue gown over a chemise of white linen. She had taken off her wimple to reveal fair hair which was curled at the front and coiled at the back. She was smiling invitingly at him.

'Golde!' he exclaimed.

'I have been waiting for you.'

'You were not supposed to arrive until tomorrow.'

'We made good time on the road.'

'When did you get to Chester?'

'Above an hour ago.'

'You have been in the castle all that time?'

'I asked to be shown to your apartment.'

'Why did you not send for me?'

'I wanted to surprise you, Ralph,' she said, moving towards him. 'Have I managed to do that?'

'Oh, yes!'

'Are you pleased to see me?'

No more words were needed. Ralph enfolded her in his arms and kissed away the long absence. Chester was a barren place without her. She had made the effort to reach the city a day earlier than planned in order to rejoin her husband. Ralph was thrilled. The unexpected pleasure of being with his wife once more was so overwhelming that he even began to look more kindly upon Idwal. Perhaps the Welshman did, after all, deserve some small credit for uniting them. It was, at least, one thing which could be said in his favour.

Canon Hubert believed in the value of meticulous preparation. Disputes over the ownership of property could be extremely complicated and the bitterness generated by the contesting parties sometimes threatened to cloud the issues at stake. To avoid confusion or distraction, it was imperative to master the underlying facts of each case well in advance. That was the procedure which Hubert always followed. Having spent some hours studying the major dispute which would come before him on the morrow, therefore, he was understandably peeved to learn that judgement in that particular instance would have to be postponed.

Annoyed at the waste of his valuable time, he immediately set off to the castle to complain to Ralph Delchard, but the latter was too happily engaged in a domestic reunion to answer his summons. Hubert was never easily deflected from his purpose. He took his protest instead to Gervase Bret.

'Come in, Canon Hubert.'

'Thank you.'

'I did not think to see you at the castle again.'

'Nor I to return here. It is not a place I would choose to visit unless I was compelled to do so.'

'You are here under compulsion?'

'Yes, Gervase.'

'Why?'

'I am moved to register a serious complaint.'

'Take a seat and tell me all.'

Hubert lowered himself on to the large stool which stood against one wall. It was a small chamber, high up in the keep, and the canon's presence made it seem much smaller. Gervase leaned against the wall beside the window. In the light of the candles, Hubert's rubicund face seemed to be glowing.

'Well?' said Gervase.

'A message was sent to me by the lord Ralph,' said the other. 'The case involving Raoul Lambert has unaccountably been dropped from our proceedings tomorrow. The postponement has caused me gross inconvenience.'

'It was unavoidable.'

'Why?'

'Were you given no reason for the change of plan?'

'None, Gervase. I have come in search of it.'

'Then the first thing you must know is that Raoul Lambert will never be able to advance his claim to the holdings in question. He was killed in the Forest of Delamere this morning during a hunting trip.'

Hubert was startled. 'Killed?' he gasped.

'His body lies in the mortuary.'

'A hunting accident?'

'No. He was murdered.'

'Saints preserve us!'

Gervase gave him a brief account of what had happened and Hubert saw that he had no real cause for protest. Death had brutally rearranged their schedule for them. What now exercised his mind were the dark motives which might lie behind that death.

'It was an attempt to assassinate Earl Hugh himself?'

'That is how it appears, Canon Hubert.'

'This is frightful intelligence.'

'It has caused great upset.'

'If the earl is not safe, then we are all at risk,' said the other with sudden alarm. 'To think that I walked through the streets alone this evening! I will not stir abroad without an armed guard in future.'

'You are in no danger.'

'I am, Gervase. So are you. So are we all.'

'Stay calm.'

'How can I when the whole city may be under threat?'

'That is highly unlikely.'

'Earl Hugh was all but assassinated this morning.'

'It does not mean that we will all have our throats cut in our beds tonight,' said Gervase reasonably. 'A murderer who chooses to strike in the forest is unlikely to search for a second victim in a city which is so well guarded as this one. Besides, there may yet be another explanation. Suppose, for instance, that this Raoul Lambert was the intended target of the attack?'

'Is that possible?'

'We should certainly consider it.'

'Indeed, we should,' agreed the canon as curiosity slowly dispelled his apprehension. 'Raoul Lambert may have had enemies about whom we do not even know. And I would hazard a guess that Welshmen would be numbered among them.'

'Why do you say that?'

'Because I have spent a long time perusing the documents relating to this dispute. The Church claims that Raoul Lambert appropriated land within the Forest of Delamere which was formerly part of its own estates. Without wishing to prejudge the case, I must say that the balance of evidence favours the Church. However,' continued Hubert, ransacking his memory, 'Raoul Lambert had additional holdings. Outliers on the Welsh border. Each one of his berewics is somewhat larger now than it was when the land was first granted to him.'

'What would you wish me to infer?'

'Nothing, Gervase. I trade in facts, not inferences. Draw what conclusions you may. Raoul Lambert was killed by a Welsh arrow. He held property which spills over the Welsh border at three or four points. In my opinion, he has no legal right to portions of his outliers.'

'So he could be a legitimate target for attack.'

'Yes,' confirmed Hubert. 'All Norman soldiers are, in a sense, legitimate targets to the Welsh but this man may have a special interest for them.' He ran a pensive hand across his chin. 'There is another singularity which I observed.'

'What is that?'

'How did he come to have such extensive holdings?'

'Earl Hugh favoured him.'

'But why, Gervase? Raoul Lambert is a huntsman. He is not a leading baron in this county.'

'Earl Hugh places great value on hunting.'

'His other huntsmen have not been so generously treated. What sets this Raoul Lambert apart from the others? Why has he been permitted to enlarge his holdings by what appears to be a series of unjust seizures? What dread offence has he caused his Welsh neighbours, so that thoughts of murder may be prompted? And have there been any earlier attacks upon him?'

'Searching questions, Canon Hubert.'

'They demand answers.'

'We will not get them from the earl himself.'

'Why not?'

'His mind is already made up,' said Gervase. 'He was the object of the assassination. That is his firm belief. And he may well be right. Earl Hugh was *there*. He felt that arrow whistle past him. We have to trust to his instinct.'

'Raoul Lambert is the one who lies in the mortuary.'

'I have not forgotten that. The points which you raise must be examined, Canon Hubert. There may yet be some link between his death and his activities on the Welsh border. I will look further into it.' He smiled and spread his arms. 'Your study of those documents was not in vain at all. It has thrown up some intriguing facts. They may yet have a bearing on what took place in the forest this morning.'

Hubert preened himself. 'I have always been thorough.'

'We have gained from your thoroughness.'

'Will you report all this to the lord Ralph?'

'Naturally.'

'I would not have it reach the ears of Earl Hugh.'

'There is no chance of that,' promised Gervase. 'We would not even be able to speak to him. Earl Hugh was to have entertained us again this evening but he has excused himself in order to attend the meeting.'

'What meeting?'

'He is holding a council of war.'

It was a complete transformation. Men who had revelled in the hall on the previous evening now sat stern-faced round the oak table. Walls which had echoed to music and laughter now eavesdropped on earnest discussion. The air of celebration had been decisively supplanted by an atmosphere of high seriousness. Important decisions were about to be taken.

Earl Hugh sat the head of the table. William Malbank, Robert Cook, Richard Vernon, Hamo of Mascy, Reginald Balliol, Bigot of Loges and Hugo of Delamere were in attendance.

Hugh's voice was low but his eyes were ominously bright.

'I will not suffer this humiliation,' he said. 'I wish to retaliate without delay.'

'Against whom, my lord?' asked William Malbank. 'We do not know who shot that fateful arrow.'

'A Welsh archer.'

'Acting on whose authority?'

'The followers of Gruffydd ap Cynan,' said Hugh. 'Because they cannot release their prince, they try to kill the man who holds him prisoner. Their motive is clear.'

'I agree,' said Hamo of Mascy. 'Trouble is brewing. That arrow was but a warning of the battle that is to come.'

'They will find us ready for them,' vowed Hugh.

'My men will be at your back, my lord,' said Hamo.

Others were quick to offer their support as well but Malbank's remained a dissenting voice. He looked round the table at the other barons and ignored the hostile stares which he was receiving.

'You are very angry,' he observed, 'and you have every right to be so. What happened in the forest was unforgivable. Raoul Lambert was murdered by an assassin's arrow which was destined for a much higher prize.' He glanced at Hugh. 'We must thank God that it missed its real target.'

There was loud endorsement for that comment. Hamo and Reginald Balliol both banged the table to indicate assent.

'Earl Hugh was spared,' continued Malbank.

'In order to strike back at my enemies,' said Hugh.

'Yes, my lord, but do it in no spirit of anger. I feel as you and the others feel, but I school myself to hold back.'

'What ails you, William? Cowardice?'

'No!' declared the other. 'I will raise my sword as readily as any man in this room when I have reason to do so. But I will not strike out in blind anger and nor should you.'

'What should we do?' taunted Hamo. 'Sue for peace?'

'Identify our foe more carefully before we go to war.'

'Wales is our foe.'

'No, Hamo. Certain Welshmen, that is all. Let us make sure who they are before we launch any attack across the border.'

'There is some sense in that,' decided Bigot of Loges. 'Commit ourselves too soon and we run the risk of spreading our forces across too wide a front. William Malbank is right. We should strike at the point where it would be most effective.'

'In Wales,' growled Hugh. 'Left to me, I'd kill every man, woman and child in that accursed country! I'd wipe it completely off the map! How dare they try to assassinate me! I'll be revenged on the whole lot of them!'

'Choose the right target for that revenge,' said Malbank.

'I will. He languishes in my dungeon.'

Even Hamo opposed that course of action. 'You must not kill their prince, my lord,' he said with alarm. 'He is our most valuable hostage. Lose him and we lose our major bulwark against the Welsh.'

'That bulwark did not prevent an assassin's attack.'

'One man was sent where an army would not have succeeded.'

'Listen to Hamo,' urged Malbank. 'We must not take out our anger on Gruffydd ap Cynan. He is their figurehead and is far more use to us under lock and key. While he is in Chester, his men are reminded daily of our superior power and advantage.'

There were murmurs of consent. Earl Hugh was irritated.

'I demand action now!' he said, slapping the table with the flat of his hand. 'God's tits! This is a council of war, not a peace negotiation. We must hit back now. We must send a raiding party to mete out punishment.'

'How and where?' asked Malbank.

'Stop trying to hinder me, William.'

'I am merely trying to help. Every knight I can muster will be at your disposal and I will be proud to ride at your side. But I would prefer to know against whom we launch our might.' He looked around the table again and saw that his argument was prevailing. 'Battles are won by a combination of power and strategy. At the moment, we have one without the other. I appeal to you, all. Shall we dissipate our power because we have no strategy? Shall we shoot our own arrows without taking careful aim?'

'Revenge is our strategy,' affirmed Hugh.

'Then let us prepare the way for that revenge.'

There was murmured discussion around the table as the barons compared notes with their immediate neighbours. Hamo of Mascy was the first to speak.

'I support William on this,' he said.

'So do I,' said Reginald Balliol.

'And I,' added Bigot of Loges, won over by persuasion.

'Send intelligencers into Wales,' said Malbank. 'Let them search for the truth behind this foul murder. And dispatch an urgent messenger to Rhuddlan Castle. If there is indeed trouble stirring, your nephew Robert of Rhuddlan will be the first to detect it.'

The notion met with general approval and even Earl Hugh recognised the wisdom of it. For once, he elected not to force his own decision upon the others.

'A messenger will ride for Rhuddlan at dawn,' he said.

'Thank you, my lord. That contents me.'

The council of war broke up and the barons dispersed. William Malbank was left alone with the earl. He felt intimidated and gave an apologetic shrug.

'I had to speak out, my lord,' he said deferentially. 'You must accept that. Careful preparation now may save a lot of unnecessary bloodshed later.'

'I agree.'

'Then you are not angry with me?'

'No, William. I am deeply grateful to you.'

'For delaying a possible attack on the Welsh?'

'No,' said Hugh with a lewd grin. 'For providing me with such delicious compensation. Raoul was not the only loss I sustained in the forest. My hawk was also killed. But not before he had won my wager.' His grin broadened. 'Send your mistress to me tonight, William. I have need of her.'

Rhuddlan Castle was a symbol of Norman domination in North Wales, a timbered fortress built on a rock outcrop to command a view across the whole valley. Protecting the road between Chester and the Welsh coast, it was a daunting reminder to the indigenous population that they were occupied by invaders. Its

107

castellan, Robert of Rhuddlan, was an experienced soldier who was constantly working to improve his defences. Nothing was left to chance. The area might be quiescent at the moment but Robert knew how quickly the Welsh could ignite. Whatever else happened, he resolved that he and his garrison would not be caught off guard.

The banging on his door awakened him at first light.

'Yes?' he called.

'The captain of the guard has sent for you, my lord.'

'What is amiss?'

'He asks that you come at once.'

'Why?'

'He said that it was urgent.'

Robert did not need to be told twice. Leaping out of bed, he grabbed his gown and wrapped himself in it before slipping back the bolt and opening the door. Only an emergency would justify disturbing his sleep. He wondered what it might be. Within a matter of seconds, he was stepping out bare-footed on to the western battlements. The captain of the guard was waiting for him with a cluster of his men.

'What is the problem?' asked Robert.

'See for yourself, my lord.'

'Where?'

'Down there,' said the other, pointing.

Robert of Rhuddlan looked out across the valley. Half a mile away, stretched out in a single line, were a hundred or more mounted warriors in full armour. It was a menacing sight. They seemed to be studying the castle with great interest, as if searching for any weak points. They were too far away to be identified but their general purpose was clear. They were an advance party of a Welsh army. After a few minutes, they swung their horses round and rode swiftly away.

One thing was obvious. They were massing for attack. When they came again, there would be far more of them.

Robert of Rhuddlan's orders were curt and peremptory.

'Double the guard!' he snapped. 'And rouse the rest of the garrison!'

Chapter Nine

The arrival of his wife invigorated Ralph Delchard in every way. Not only was he up early on the following morning with love in his heart and energy in his limbs, he felt that his mind had been stimulated as well. Gone was the mood of creeping sadness which always gripped him whenever he and Golde were apart and hampered his relationship with his colleagues. Ralph was now liberated. He could think clearly for the first time since he had come to Chester.

When he encountered Earl Hugh in the courtyard, Ralph beamed happily. His greeting was excessively cordial.

'You seem to be in good spirits,' observed Hugh.

'I am, my lord. My wife arrived last evening.'

'So I understand, and she is most welcome. I am sorry that she joins us at a time when we are distracted by events in the Forest of Delamere. No matter,' he said with a confiding grin, 'I can see that she warmed your bed for you. I, too, had a lively night. There is nothing quite like a woman to provide solace in times of trouble.'

'Nothing quite like a loving wife,' corrected Ralph.

'I will settle for a woman. Any woman.'

'We must agree to differ.'

'You would change your mind if you enjoyed the bounty that fell to me last night,' said Hugh. 'A fine, fiery wench in every way. Malbank's loss was my gain.'

His meaning was clear. Not wishing to hear any more about his amorous adventures away from the marital couch, Ralph changed the topic of conversation at once.

109

'I have been thinking about the death of Raoul Lambert.'

Hugh scowled. 'It was a cowardly murder!'

'Yet obviously planned, my lord.'

'In what way?'

'If you were the chosen target – and for the time being let us assume that you were – then you had to be attacked at a vulnerable moment. The forest was the ideal place. You would be among friends and completely off guard. An assassin would never have such a good opportunity here in the city.'

'What do you conclude?'

'We must look for someone familiar with your movements.'

'I could have been watched.'

'But there is no pattern to your hunting,' said Ralph. 'You ride out when the mood seizes you and choose what game appeals to you on any particular day. The forest is vast. You traverse different parts of it every time you venture out.'

'So?'

Ralph was blunt. 'You have a traitor in your ranks.'

'Out of the question.'

'Not the assassin himself, perhaps, but his confederate.'

'The night with your wife has befuddled your brain.'

'Think it through, my lord,' recommended the other. 'A hunting party leaves the castle early in the morning. Will an assassin be lurking in the city in order to follow you? It seems unlikely. He would surely be seen on your trail. It would be much easier for him to conceal himself in that part of the forest which you had decided to hunt in.'

'Go on.'

'Then he could bide his time until opportunity arose.'

'You have shifted your ground, Ralph,' said Hugh with a curl of his lip. 'Yesterday, you were telling me that a member of my own hunting party actually shot the arrow at me.'

'That is still a possibility.'

'Only in the realms of fancy.'

'The assassin needed help,' said Ralph doggedly. 'If he was not a member of your entourage, then he must have been forewarned by a co-conspirator.'

'Stop chasing moonbeams.'

'Hear me out, my lord.'

'I do not need to,' said Hugh dismissively. 'Your theory has a fatal flaw in it, Ralph.'

'What is that?'

'Nobody in my entourage knew our destination until we breakfasted on the morning itself.'

'Then listen to my final guess,' suggested Ralph. 'And remember, I am a detached observer. I view the situation dispassionately from the outside. No personal loyalties blur my vision. I realise that you do not enjoy that advantage.'

Hugh was sceptical. 'And what is this final guess?'

'It will offend you, my lord.'

'Tell me all the same.'

'It concerns Raoul Lambert.'

'Go on.'

Ralph waited until a detachment of soldiers marched past on their way to relieve the guard. Under the earl's cynical gaze, he took a deep breath before developing his argument.

'My feeling is this,' he began. 'Raoul Lambert was, I suspect, the designated victim, after all. Let me finish, my lord,' he pleaded as his companion mouthed a protest. 'We both have archers at our command. We know how long and how painstakingly they will practise. Accuracy is a matter of honour to them.'

'So?'

'They rarely miss a target from short range.'

'The Welsh archer contrived to miss me.'

'No, my lord,' said Ralph, 'his aim was good. An arrow which misses one person will rarely kill another with such precision. It is far more likely to wound him. Yet you say that your huntsman was virtually killed outright.'

'That is so.'

'Then grapple with this notion,' advised Ralph. 'Raoul Lambert was not merely the chosen target in the forest. He was also the man who betrayed your movements to the assassin.'

'Then why was he killed?'

'As a stark warning to you.'

'The assassin murdered his own confederate?'

'He removed someone who had already served his purpose.'

'Raoul?' spluttered Earl Hugh. 'He was no traitor. It is an insane suggestion. You never even met the man.'

'Not face to face, my lord, I grant you. But I know him from the documents we brought with us. He appears a great deal in those. Gervase made his acquaintance that way and so did Canon Hubert. Between the three of us, we know your huntsman far better than you think.'

'He would never be in league with a Welsh assassin.'

'Even though his holdings intruded into Wales?'

'He hated the Welsh.'

'That would not stop him taking their money,' said Ralph. 'We both fought at Hastings, my lord. Remember how many of those French and Breton and Flemish mercenaries of ours must have hated Duke William. Yet they fought under his banner.'

'Raoul was my close friend!'

'Then he was in the ideal position to betray you.'

'Never! The idea is ridiculous!'

But Ralph could see that he had planted a tiny seed of doubt in the other's mind. It was enough. He backed off.

'Excuse my ravings, my lord.'

'That is what they are.'

'Put them down to the excitement of seeing Golde again.'

'She must be a remarkable woman.'

'She is.'

'I long to meet this paragon. Well,' he said, anxious to end a conversation which had left him jangled, 'you have work awaiting you at the shire hall. I will let you go to it.'

'One moment, my lord.'

'No more lunatic suggestions – please!'

'This is a request from an archdeacon.'

'Frodo?'

'Idwal, Archdeacon of St David's.'

Earl Hugh tensed. 'A Welsh churchman?'

'In every sense, my lord. He came in search of you last evening but you were not available to consider his appeal.'

'What appeal?'

'An hour with Gruffydd ap Cynan, Prince of Gwynedd.'

'He will not have the tenth part of a second with him!' roared Hugh with fists bunched. 'Nobody is allowed near my prisoner, especially Welsh spies in clerical garments. If this Idwal wishes to visit my dungeons, I will find him one of his own in which to preach. His appeal is denied outright.'

'I warned him that it would be.'

'The Welsh are our enemies.'

'Yet they have learned to live in submission.'

'They tried to kill me.'

'That is still open to dispute.'

'They did, Ralph!' yelled the other. 'I will not have anyone say otherwise.'

'Then I withdraw my foolish suggestions.'

Hugh was adamant. 'I was the victim of an assassination attempt. That demands a forceful reply from me.'

'What action are you taking, my lord?'

'I am marshalling my forces in readiness,' said the other. 'If they wish to fight, they will have a battle they will never forget. A messenger left for Rhuddlan Castle at the crack of dawn. My nephew needs to know what has been happening here and I am anxious for his news about any early signs of revolt.'

'Do you really believe that the Welsh will attack?'

'I am certain of it, Ralph.'

'Even though you hold their prince here?'

'They may have found another leader.'

'It seems improbable, my lord.'

'I know these people,' insisted Hugh. 'I have lived side by side with them for years. I sense their moods. Warfare is imminent, believe me. The attempt on my life was but the first signal of hostilities to come.'

'Is that the message you sent to Rhuddlan?'

'Yes, Ralph. I warned them to beware.'

The messenger had chosen the swiftest horse in the stables and ridden him out of the city at a canter. It was a long way to Rhuddlan and his mount had to be paced carefully. There might be times when he would need to coax extra speed out of him or ride hell-for-leather to escape from outlaws. He had spurned an escort. One man alone, he assured his master, would move faster and attract less attention.

The weather favoured him. It was a clear, dry day with a cooling breeze. The track was firm beneath the horse's hooves. There were no obstacles ahead of him and no sign of pursuit behind him. When he crossed the border into Wales, he felt no warning impulses. Those who toiled in the fields barely gave him a glance. Those he passed in hamlets and villages had too much to do even to notice him. Tranquillity reigned on all sides. The messenger was relieved to see that Earl Hugh's dire predictions were unfounded.

He was almost halfway to his destination when he met the obstruction. A wagon had overturned on a downward slope and spilled its mean cargo on the ground. An old man and his wife were struggling to push the wagon upright but their strength was patently inadequate. As he rode closer, he could see the sweat that was glistening on the old man's face. He took pity.

Bringing his horse to a halt, he dismounted. 'Let me help you,' he offered.

The man and his wife gave tired smiles of gratitude.

'The three of us should be able to manage it.'

He took up a position and got a firm grip on the wagon. Before he could lend his strength to theirs, however, he felt a searing pain as a long knife was plunged deep into his back. When he tried to turn, he was buffeted to the ground by the old man's stout forearm. Danger had come when he least expected it. He had ridden into a clever trap.

His message would never reach Rhuddlan.

*   *   *

114

They saw the change in him at once. As soon as Ralph Delchard walked into the shire hall, Canon Hubert and Brother Simon noted the spring in his step and the unassailable buoyancy in his manner. They understood its cause. Golde had arrived. Hubert was pleased. If his wife could lift his spirits so markedly, then she was a most welcome visitor to Chester because they would all benefit.

Simon was ready to enjoy that benefit without dwelling on its implications. Marriage was a terrifying mystery to him and he never dared even to imagine what strange practices took place between a man and his wife in the privacy of their bed. Celibacy was his chosen path and he thanked God daily for the protection it gave him from what he saw as the contaminating touch of a woman. Ralph was in high humour. That was all that mattered. Simon was satisfied that his colleague would lead the commission with more gusto and efficiency than he had managed on their first day.

It was a testing session in the shire hall. Their work was beset by problems from the start. The death of Raoul Lambert made it impossible for them to proceed with the dispute in which he figured so largely. Witnesses who had been summoned to give evidence on his behalf or on that of the Church were turned away with apologies. The disputants in the case which replaced the one postponed were late arriving and unprepared for a legal confrontation which was forced upon them before they were ready. They begged for more time to compose themselves.

Delay followed delay, setback ensued setback. But Ralph Delchard refused to be upset or even irritated. He carried out his duties with unruffled calm and his geniality helped to sustain his colleagues. Even Gervase Bret succumbed to pique when a disputant in one case blithely announced that she had decided not to bring a vital charter with her because she could remember exactly what it said. Ralph's whispered comments soon had Gervase smiling tolerantly.

Attenuated by mishaps, their day nevertheless did yield some progress. Two minor disputes were settled and a third was in sight of completion when they adjourned. They could look back on their efforts with some satisfaction. Hubert took the opportunity to probe Ralph for information about the matter which was still at the forefront of his mind.

'I was deeply alarmed to hear of the foul murder.'

'So were we all,' said Ralph.

'Gervase and I discussed it last evening.'

'Yes, Hubert. Your comments were very apt. Gervase passed them on to me over breakfast. You and I seem to have been thinking along the same lines.' He smiled. 'For a change.'

'What does Earl Hugh say?'

'He will not listen to any of our ideas. Nothing will shift him from the view that an attempt was made on his own life as a prelude to a Welsh uprising.'

'That is my own secret fear, my lord!'

'And mine!' said Simon.

'Your fears are groundless.'

'I wish that I could believe that,' said Hubert, 'but my instinct rules against it. Bishop Robert and Archdeacon Frodo are equally unnerved. They know the Welsh.'

'So do I,' said Ralph airily. 'I have fought against them enough times. They are hardy warriors but they will not go to war for the sake of fighting. The Welsh mind is crafty and calculating. Before they would even consider an attack on Chester, they would first introduce some men slyly into the city. Artful spies who could prepare the way for them.'

Hubert's eyes bulged. 'Archdeacon Idwal!'

'He has too much integrity to be a spy,' said Gervase.

'*Welsh* integrity,' said Hubert meaningfully.

'Leave Idwal out of this,' said Ralph. 'Intelligencers are stealthy and no man has less stealth than our archdeacon. His idea of open warfare would be to talk us all to death. He is not the problem here.'

Simon trembled. 'He is if you lodge under the same roof.'

'No,' said Ralph, warming to his subject, 'the real source of interest is this Raoul Lambert.'

'Yes,' agreed Gervase. 'I have been making a few inquiries

116

about him. Everyone at the castle knew him. Honest, reliable, skilled at his trade. That is how most remember him.'

Ralph nodded. 'That was Earl Hugh's epitaph. According to him, Raoul Lambert was a man with no enemies.'

'None within the city, perhaps,' said Gervase, 'but he may have been less popular on the Welsh border. It is a pity that he will not appear before us for examination. I would have pressed him to explain how his berewics increased steadily in size over the past couple of years.'

'Unjust seizure!' asserted Hubert. 'This county has a deplorable record of it. And the worst culprit is Earl Hugh himself. Raoul Lambert was only following his example.'

'There is certainly a curious bond between the two men,' opined Ralph, 'and it was not just a mutual interest in hunting. Did you discover what that bond was, Gervase?'

'No, Ralph, but I did learn something else.'

'From whom?'

'The town reeve,' said Gervase. 'A most obliging fellow. I made a point of arriving here this morning early enough to talk at length with him. He is a fount of wisdom with regard to matters concerning Chester and its environs. He knew our huntsman and spoke well of him. Like everyone else, he was shocked to learn of the murder. Raoul Lambert will be mourned. But the reeve did recall certain events which may cast a slight shadow over Lambert's reputation.'

'Dark deeds in his past?' said Ralph hopefully.

'Not necessarily,' warned Gervase. 'He may be innocent of any involvement. The town reeve certainly thought so. This is what happened. Two of the berewics held by Raoul Lambert encroached on Welsh soil. In both instances, there was strong local resistance.'

'What form did it take?' asked Hubert.

'Verbal abuse then threats of violence.'

'How were the cases resolved?'

'In the most abrupt way,' explained Gervase. 'One of the men who protested was drowned in mysterious circumstances in the River Gowy. There was talk of suicide.'

117

'And the other case?'

'The man whose land had been taken simply disappeared. He set off for Chester to register his protest with Earl Hugh and was never seen again. To this day, nobody quite knows what happened to him.'

'Do you think that our huntsman did?' said Ralph.

Gervase shrugged. 'I am not sure. In both instances, he was the beneficiary. Protest was effectively stifled. There were vague rumours that he may have been implicated.'

'Rumours prove nothing,' Simon pointed out.

'True,' said Gervase. 'At their best, they amount to hearsay evidence and that is notoriously unreliable. But I would say one thing. The elements which characterise the disputes in which Raoul Lambert was involved are repeated time and again in other cases that will come before us. It is almost as if he set a pattern for others to follow.'

'Yet he was no baron of high rank,' said Hubert, frankly bewildered. 'How did he achieve such pre-eminence? What made this huntsman stand out above all others?'

'Find that out,' concluded Ralph, 'and we will know why he was murdered in the Forest of Delamere.'

It was a simple funeral. Barely half a dozen people were gathered in the church to hear the white-haired Father Ernwin sing Mass for the souls of the departed. Most of the congregation were too stunned to listen to the words and none understood the melodious Latin. All that they knew was that two men were going into their grave before their time. The crude wooden coffins held mutilated bodies which bore vivid testimony to the ruthlessness of the Earl of Chester. That thought subdued all who were present.

Gytha sat on the front bench in the tiny nave, cradling her brother who was too frightened either to look or to listen. To comfort Beollan, she had to control her own grief and that required a supreme effort. It was only when the coffins were finally lowered into the ground and earth was tossed on to them that the loss of her father and elder brother hit her with its full impact. Her control suddenly vanished. She burst into tears, began to sway violently, lost her footing and all but fell into the grave after them.

It was Beollan who showed strength then, putting an arm round her to steady her and muttering words of comfort. Gytha slowly recovered. When the service was over, the ancient priest braved the long walk to escort them all the way back to the cottage and offered what little consolation he could. He promised to call again the next day to see how they were faring. Gytha and Beollan were left alone. An hour passed before either of them could even speak.

Gytha broached a subject which she had put aside after the discovery of the bodies in the ditch. It could not be ignored any longer.

'Beollan.'

'Yes?' he murmured.

'Tell me what really happened that day.'

'I have, Gytha. I lost sight of them.'

'No,' she said quietly. 'That is not the truth. You are still hiding something from me. There will be no secrets in this house. I must know. Tell me everything. I am not going to blame you or chastise you.'

'There is nothing to tell.'

'Yes, there is. I saw you speak to Master Bret when he came to see us. You told him the truth. I could see it in his face. He knows what I have a right to know. I am your sister.' She took him by the shoulders to stare deep into his eyes. 'Why are you so guilty? What did you do that day?'

The memory brought tears to the boy's eyes and he tried to turn away, but his sister was determined to wrest the truth from him. She held him firmly and saw his resistance fade.

'What did you *do*, Beollan?'

'I ran away,' he whimpered.

'When?'

'When the earl's hawk was killed. We were hiding in a ditch and I bolted like a coward.'

'That was not cowardice.'

119

'They were caught and I escaped, Gytha.'

'I thank God for that small mercy!' she sighed. 'Think how much worse it would have been for me if all three of you had been captured. Your age would not have saved you, Beollan. You would have been hanged with them.' She gave him a hug. 'I love you and I do not blame you. God has spared you for a purpose. You were right to run.'

'I feel so ashamed.'

'There is no cause.' She released her hold. 'What else did you tell Master Bret?'

'That I saw someone sneaking away in the forest.'

'Sneaking away?'

'Carrying a bow.'

'The archer who shot that arrow!' she decided. 'He was the one who should have been hanged from that tree. Not Father and our dear brother Arkell. They were innocent. Master Bret will know that now. You were a witness.'

Beollan nodded and squeezed her arm affectionately. He had expected his sister to be angry with him, but she was instead kind and understanding. It made all the difference. He was closer to her than he had ever been before and felt able to part with one last secret.

'There is something that I have not told anyone,' he said.

Chapter Ten

Towards the end of another day, Robert de Limesey carried out his routine inspection of the work being done on his beloved cathedral. There was little perceptible change behind the scaffolding but he felt somehow reassured each time he visited the scene. It was heartening to reflect that while he was conducting services within the cathedral, a team of able men was improving the outer fabric of the building. The blessed time would come when the scaffolding was finally removed and the bishop could view the renovations in their full glory.

The place was deserted now. Ropes dangled idly and pulleys were silent. Stone lay about on the grass in abundance, some of it already dressed to shape and ready to be hoisted up into position, some of it fresh from the quarry, waiting for the mason's hammer and chisel to fashion it appropriately. Bishop Robert loved to watch the craftsmen at work, taking an ugly lump of stone and slowly releasing its hidden beauty until it was fit to adorn the cathedral church of St John.

He was still musing on the majesty of the architecture when Archdeacon Frodo came padding across the grass.

'Is there anything to see, Bishop Robert?' he asked.

'Progress. Slow, steady, unhurried progress.'

'I will be glad when the stonemasons finish,' said the other. 'They have a noisy occupation. We will never hear the angels sing above the din of those hammers.'

'Listen more carefully, Frodo.'

The archdeacon smiled. 'I will,' he said. 'But I bring word

121

from Father Ernwin. The funeral was held this afternoon and he sends thanks for the permission you kindly gave.'

'I could hardly refuse it. Those two men who were hanged in the forest may have been poachers but they are still entitled to a Christian burial. It would have been sinful to leave them in a ditch to rot.'

'That is what Earl Hugh intended.'

'I am glad we were able to frustrate that intention.'

'It was one of the commissioners who found the bodies.'

'So I understand,' said the bishop. 'Master Gervase Bret. A young man of true Christian impulse. Canon Hubert has nothing but praise for his colleague and I can see why. He offered help to a family who were spurned by everyone else. Out of pure compassion, he turned Good Samaritan.' He heaved a sigh. 'It is a sad business, Frodo. But at least the bodies are now buried safely in the ground. They have been laid to rest. The surviving members of the family can now begin to mourn.'

'Father Ernwin said the same in his message.'

'He is a good shepherd and tends his flock well.' He glanced around to make sure that they were not overheard. 'Frodo,' he said quietly, 'I am sure that you appreciate how important it is to keep this from Earl Hugh.'

'You may rely on my discretion.'

'I always do.'

'Father Ernwin also understands the situation.'

'Good,' said the bishop. 'When he had their corpses tossed in that ditch, Earl Hugh meant them to lie there as a hideous warning to others. He would be highly displeased to hear that they had been recovered by their family and given a decent burial.'

'He will hear nothing from my lips,' promised the archdeacon, 'but then, he is too busy to listen to anything that we might have to say. The murder of Raoul Lambert has blocked out all else from his mind.'

'It troubles me as well, Frodo.'

'There will be severe repercussions.'

'We have already suffered one of them,' noted the bishop. 'Our appeal against Raoul Lambert's annexation of Church property will now go unheard. And you will have to forgo the pleasure of exposing his rapacity to the commissioners in the shire hall.'

'Some of our property may yet be returned, your grace.'

'I pray that all of it will.'

'Leave that to me and to the commissioners.'

'I will, Frodo.' He washed his hands nervously in the air. 'What is the true story, do you think?'

'True story?'

'Of the murder in the forest. Was it, in fact, do you suppose, a bold attempt on the life of Earl Hugh?'

'I can only guess,' said Frodo. 'Though I have talked with two people who were in the hunting party and they are firmly of the opinion that it was a bungled assassination. It has enraged Earl Hugh beyond measure.'

'That is not difficult to do.'

'This time his fury has just cause.'

'How has it expressed itself?'

'In prompt action,' said the archdeacon. 'When I went into the city, I saw extra guards at the gate. They let nobody through until they had checked his identity and purpose. It was the same at the castle. Soldiers are everywhere. The show of military strength is quite daunting.'

'And unsettling,' admitted the bishop. 'Earl Hugh would not stiffen his defences in that way unless he feared some kind of attack. And there is only one place from which that would come.'

'Wales.'

'Yes, Frodo. I begin to tremble.'

'Why, your grace?'

'Because I suddenly fear for my cathedral.'

'It is in no real danger.'

'How do you know that?'

'Chester has a large garrison.'

'But they are inside the castle,' said Robert anxiously. 'They have stone walls to protect them. We do not. We are outside the city with no fortifications to hide behind.'

'We have God to watch over us.'

'Yes, Frodo, but even He might not be able to stop a marauding army from over the border. It would not be the first time that a cathedral was sacked in Chester.'

'That will not happen, your grace.'

'It might.'

'Only as a remote possibility.'

'While that possibility exists, I continue to fret.' He looked up wistfully at the building. 'An immense amount of love and devotion has gone into the construction of this cathedral, quite apart from the money and the effort that have been lavished upon it. I hate the thought that it could all go up in smoke. I would be devastated.'

'So would I, your grace,' said the archdeacon, 'but I am confident that we will never be in that predicament. Earl Hugh is reacting to a threat which may not even be there. The Welsh have been peaceful neighbours ever since their prince was imprisoned in the castle. They would never endanger his life by mounting an attack.'

'How can you be so certain?'

'The Welsh are very predictable.'

'Are they?' returned the other. 'I disagree. Look at Archdeacon Idwal. He is as predictable as a mad dog. If he is typical of the Welsh, then we are all doomed!'

Brother Gerold listened to the request with the utmost sympathy, but he saw no point in offering his visitor false hope. His shoulders hunched into an apology.

'There is not the slightest chance, I fear.'

'How do you know until you ask him?'

'Because I am privy to his mind, Archdeacon Idwal,' said the monk. 'Earl Hugh would not let you near his prisoner.'

'A single hour is all that I seek.'

'I am sorry.'

'Half an hour?' bargained Idwal. 'Ten minutes? Five even? I would settle for any length of time with Gruffydd ap Cynan.'

'You will have to settle for none at all.'

'This is monstrous!'

'It is Earl Hugh's decree.'

'Then get him to revoke it.'

Gerold smiled. 'That is like asking me to turn the River Dee into red wine. Earl Hugh will not be persuaded.'

'But I was told that you had influence with him.'

'In some small way.'

'Bishop Robert gave me to understand that you were the one person in the castle to whom he paid serious attention.'

'At times.'

'Then let this be one of those times.'

'My plea would be ignored.'

'At least make it on my behalf.'

'It would be treated with utter contempt.'

'Then I will make the plea myself,' vowed Idwal, temper flaring and arms gesticulating wildly. 'Others may quake before Earl Hugh of Chester but I do not. He may have an army but I have the might of the Welsh Church at my back. Contrive an appointment for me, Brother Gerold. I will be heard.'

'Not by Earl Hugh.'

'But I am an archdeacon!'

'Even a bishop would not gain his ear at this time.'

Idwal stamped his foot in exasperation. The two of them were standing in the half-dark at the rear of the chapel. Idwal's arrival had been unannounced but he was treated with courtesy by Brother Gerold. That courtesy seemed to ruffle rather than please the visitor, who was forced into a change of strategy.

'Carry a message to him,' he urged.

'To Earl Hugh?'

'No, Brother Gerold. The only message I would like to send him would burn the hands off anyone who carried it. I talk of sending word to Gruffydd ap Cynan.'

'That would not be allowed.'

'Why not?'

'It is not for me to say.'

125

'Could you not take a simple letter to him?'

'No, Archdeacon Idwal.'

'Not even as a favour to me?' coaxed the other, producing a sweet smile of persuasion. 'I would view it as an act of Christian fellowship and remember you in my prayers.'

'I would be touched.'

'Then you agree?'

'No,' said Gerold. 'Communication of any kind with the prisoner is forbidden.'

'Surely the chaplain is entitled to visit him?'

'Only to offer what spiritual sustenance I may.'

'There is your opportunity,' declared Idwal. 'Next time you are alone in the dungeon with him, give him my letter in secret. It is only a message of greeting but it may bring some small cheer to the Prince of Gwynedd. Will you do this?' He saw the chaplain shake his head. 'Why not?'

'It would be wholly improper.'

'What harm could it do?'

'Untold harm. Earl Hugh would be furious.'

'Only if he learned about it and he will not.' Idwal brought his smile back into action. 'Please, Brother Gerold. My country-man suffers enough punishment as it is. Do not deprive him of all contact with his nation. Carry my message to him. Show pity. Who will ever know about it?'

'I will,' said Gerold firmly.

'*Iesu Mawr!* How can you refuse me?'

'There are rules.'

'Break them, mun! It is your Christian duty.'

But the chaplain's view of Christian duty differed greatly from that of the Welshman and he politely declined to smuggle any messages to the prisoner. After ridding himself of another torrent of protest, Idwal accepted that he would not be allowed to see the prince. He gave a moan of resignation then let his gaze move slowly round the chapel.

'This place has the feeling of being used,' he said with grudging approval. 'Soldiers are not the most devout men. Some of them only remember God when they need His help on the eve of a battle. I have been in castles where the chapel is empty most of the time.'

'That is not the case here.'

'Even with a heathen like Earl Hugh in charge?'

'He is no heathen but a true Christian.'

'I prefer to judge him by his actions.'

'Then know what they are,' said Gerold briskly. 'He has endowed churches and encouraged the spiritual life of the whole city. Earl Hugh is a willing student of the scriptures. He has many close friends in the Church and in the monastic community. Chief among them is Anselm.'

Idwal was astounded. 'Anselm of Bec?'

'The same.'

'*He* is a friend of Earl Hugh?'

'They exchange letters regularly,' explained Gerold. 'The earl draws great strength from that friendship. It is to Anselm he turned when he conceived the idea of founding an abbey in Chester.'

'But that is Bishop Robert's ambition as well.'

'He may be involved,' said Gerold easily, 'but an abbey will only come into being with the weight of Earl Hugh behind it. Do you still call him a heathen?'

'No,' said Idwal, his interest quickening. 'I am pleased to hear that he has been so generous towards the Church. Has he bestowed any gifts upon this chapel?'

'Several. His purse is always open to us.'

'Have you purchased anything of special value?'

'Special value?'

'Yes, Brother Gerold. Relics of a saint, perhaps?'

'Why do you ask?'

'Idle curiosity,' said Idwal, eyes roaming. 'A man of Earl Hugh's wealth could afford to buy almost anything that caught his interest.'

'We have a few relics,' admitted Gerold, 'but they are kept under lock and key. Like the prisoner.'

Idwal's anger rekindled at once and his voice crackled.

'You may rue the day you stopped me from seeing Gruffydd

ap Cynan,' he said with vehemence. 'Remember that if war does break out. I would have convinced the Prince of Gwynedd that peace is to the advantage of the Welsh. He might have ordered his men to lay down their arms.'

'How can he when he is not in contact with them?'

'There are some things that even the deepest dungeon will not hold in,' said Idwal with a strange smile. 'You said earlier that it would be easier to turn the River Dee into red wine than to change Earl Hugh's mind for him.'

'That is true.'

'In rejecting me, you may unwittingly have achieved that miracle, Brother Gerold. I hope that you are ready to take the blame. Enough blood may soon be spilled to turn the River Dee the colour of red wine. Be warned!'

In the absence of Earl Hugh, his wife took on the duty of extending warm hospitality to the guests. Ermintrude was a gracious hostess. At the earlier banquet, she had been very much a marginal figure, seated beside her husband out of loyalty rather than personal enjoyment and taking the earliest opportunity to quit the room when the revelry began to tip over into mild riot. In the hall that evening, over a delicious meal with Ralph Delchard, Golde and Gervase Bret, she really came into her own and emerged as a kind and considerate woman of no mean intelligence. Ralph was soon asking himself again how such a beautiful and stately creature could bear to be married to such an ogre.

'I am sorry that Hugh is unable to join us,' she said, 'but he has important affairs to discuss elsewhere. It gives me the opportunity to welcome you properly to Chester Castle and to offer a particular welcome to you, Golde.'

'Thank you, my lady.'

'Your husband has missed you sorely.'

'So he has told me,' said Golde.

She caught Ralph's wink and smiled in response. Golde was wearing her finest apparel but it seemed almost drab beside the elegant chemise and gown worn by Ermintrude. Earl Hugh did not stint on his wife's wardrobe. The gold circlet which held her lustrous black hair in place was worthy of a queen. It glinted in the candlelight and set off her whole face. Golde was fascinated by it.

'How did you meet your husband?' wondered Ermintrude.

'By accident, my lady. In Hereford.'

'Gervase and I were there on royal business,' said Ralph. 'It was one of the most difficult assignments we have ever had wished on to us, my lady.'

'Difficult and arduous,' recalled Gervase.

'But not without its compensations,' observed Ermintrude with a glance at Golde. 'How else would you have made the acquaintance of your future wife?'

'I would not have done so,' confessed Ralph. 'If Golde had not rescued me from my lonely existence, I would have spent the rest of my days as a crusty old bachelor.'

'There is nothing crusty about you,' said Golde. 'And you are the kind of man who never really grows old.'

'I am childish?' he teased. 'Is that your meaning?'

'No, Ralph. I was praising your youthful energy.'

'We have all been victims of that,' said Gervase.

Ermintrude led the gentle laughter. It was a world away from the heady banquet on the day of their arrival. All four of them talked amiably together in a relaxed atmosphere. There was no strain or awkwardness. Golde was drawn to her hostess. Ermintrude was regal yet approachable and she showed an easy tolerance of Golde's occasional moments of hesitation over her Norman French. It was the language she used more often than her own now and her sister had taunted her about it during her recent visit to Hereford.

One part of her past Golde was resolved not to surrender. When wine was brought to the table, she put a hand over her cup and looked up at the serving man.

'I would prefer beer, please.'

He was mystified. 'Beer, my lady?'

'Do you have such a thing in the castle?'

'Of course, but . . .'

'Fetch some beer at once,' said Ermintrude. 'Our guests will

129

want for nothing.' She turned to Golde. 'Though it is an odd request from a lady.'

'Not from one like me,' said Golde.

'Her first husband was a brewer,' said Ralph. 'When he died, Golde inherited a prosperous business and took over the running of it herself. She was providing all the beer for Hereford Castle when I chanced upon her.'

'Did she convert you to the drink?' asked Ermintrude.

'Never, my lady! It tastes like muddy water to me.'

'Your wine is too sweet for my palate,' said Golde.

'I drink both with equal pleasure,' volunteered Gervase, raising his cup. 'Wine or beer. Both are enjoyable.'

The serving man reappeared with a jug of beer and poured some into Golde's cup. He hovered while she tasted it. Her face puckered in disapproval. Ermintrude was alarmed.

'There is something amiss?' she asked in concern.

'No, my lady.'

'I can see that you do not like it.'

'I like it well enough,' said Golde, recovering quickly. 'It caught me unawares, that is all. I am used to something a little stronger. Something with more body. But this is perfectly good,' she insisted, taking a long sip. 'Yes, it is very acceptable.'

Ermintrude was not convinced. She snapped her fingers and Durand appeared out of the shadows that bordered the hall. The dwarf came trotting over to cringe before her.

'Yes, my lady?'

'Did you taste this beer?'

'No, my lady.'

'Why not?'

'Nobody ever drinks it at table.'

'Your orders are to taste *everything*, Durand. Even if it is not customarily served. I will have to mention this lapse to my husband.'

'Yes, my lady,' said the dwarf, bowing obsequiously but oozing resentment at the same time. 'Let me take the jug away and I will taste it for quality.'

'Do that.'

'I will, my lady.'

Durand gave a signal to the serving man who followed him out with both the jug and the half-filled cup which had been set before Golde. Conversation resumed in earnest. When the taster returned after a couple of minutes, he was bearing a clean cup and a fresh jug of beer.

'I think you will find this more to your satisfaction, my lady,' he said, placing the cup before Golde and filling it with beer. 'Please try it.'

Golde did and nodded in gratitude. The beer was still not of the highest quality but the second cup was an improvement on the first. Durand left the jug and backed away once more into the shadows, listening to what was said and memorising it for his report to Earl Hugh.

As the meal wore on, the talk became more personal and confidences were more readily exchanged. Ermintrude was intrigued to know how Ralph and Gervase had become commissioners and they were entranced by her description of her husband's romantic courtship of her.

Earl Hugh had changed out of all recognition.

'Memories are precious things,' said Ermintrude with a sigh of regret. 'That is why I cherish them so much.'

After conferring for most of the evening with the leading barons, Hugh d'Avranches called for torches to light his way on an inspection of the defences. He checked that sentries were posted at regular intervals along the battlements and that the gate was secured. Night was a time when extra vigilance was required. The sentries were too frightened to relax. They knew the penalty for being slack in their duties. Throughout the hours of darkness, they would remain alert and watchful.

Accompanied by six of his men, Earl Hugh left the castle by the postern gate to confirm that the city walls were being patrolled with equal diligence. Mounting the steps in a blaze of light, he marched along the battlements until he came to the main gate. It was well guarded. The stout timbers were proof

131

against any but the most concerted attack and he resolved that no enemy would ever get close enough to batter a way in.

He was still high on the city wall when he heard the thunder of hoofbeats. A dozen or more horses were conjured out of the gloom. Sentries drew their weapons and additional men came running up the steps. As the horses were brought to a halt outside the gate, the captain of the guard challenged the newcomers.

'Who is below?'

'Messengers from Rhuddlan,' called a voice.

'Why are there so many of you?'

'To ensure safety on a dangerous road.'

'This is Hugh of Chester who speaks,' said the earl, taking charge of the situation. 'Stand forth that I may see you more clearly and identify you.'

He leaned over the wall as the spokesman nudged his horse forward into the pool of light cast by the torches. Hugh could see from his armour and bearing that the man was no impostor.

'Did you meet with trouble on the way?' he asked.

'Yes, my lord, but we outran the pursuit.'

'What have you brought from Rhuddlan?'

'An urgent message to be delivered into your hands.'

'Did my own messenger arrive before you left?'

'No, my lord.'

'Are you sure?'

'Quite sure,' said the spokesman. He gave a command and one of his companions towed a horse forward into the light. Across its back was the body of the messenger whom Hugh had dispatched from Chester at dawn.

The spokesman indicated the corpse with a forlorn gesture.

'We found him by the wayside, my lord,' he explained. 'Stabbed in the back. He never got anywhere near Rhuddlan.'

Chapter Eleven

Morning found the castle in complete turmoil. Sentries were being increased in number and weapons sharpened, extra supplies of food were being brought in, men were herding sheep into a pen and drawing water from the well to fill barrels all around the bailey, and soldiers rushed to and fro in a frenzy of activity. It was almost as if they were preparing for a long siege. Earl Hugh was in the midst of it all, barking orders, pointing an imperious finger and cursing anyone he felt was slow to respond to his curt commands.

The castle gate was shut and barred. Nobody was allowed in without good reason and nobody was allowed to leave without express permission. Ralph Delchard was the first to protest. With Gervase Bret at his side, he accosted their host in the middle of the courtyard.

'We have just been turned back at the gate, my lord!'

'On my instruction, Ralph.'

'But why? We have business in the shire hall.'

'Not today.'

'Claimants have been summoned, witnesses called.'

'Your deliberations have been cancelled until further notice,' said Hugh peremptorily. 'The town reeve has been given notice of this and will turn away anyone who comes to the shire hall in search of you.'

'We had no warning of this.'

'You are receiving it now.'

'Why were we not consulted?' demanded Ralph angrily. 'We are the King's agents. Our business has royal authority. It cannot be arbitrarily suspended on a whim of yours.'

'What Ralph means,' said Gervase, seeing the rancour in Hugh's eye and adopting a more reasonable tone, 'is that this interruption is highly inconvenient.'

'It was forced upon me, Gervase.'

'By whom?'

'The Welsh archer who tried to kill me in the forest. The warriors who came out yesterday to assess the defences of Rhuddlan Castle. The murderer who stabbed my messenger in the back on the road to Rhuddlan. The villains who tried to intercept the couriers whom my nephew, Robert, sent to me. The army that is gathering on the other side of the border.' He glared at Ralph. 'Do I need more justification than that?'

'No, my lord,' said the other, assimilating the news. 'I had no knowledge of these other worrying incidents.'

Hugh was bitter. 'Well, now you do. So perhaps you will stop telling me that Raoul Lambert was struck down on purpose and that my fears of a Welsh rebellion are groundless. Talk to the men who came last night from Rhuddlan. They will soon convince you that the danger is real.'

'We both accept that, my lord,' said Gervase.

'Yes,' added Ralph, cowed into a murmur.

'My first task,' said Hugh with a sweep of his arm, 'is to protect this city from attack. Precautions have to be taken and restrictions imposed. We all suffer inconvenience but there is no other way. Until we see what the Welsh intend to do, Chester must lock itself indoors.'

'Can we be of any assistance, my lord?' offered Ralph.

'Only by keeping out of my way.'

Hugh let out a bellow of rage at two soldiers who accidentally dropped the basket of stones they were carrying up the steps to the battlements. He charged off to berate the men. The commissioners took the opportunity to drift away in order to confer in a quiet corner.

'What do you make of this?' asked Ralph.

'Earl Hugh seems to expect a full invasion.'

'When he holds the Prince of Gwynedd in his dungeon? He

134

boasted to me that Chester was safe from attack as long as Gruffydd ap Cynan was in captivity.'

'That view will have to be revised.'

'So it seems.'

'Canon Hubert and Brother Simon will be greatly alarmed by this turn of events,' said Gervase. 'Should we send word for them to come here?'

'They would refuse to do so. I believe that they would rather endure an attack from Wales than turn to Hugh for protection. They think him a species of devil.' He watched the irate earl, howling at some sentries. 'When I see him like this, I am inclined to agree with them.'

'Where does this leave our notions about Raoul Lambert?'

'In tatters, Gervase.'

'I wonder.'

'We were wrong and Hugh was right.'

'That is how it may appear at the moment.'

'That is how it *is*, I fear.' Ralph thought of his wife. 'Golde will be alarmed by all this activity. I had better go back and explain what is happening.'

'She came to Chester at a bad time.'

'Is there ever a good time to visit this accursed city?'

Ralph departed on that note of cynicism and Gervase was able to take a closer look at what was happening all around him. Earl Hugh was a most effective general. The speed and thoroughness of his preparations were impressive. Gervase was still admiring the sense of controlled urgency when he became aware of a man at his elbow. The sentry was in his hauberk, eyes set apart by the thick iron nasal of his helm.

'Master Bret?' he asked.

'Yes?'

'You have a visitor.'

'Who is it?'

'You will have to come to the gate to find out,' said the man. 'We have orders to admit nobody to the castle. And you must not go far outside it yourself. But the visitor implores you to come.'

'Is it Canon Hubert? Or Brother Simon?'

'Neither.'

'Then who?'

'A young woman.'

Gervase was surprised. He knew no young women in Chester. Mind racing, he followed the sentry back to the gate. When he was allowed to leave by the postern, a familiar face was waiting to greet him with a weary smile.

'Gytha!' he exclaimed.

'Thank you for agreeing to see me.'

'What are you doing here?'

'I had to see you,' she said.

'Did you walk all the way to Chester?'

'Yes.'

'It will have taken an age. What time did you leave?'

'Well before dawn.'

'It must be important, then.'

'I think it is.'

Several people were milling around the gate, arguing with the sentries and pleading to be let in. Gervase took her by the arm to move her away from the hubbub. When they paused in the doorway of a house, he was able to take a considered look at her. Flushed and exhausted, she still had an extraordinary resemblance to Alys. Gervase's blood coursed and he was momentarily confused, not sure whether he was doting on his betrothed or showing an improper interest in a vulnerable young woman. Gytha's embarrassment suggested that she, too, was grappling with warm feelings which caused her some concern.

'How is your brother?' he inquired.

'He is better now that the funeral is over.'

'Over? Already?'

'Father Ernwin saw no reason to delay it.'

'I applaud his wisdom.'

'He has been very kind to us.'

'Was it an ordeal for you?'

'Yes.'

'I am sorry I was not there to comfort you.'

She looked up at him. 'So am I,' she said softly, 'but you have already done so much for us.'

'I wish that I could have done more, Gytha.'

Their eyes locked and both felt the pull of attraction.

'I am very grateful,' she said at length. 'We both are. Beollan and me. You had no obligation to help us.'

'Yes, I did.'

'Why?'

'You were in distress.'

'But we were complete strangers to you.'

'It makes no difference.'

Their eyes met again but she was suddenly afraid of the intensity of his gaze and the surge of her emotions. She lowered her head shyly. Gervase wanted to reach out to console her but fought against the impulse, reminding himself that there was a narrow dividing line between offering comfort to a lovely young woman and deriving pleasure from any contact with her. He had pledged himself to Alys and knew that he had to resist the fleeting appeal of Gytha.

'Why did you come?' he asked.

'To tell you the full story.'

'Story?'

'Of what happened in the forest the day that my father and brother were killed. I have talked to Beollan.'

'He has spoken to me himself.'

'But you did not hear the whole story,' she said, 'and I felt it important that you should. It may help. Besides . . .'

She raised her head to look at him once more.

'Well?'

'I wanted to see you again,' she said simply.

'I'm glad that you came.' He touched her shoulder with his fingertips then became serious. 'What did Beollan tell you?'

'He saw an archer sneaking away in the forest.'

'He caught a glimpse, he said.'

'It was more than that. The archer ran within a few yards of him. Beollan had a close look.'

137

'And?'

'He misled you.'

'Did he?'

'What you believed he saw was a Welshman with a bow in his hand, making his escape through the trees.'

'Yes,' said Gervase. 'That is what I assumed.'

'Beollan held back one vital detail.'

'What was that, Gytha?'

'The archer was a woman.'

Birdsong rang through the Forest of Delamere to celebrate a bright and peaceful morning. Deer grazed safely, pigs were foraging eagerly and smaller animals were free to roam and nibble wherever they wished. Leaving her pony tethered, she walked leisurely through the undergrowth and let the sun play fitfully on her face as it poked its way through a fretwork of branches. When she came to the edge of a clearing, she was more circumspect, pausing to make sure that all was well before emerging from cover.

The old woman was outside her hovel, trying to milk the fractious goat which was tied to a stake and cursing it aloud whenever it shifted its position again. Her visitor approached across the grass with a welcoming smile. When the old woman saw her, she gladly abandoned her chore and gave the goat a valedictory slap. The two friends spoke in Welsh.

'Good morning!' said the newcomer.

'It is good to see you again.'

'No problems, I hope?'

'None, Eiluned.'

'I am glad. I would hate to have put you in danger.'

'Do not fear for me,' said the old woman. 'I have learned to look after myself.'

'I know.'

'What about you, Eiluned?'

'I got back safely. They were very pleased.'

'You are a brave girl.'

Eiluned smiled. She was a stocky young woman with dark

brown hair and eyes of a matching hue. Her face was pleasant rather than pretty and her attire was plain. There was a quiet determination in her manner and she neither spoke nor moved like a woman seeking the admiration of men.

She glanced across at the half-made basket which stood outside the cottage. A low stool was set beside it.

'What did you do with my basket?' she asked.

The old woman grinned. 'I threw it away.'

'Was it so bad?'

'You would never be able to sell such poor workmanship.'

'I would never be able to finish the basket in the first place,' said Eiluned. 'After a couple of hours, my fingers were aching. It is more difficult than it looks. I was grateful when the soldiers finally came and went. Then I was able to put the basket aside.'

'It served its purpose.'

'Very well.'

The old woman led the way into her fetid hovel. It was a wooden hut with a thatched roof in need of repair and a sunken floor. The small window admitted scant light and air. A few mean sticks of furniture stood around. The old woman waddled across to the rough mattress on the floor and knelt down beside it. She groped around in the straw on which the mattress was laid and pulled out a bow. Taking it from her, Eiluned stroked the weapon fondly then helped her companion up from the floor.

'No arrows?' said the old woman.

'I shot the only two I needed.'

'You must have been sure of your aim.'

'My father taught me well,' said Eiluned, pleased to have the bow in her hands again. 'He brought me up as the son he never had. Other girls learned to cook, sew and make baskets. I practised with a dagger and a bow.' Her jaw tightened. 'I am glad that my skills can be put to such good use. Had he lived, my father would have been proud of me.'

She came out into the fresh air again and inhaled deeply.

'What will happen now?' asked the other, following her out.

139

'I cannot tell you.'

'Why not?'

'The less you know, the better for all of us.'

'If you say so.'

'I do.' She gave the old woman a brief hug. 'Thank you again for your help. You saved my life. I will not forget.'

'Goodbye, Eiluned.'

'Goodbye.'

'Will you come again?'

'No.'

'I am always ready.'

'We will not put you in such danger again.'

Eiluned walked to the edge of the clearing and turned.

'Good luck!' called the old woman.

'We may need it,' murmured the other. With a farewell wave, she darted swiftly off into the trees and was soon lost from sight.

Ralph Delchard took a long time to get used to the notion.

'A female archer!' he exclaimed. 'Never!'

'That is what the boy saw,' said Gervase.

'It is what he *thought* he saw. But how much credence can we place on the word of a frightened lad? He was in a panic when he fled from the others in the forest. He would have been too terrified to notice anything.'

'I disagree, Ralph. I spoke with him.'

'Then why did he not mention this fantasy of his before?'

'It is not a fantasy.'

'A woman using a bow and arrow? No, Gervase!'

'It would not be the first time in these isles,' the other reminded him. 'Warrior queens have ruled here in ancient times. They took up arms and rode out to battle in their chariots.'

Ralph was scornful. 'Is that what this archer is supposed to have done? Ridden up in her chariot and fired a deadly arrow as she raced past? You insult my intelligence, Gervase.'

'I was astonished myself at first,' confessed his friend, 'but

Gytha swore to me that that was what her brother said. The reason Beollan did not tell me the truth earlier is obvious. He did not trust me enough. Why should he? I am staying under the roof of the man who ordered the death of his father and brother. He was bound to be suspicious of me.' Gervase was convinced. 'The archer was a woman, Ralph.'

'That is patent nonsense.'

'Why?'

'Because it takes strength to pull a bow.'

'It takes strength to do all the household chores that most women do each day. The weaker sex is not as weak as you suppose. Beollan really did see a woman with a bow.'

'Only in his imagination.'

'Why should he invent such a tale?'

'To confuse us still further.'

'No, Ralph. The boy has sharp eyes. He was trained as a lookout. He would not make a mistake.'

'He did on this occasion. Women do not shoot arrows.'

'Is it any more difficult than brewing beer?'

Ralph was checked. He had forgotten Golde. Only a robust woman could have run the business as effectively as his wife had done in Hereford. She would not have survived in such a tough, competitive trade if she had been meek and mild in her approach. Both in mind and body, Golde was undeniably strong.

They were in Gervase's apartment at the castle. Sounds of activity rose up from the bailey. Ralph crossed to the window and looked down at the busy scene. When he saw quivers of arrows being set out in readiness at intervals along the battlements, he turned back to Gervase. He shifted the ground of his argument slightly.

'Great skill is needed in archery,' he said.

'Women can acquire skills as easily as men.'

'A bow is a deadly weapon, Gervase.'

'That was proved in the forest.'

'Not by any female archer,' maintained Ralph. 'Skill must be matched with an instinct to kill. Women are brought up to nurture life, not to take it. Look at Golde. She has power enough to kill but has far too gentle a disposition ever to use that power.'

Gervase smiled. 'I am not so sure about that,' he teased. 'Judging from her expression at the table last night, I think she would cheerfully have murdered the brewer who provided that dreadful beer.'

'She would have drowned him in his own brewhouse!'

'I rest my case.'

'Be serious, Gervase,' returned the other. 'There is every difference between a momentary impulse such as Golde felt and a calculated act of murder. What sort of woman would have the nerve to assassinate someone?'

'One with a strong motive. It has happened many times before, Ralph. Emperors and kings have fallen victim to wives or discarded mistresses.'

'They did not lurk in the forest with a bow and arrow.'

'No,' conceded Gervase. 'Women tend to favour poison or a stealthy dagger over archery, but the result is the same.'

Ralph could manage no reply. He wrestled with his doubts for a few minutes before looking across at his friend.

'Are you completely persuaded about this?' he said.

'Gytha would not lie to me.'

'Supposing her brother lied to *her*?'

'To what end? Beollan told her honestly what he saw.'

'A woman running away.'

'Leaving two men to pay for the crime she had committed,' said Gervase. 'His father and brother were executed, Ralph. Hanged by the neck then hacked to pieces. Do you think that Beollan will ever forget the archer who was responsible for their deaths? They unwittingly covered her escape.'

'Only on the first occasion.'

'First?'

'When the hawk was killed,' said Ralph. 'What about the second incident when Raoul Lambert fell to an arrow? If, as you argue, the same archer claimed both victims, how did she escape the second time when there was nobody to divert attention from her? You heard Earl Hugh. They searched under every bush in that part of the forest and found nothing.'

'Yes, they did.'

'What?'

'Two women making baskets outside a cottage.'

'So?' The truth slowly dawned on him. 'You think . . .'

'It is only a guess, Ralph, but it has taken firm hold on my mind. What better way to elude capture? The soldiers were searching for a male archer. They would not look too closely at a woman who was working away at a basket. If you were hunting a wild boar, would you stop to look at rabbits?'

'No.'

'She outwitted them.'

Ralph pondered. 'You may be right,' he said at length.

'What other explanation is there?'

'None.'

'Then we are faced with a dilemma.'

'In what way?'

'Do we divulge this intelligence to Earl Hugh or not?'

'I think not,' decided Ralph. 'I would love to see the expression on his face when I tell him that his huntsman was killed by a woman, but I will forgo that pleasure until we are quite certain of our facts.'

'That is my feeling as well,' said Gervase. 'Apart from anything else, I want to protect Gytha and her brother.'

'Hugh would haul the pair of them in for interrogation and I would not wish that on anybody. I have seen his methods.'

'There is another consideration, Ralph. Their parents were buried in secret yesterday at their parish church.'

'Hugh ordered that the bodies lie in a ditch.'

'Exactly. If he learns the truth, he is likely to have them dug up and thrown back where he left them.'

'We are agreed on one thing then. Hugh hears nothing.'

'Until we verify the facts.'

'And how do we do that, Gervase?'

'We go to the cottage where those two women made baskets,' said the other. 'That is where we must start.'

'How on earth would we find the place alone?'
'We would not, Ralph. We need a guide.'
'Brother Gerold?'
'Not this time,' said Gervase. 'We must seek help from someone who lives in the Forest of Delamere itself. Someone who is indirectly involved in this business. Someone with her own reasons for finding out the truth.'

The affection in his friend's voice made Ralph smile.
'Would her name be Gytha, by any chance?'

Gruffydd ap Cynan, Prince of Gwynedd, finally lost his patience. Picking up the little stool, he used it to bang on the door of his cell, yelling at the top of his voice at the same time. The noise brought two of his gaolers hurrying down the dark passage towards him.

'Stop that noise!' ordered one of them.
'Or we'll stop it for you!' warned the other.
'What has got into him?'

When they peered through the grille in the door, their prisoner backed away and tossed the stool aside. He pointed upwards and gestured for them to unlock the door. They shook their heads. Snatching up the stool again, he hurled it at the door with all his might and it splintered against the stout timber. One of the guards turned to his companion.

'He's run mad. Fetch Earl Hugh.'
'Try to calm him down,' said the other, hurrying away.
'I'll calm him down!' muttered the first man, fingering his sword. 'If he keeps up this clamour, I'll calm him down for good. Do you hear that, Gruffydd?' he shouted. 'We like peace and quiet down here.'

The prisoner came to the grille and issued a stream of abuse in Welsh. His gaoler laughed then spat contemptuously at the floor. Gruffydd ap Cynan ranted even more wildly.

Earl Hugh eventually came to see what the commotion was about. Bearing a flaming torch, he strode along the corridor with a howl of anger. Four soldiers marched at his heels.

'Open the door!' he ordered.

'He's in a dangerous mood,' warned the gaoler.

'So am I. Do as I say!'

The door was unlocked and the prisoner tried to rush out, but Earl Hugh forced him back with the naked flame. Walking into the noisome cell, he stood over the Welshman and glowered at him. Gruffydd ap Cynan was not afraid. He met his captor's gaze without flinching.

'What is the trouble here?' demanded Hugh.

'He is complaining, my lord,' said the gaoler, 'because we haven't taken him for exercise today. I don't understand a word of his language but that's what he seems to be saying. He wants to stretch his legs and breathe in some clean air.'

'He is a prisoner here and not a guest,' snarled Hugh. 'And he will certainly not enjoy the freedom to stroll about in the bailey as long as his countrymen threaten us.' His hands moved in graphic gestures. 'Do you hear that, you Welsh pig?' he said, holding the torch near Gruffydd's face. 'You will stay locked up down here. No light, no exercise and no privileges of any kind.' He wagged a finger. 'And no more complaints or I will get really angry.'

Gruffydd ap Cynan knew little of the language in which he was being addressed but his captor's meaning was clear. He stood there in dignified silence as his visitors went out and locked the door after them.

The gaoler followed Earl Hugh along the corridor.

'What will we do if he gets violent again?'

'Put him where he belongs – in chains!'

Chapter Twelve

The more Golde saw of the Lady Ermintrude, the more she warmed to her. It was not simply the bonding of two women in a largely male environment, though that was a definite factor in a shifting military situation. There was a deeper kinship, unrecognised at first by either of them, then undeclared when it did slowly impinge upon their consciousness. They sought each other out, talked, compared, speculated together, and developed, in a surprisingly short time, a real friendship. Neither of them dared to probe the roots of that friendship which was, by its very nature, only temporary. They just enjoyed it while they could, like two strangers marooned on a desert island, united in adversity and making light of any individual differences.

Ermintrude was tolerant of her guest's occasional stumbles in Norman French and Golde made allowances for the sometimes jarring values of a woman brought up in a dominant aristocratic culture which she, as a Saxon, had come to hate. Golde was helped by the fact that her companion had none of the arrogance and high-handedness so often associated with conquest. If anything, there was a faint air of apology about the Lady Ermintrude, as if she was graciously aware that she was trespassing on someone else's property.

'Tell me more about brewing,' she invited.

'Oh, my lady!' said Golde. 'We should be here all day.'

'Listening to you is far more interesting than watching the soldiers exercising in the yard. I am intrigued by the idea of your actually taking over your husband's business when he died. Did you have a natural inclination for the trade?'

'Not in the least.'

'How, then, did you come to master it?'

'Of necessity,' said Golde with a sad smile. 'My first husband was not wealthy and I had a younger sister to provide for as well as myself. Brewing was a means of survival, my lady. I had picked up the rudiments of it from my husband but I never thought to make a living from it.'

'Yet clearly you did.'

'In time.'

'Your beer must have been of a high quality if you supplied it to Hereford Castle.'

'It was, my lady. But only after I had learned the trade by a process of trial and error. Hereford had other brewers and they mocked the glaring mistakes I was bound to make at first. But I rarely made the same mistake twice and their sniggers soon turned to irritation when I began to take customers from them.'

Ermintrude was delighted. 'You got the better of men at their own trade?'

'And women,' explained Golde. 'I was not the only female brewer in the city. It is a job that requires patience and intuition. Women tend to have an abundance of both.'

'Yes,' said Ermintrude, lowering her eyelids and clasping her hands in her lap. 'Patience is indeed a virtue. I have struggled to show it myself. As for intuition,' she added with a dismissive shrug, 'that has always been beyond me.'

'Surely not, my lady!'

'I lack instinct, Golde.'

'That is patently untrue.'

'On the surface, perhaps. Deep down, it is another matter.'

'Yet you are so responsive to others,' said Golde, taken aback by the confession. 'You seem to know exactly what your guests want before they can even guess at it themselves.'

'That is easy. One can be trained to do that.'

'What is it that you are unable to do, my lady?'

148

'Make the right decisions.'

There was a dull finality in her voice which signalled the end of that phase of the conversation. Though Ermintrude retained her usual poise, there was a hint of real suffering behind the impassive mask. Golde waited until her hostess was ready to speak again. They were in the latter's apartment, high up in the keep but well within earshot of the constant activity down in the bailey.

Ermintrude cast a rueful glance at the window. 'Do you mind being married to a soldier?' she asked.

'Ralph's fighting days are behind him, my lady.'

'Then why does he keep himself in such fine condition?'

'Out of a sense of pride.'

'No, Golde. It springs from an eternal readiness. We are both married to Norman soldiers and they are a breed apart. Such men never retire from the field. Warfare is in their blood. They cannot escape it.'

'Ralph has managed to do so,' said Golde.

'Has he?'

'More or less.'

'I heard that he fought a duel in Herefordshire.'

'That was different, my lady.'

'He bore arms again. Wherein lies the difference?'

'It was the only way to resolve a crisis.'

'That is the common excuse for all battles,' said Ermintrude with a weary smile. 'They resolve one crisis then create a dozen others. And so it goes on. I have watched my own husband being drawn into one unnecessary engagement after another. Hugh is an inveterate soldier. He cannot help it. The blast of war is like a love song to him.' She looked Golde directly in the eyes. 'I suspect that Ralph Delchard is a man of similar stock.'

'No, my lady!' protested Golde loudly, shocked at the comparison of her husband with a man she considered to be grotesque and uncouth. 'I am sorry,' she said, realising that her reaction might well cause offence to a loyal wife. 'I know that Ralph came to England as a soldier, but he has now chosen a more peaceful way of life.'

149

'Not if he travels around the country.'

'What do you mean?'

'Danger lurks everywhere. Ride any distance and, sooner or later, you are likely to have to defend yourself from attack. Even with their escort, Ralph and Gervase must surely have been the intended prey of outlaws.'

'Yes,' admitted Golde. 'On our way to York.'

'Did your husband have to draw a weapon in the city?'

'Only to ward off some lions.'

'Lions?'

'Two of them, my lady. Ralph was trapped in a cage with them. He fought to save his own life.'

'He may well have to do that again.'

'Again?'

'Can you not hear that din down below?' said the older woman. 'They are preparing for battle. Chester is very close to the Welsh border and there are thousands of roaring lions on the other side of it. What will happen if they launch an assault on this castle?'

'There is no chance of that, surely?'

'Hugh seems to think so.'

'Ralph believes it highly unlikely.'

'But he, with respect, has only been in Cheshire a short while. My husband has been here for several years. He knows the Welsh of old.' She scrutinised Golde's face again. 'In the event of a battle, what will Ralph do? Stay in his apartment with you? Or take up arms and join in the fray?'

Golde blushed as she accepted what the answer must be.

'I did not mean to upset you,' said Ermintrude with a soft hand on her wrist, 'but it is as well to face the truth about one's husband. It makes for a certain amount of discomfort but it spares you the shock of unpleasant discoveries.'

It was as close as Ermintrude was prepared to go towards the subject of her husband's rampant infidelities and she immediately backed away again.

'Ralph Delchard is a fine man,' she said enviously. 'You chose well, Golde.'

150

'He likes to think that he did the choosing.'

'And did he?'

'It was a mutual decision.'

'The only kind with any true validity.' Her manner brightened. 'I wish that I had been a brewer.'

Golde was amazed. 'You, my lady?'

'Yes. I would love these delicate hands of mine to have learned something other than merely how to sew a fine seam. I do admire your enterprise.'

'I was forced into the trade.'

'Nevertheless, you succeeded. Against all the odds. You did something useful, Golde. At the end of the working day, you must have had great satisfaction.'

'I did,' agreed the other, 'but I also had the abiding smell of beer in my nostrils, my apparel and my hair. Brewing follows you home at night, my lady. I would much rather have been able to pass the time sewing a fine seam.'

The noise outside took on a fresh urgency. Golde tensed.

'Have no fear,' said Ermintrude soothingly. 'My husband has the situation in hand. He is at his best in these situations.'

Golde nodded. 'So is Ralph,' she admitted to herself.

Rules which applied to the citizens of Chester were waived for two royal commissioners and the six knights who escorted them. The gate was duly opened and the party rode out at a brisk trot towards the Forest of Delamere. Aware of the risk they were taking in being abroad in such troubled times, they remained watchful. Ralph Delchard still had doubts that a Welsh attack was imminent and evinced no fear, but Gervase Bret was much more cautious. They had been in the saddle for half an hour before he stopped inspecting every bush and tree in case it was a potential hiding place.

'Do not fret, Gervase,' said Ralph as they cantered along a forest path. 'We are safe enough, I warrant you.'

'And how safe is that?'

'You have seven strong swords to protect you.'

'Earl Hugh had fifty but it did not stop someone from firing an arrow at him. Or at Raoul Lambert.'

'Is that what you are afraid of?' teased Ralph. 'A female with a bow? Well, I do not blame you. It has happened before and the wound was fatal.'

'What wound?'

'Yours, man. When Alys strung her bow and shot a dart of love at you, Gervase Bret was felled on the spot. You were a shrewd and conscientious young lawyer until you were struck down by her missile. No wonder you fear the sound of a bowstring!'

Gervase grinned. 'You make a jest of everything.'

'It soothes the nerves.'

'Yours or mine?'

'Both.' Ralph nudged him. 'Do you miss Alys?'

'Very much.'

'Does this Gytha remind you of her?'

'Yes,' said Gervase, involuntarily, then tried to cover his confusion by gabbling. 'Not that there are any real points of comparison. Gytha comes from humble stock and has led a life of drudgery while Alys has been more fortunate. There is a slight physical resemblance between them but it is negligible. No, Ralph, she does not really remind me of Alys. No other woman could do that. Alys is unique.'

'So are you.' Ralph gave him an affectionate punch. 'That is why the pair of you are so well matched.'

'I could say the same of you and Golde.'

'Hardly! That is a case of the attraction of opposites.'

'Not from where I stand.'

'Then you have been misled, Gervase. We came together in spite of ourselves. My brains and Golde's beer made an irresistible combination.'

His laughter disturbed some nearby rooks which took to the air with a fanfare of protest, leaving the bough on which they had been perched vibrating for a full minute. Gervase abandoned the badinage with his friend in order to concentrate on his pathfinding. Having only been to Gytha's cottage once, he was not entirely certain that he could find it again, but his memory was sound and he soon began to identify tiny landmarks.

After a long ride without incident, they eventually came out into the clearing where the hovel stood. There was no sign of Beollan but Gytha immediately poked her head out of the dwelling. Alarmed at the sight of the armed soldiers, she relaxed when she recognised Gervase, and his warm smile of greeting reassured her. Gytha came out of the door and Ralph was able to make a full appraisal of her before emitting a low murmur of approval. His soldiers were also struck by the unexpected sight of a lovely young woman emerging from such a mean hovel.

Gervase introduced Ralph Delchard to her and she eyed him warily. His candid smile of admiration was rather disturbing.

'What do you want?' she asked.

'Your help,' answered Ralph, astonishing her with his knowledge of her language. 'And we have ridden a long way to ask for it, Gytha.'

'You do not need to tell her that,' said Gervase. 'Gytha has walked to Chester and back twice already this week. She knows exactly how long a distance it is.'

'How can I help you?' she wondered.

Gervase explained that they were looking for a woman in a certain part of the forest but had no idea who she was. He gave the few facts about her that he possessed but did not divulge their reason for wishing to see her. Gytha guessed that they wanted to question the woman about something and she became defensive, instinctively opposing the wishes of Norman soldiers. It took time for Gervase to persuade her of the importance of their mission.

'I do not know this person,' she said bluntly.

'Can you at least take us to that part of the forest?' coaxed Gervase. 'We would be very grateful.'

'Beollan would be a surer guide.'

'Where is he?'

153

'Putting flowers on the grave. I have just come back from the churchyard myself. Beollan will soon follow.'

'Let us meet him on the way.'

Gervase dismounted and offered his horse to her but Gytha was too embarrassed to accept his invitation in front of the others. Instead, she set off purposefully and they trailed along behind her, Gervase still on foot, Ralph watching the bob of her head and the beguiling swing of her hips. When they met Beollan near the church, he was frightened by the sight of the soldiers and all but bolted. His sister had to grab him to keep him there and the two of them had a conversation that was far too breathless and hasty for Ralph to understand. He turned to Gervase for elucidation.

'Beollan will take us,' said the latter. 'As long as we can guarantee his safety and that of Gytha.'

'I will do more than that,' conceded Ralph, taking a purse from his belt and extracting a coin. 'If he leads us to the woman in question, there will be a reward.'

He held up the coin and Beollan's hesitation vanished.

With Gytha beside him, the boy loped along a series of trails that were sometimes so narrow and overhung with leaves that they had to plunge into dark tunnels before emerging once again into sunlight. Brother and sister seemed tireless as they covered mile after mile. When they reached a patch of open land, Beollan finally paused for breath, hands on his knees as he bent double. Gytha exchanged a few panted sentences with him then turned to the others.

'The cottage is nearby,' she said, pointing a finger. 'An old woman lives there alone. Beollan is not sure if she is the person you seek but she is the only one in this part of the forest who answers the description you gave.'

'Thank you, Gytha,' said Gervase.

'One thing more.'

'Yes?'

'She is Welsh.'

Ralph Delchard could not resist another jest.

'Does she have a bow and arrow?'

*   *   *

154

Having held his council of war, the Earl of Chester now sought the blessing of the Church. It was not easily forthcoming.

'I oppose violence of any kind,' said a querulous Bishop Robert. 'Start another war and where will it end?'

'In victory for us,' Hugh assured him.

'At what terrible cost, my lord?'

'That remains to be seen.'

'Many lives will be lost.'

'Even more will be saved,' said the earl. 'As I see it, a stark choice confronts us. We either wait until the Welsh launch an attack on us here or we strike first and rout them before their assault has gathered momentum.'

'Neither course of action commends itself to me.'

Hugh was sarcastic. 'What do you propose as an alternative, Robert? Abject surrender? Or do we abandon the city and retreat with all the belongings we can carry?'

'I fear for my cathedral,' said the other.

'I fear for my county!'

Earl confronted bishop in the hall at the castle. Robert de Limesey had repaired there in haste to implore that his beloved cathedral be saved from possible demolition only to find Hugh in warlike mood. Unable to condone military action, the bishop only succeeded in enraging the earl and decided to bow out of the debate altogether.

Archdeacon Frodo immediately came to his rescue by taking his place in the discussion, beginning with a conciliatory smile then speaking with quiet respect.

'My lord,' he said, rubbing his palms together, 'the decision lies with you. We acknowledge that. The Church can only advise and we do that with the deference that is due to you. Bishop Robert and I are extremely conscious of the debt which we – and the whole city – owe to you for protecting us so well over the years. Your policy has been as wise as it is effective.'

'I am glad that you appreciate that,' growled Hugh.

'We do, my lord.'

'Then why does Robert come bleating about his cathedral?'

155

'The bishop is merely representing our point of view,' said Frodo softly, 'and I am sure that Brother Gerold would endorse it. He would no more wish to see Chester cathedral destroyed than watch his own chapel razed to the ground.'

'That will never happen!'

'We pray that it will not.'

'There will be no threat to the chapel or the cathedral if we strike first and put the Welsh army to flight. They will be completely disabled.'

'For the time being, my lord.'

'What do you mean?'

'The Welsh have been disabled many times but they have a strange capacity for rebuilding their forces. No matter how many battles you win, the war somehow drags on. That is what concerns Bishop Robert and myself.'

'Who asked for your opinion, Frodo?'

'It is irrelevant here,' said the other with another smile of appeasement. 'Authorised by Bishop Robert, I merely offer the Church's view. We are doves of peace, my lord.'

'I am a hawk of war.'

'There are more of us in the sky. From what I hear, the Church is not alone in advocating restraint. Your own close advisers warned against intemperate action.'

'That was before my messenger was killed on the road to Rhuddlan Castle.' Hugh took a step towards him. 'Who told you of our secret deliberations?'

'Such things are difficult to keep private, my lord.'

'Is there a Church informer among my barons?'

'There are several Christians.'

Hugh was stung. 'I am one myself, Frodo.'

'That is why we feel able to appeal to you.'

'In the spirit of Christian fellowship,' added Robert. 'Before you commit yourself to war, consult with Brother Gerold. He will surely take our part. Yet one more dove.'

'The hour of the hawk has come,' insisted Hugh, striding round the table to take up a position in front of his chair. 'This whole business began with a hawk being brought down from the sky. Doves of peace cannot avenge that outrage nor can they atone for the murder of Raoul Lambert. It is time to remove the hoods from the hawks of war.'

'Do that and you lose all control,' cautioned Frodo.

'It is the only way to *impose* control.'

'Bishop Robert and I view it differently.'

'I have grown accustomed to your poor eyesight.' The earl waved a contemptuous arm. 'Away with the pair of you! If you will not bless our mission, do not hinder it. Scurry back to your precious cathedral and protect it with an odour of sanctity.'

'That remark is blasphemous!' cried Robert.

'Earl Hugh has our best interests at heart,' said Frodo, jumping in to calm down his quivering companion. 'We must understand that, your grace. It is unfair of us to expect him to obey our dictates when we know little of the true situation here. What we can, however, suggest is this.' His third smile was the most obsequious yet. 'A middle way.'

Hugh was sceptical. 'Between what?'

'Outright war and inaction.'

'Middle way?'

'Negotiation, my lord. Using your prime weapon.'

'My army.'

'No,' corrected Frodo. 'The man who rots in your dungeon. Gruffydd ap Cynan. He can prevent this battle.'

'He is the cause of it!' howled the earl.

'Cause and symptom.'

'Do not split hairs with me, Frodo.'

'Is it not at least worth trying?' pleaded the other. 'If one man can avert a war, why let hundreds of others die in it? Reason with the Prince of Gwynedd. Strike a bargain.'

'I already have. He is my prisoner.'

'Then extract information from him, my lord.'

'How can we when we do not speak his foul language?'

'Use an interpreter.'

'Yes,' said Robert. 'Someone who is cunning enough to charm the truth out of him. Set a thief to catch a thief. Instruct a Welshman to lure a Welshman.'

Hugh was unconvinced. He ran a hand across his jaw.

'There is no man to whom I could entrust this task.'

Robert and Frodo had a muttered conversation. The bishop had obvious reservations but was eventually persuaded by his archdeacon. The latter turned back to the earl.

'A curious coincidence,' he said.

'You speak the language yourself?'

'No, my lord. But we have the Archdeacon of St David's staying with us at present. Let him examine the prisoner.'

'Never! They would simply conspire against us.'

'Not if a third person were present.'

'Third person?'

'Yes,' said Frodo, gently. 'Master Gervase Bret. He can understand Welsh but he is not sufficiently fluent in the language to question Gruffydd on his own. What he can do, however, is to act as our witness. That is our counsel, my lord. Employ this Archdeacon Idwal to talk to the prisoner under the supervision of Gervase Bret.' He spread his arms in a gesture of persuasion. 'The whole city may benefit from such a conversation.'

The moment he set eyes on her, Gervase experienced a thrill of certainty. When they came out into the clearing, the old woman was seated on a tree stump, gazing idly around while her nimble fingers worked at her basket. She was in no way alarmed by their arrival and gave them a vacant grin.

'Thank you, Beollan,' said Gervase.

'Is this the right place?' asked the boy.

'I believe so.'

'Can we go now?'

'Wait until we have spoken to her.'

Beollan and his sister withdrew into the trees as the visitors closed in on the old woman. Her hands continued to work away at the basket with unhurried precision. Ralph ambled across to her and barked a question but she simply mimed incomprehension. When Gervase spoke to her in Welsh, however, she stiffened at once and her fingers froze.

'Good day to you!' he said.

'And to you, young man.'

'That is a fine basket you have there.'

'I have been weaving them all my life.'

'Is your daughter as adept at it as you?'

'I have no daughter,' she said.

'What of your neighbours?'

'I work alone.'

'Always?'

She nodded grimly. 'Always.'

'Then who sat beside you the other day when soldiers came in search of an archer?' he asked, watching her carefully. 'If she was neither daughter nor neighbour, who was she?'

'I do not know.'

Gervase's gaze was penetrating and she slowly began to wilt beneath it. When she looked at the others, she saw that she was surrounded by hostile glares. She shifted uneasily for a moment then rose to her feet to put her basket aside.

'There was someone,' she confessed.

'Who was it?'

'I have no idea, young man. She came running out of the forest and begged me to let her sit beside me and work at another basket. She gave me money. What was I to do?'

'Was she carrying anything?' pressed Gervase.

'I forget.'

'Try to remember.'

'It is gone,' said the old woman evasively.

'Then let me jog your memory. I believe that she may have had a bow and arrow with her.'

The sharp intake of breath gave her away. Gervase had no need to pursue his questioning. She capitulated at once and became eager to co-operate.

'You are right, young man,' she said. 'She did have a bow and arrow. What is more, she hid them in my cottage so that the soldiers would not catch her with the weapon. They are still there,' she said, hobbling into her home. 'I will fetch them instantly.'

159

'Well done, Gervase!' said Ralph.

'Now do you believe that it was a female archer?'

'I do.'

'The old woman was an unwitting accomplice,' said Gervase. 'How was she to know that the visitor who sat beside her weaving a basket had just committed murder? She probably could not believe her good fortune when she was offered money for letting the girl sit out here beside her.'

'Why was the bow and arrow left here?'

'For safety, Ralph. If she had been caught with them in her possession, the game would have been up. Far better to conceal them here. Who would expect to find a bow and arrow in such a place? The archer will no doubt return for them in due course.'

'We will be waiting for her.'

'That bow and arrow are the most valuable clues yet.'

'Yes.' Ralph nodded at the hovel. 'What on earth is keeping the old woman? Is she writing her will in there?'

'I will go and see.'

Gervase approached the hut and knocked gently on the door before ducking his head to step into the single, cluttered, evil-smelling room. Ralph followed him and looked over his shoulder. Both gasped in utter amazement when they saw that the place was empty.

The old woman had mysteriously disappeared.

Chapter Thirteen

Ralph and Gervase were too stunned at first even to speak. After exchanging a silent glance of dismay, they began a frantic search of the grim habitation. Gervase treated the woman's mean belongings with a degree of courtesy, moving them aside with care, but Ralph had no compunction about hurling them about indiscriminately to relieve his anger. The hut was soon in even greater chaos than when they first entered and the cloud of dust they created made them choke.

It was when Ralph flung aside a pile of baskets that the mystery was solved. There was a low door in the wall of the hut, small enough to be easily concealed but large enough to allow someone to crawl through it. Evidently, the woman had made her escape through the door and pulled the baskets over the exit to buy herself some time. Both men were profoundly shocked. They had taken her for a harmless old crone but she had outwitted the pair of them.

Gervase Bret had a grudging admiration for her but Ralph Delchard was livid. Finding his voice again, he stormed out of the hovel to address his soldiers.

'After her!' he ordered.

'Who?' said one of the men.

'The old woman.'

'She went into the cottage, my lord.'

'And out again through a door at the back.'

'We did not see her leave.'

'No more did we but she has gone. Run her down!'

'Which way did she go, my lord?'

161

'How should I know? Look for her.'

'Yes, my lord.'

'Spread out!' yelled Ralph, waving his arms. 'And search very carefully. She was clever enough to deceive us once. It must not happen again.'

'No, my lord.'

'Do not come back without her!'

The men divided into three pairs and set off in different directions, using their swords to hack their way through any obstructions and disturbing nesting birds and wildlife. The commotion brought Gytha and Beollan out of the trees and they watched in bewilderment from the edge of the clearing. They could not believe that the basket-weaver had somehow eluded the grasp of eight men.

When Gervase came out of the hut, Ralph was still fuming.

'Duped by a ridiculous old woman!'

'She was shrewder than either of us imagined,' said Gervase. 'But one thing seems clear. She did not unwittingly help the archer. She was probably her sworn confederate.'

'Full of the same low cunning.'

'I can see that your pride has been wounded, Ralph.'

'It has,' said the other with feeling. 'I would hate it if I were beaten in a fair fight with a man. But to be tricked by a woman like this! What sort of brutish people are the Welsh? Using their womenfolk as spies and assassins. It is against all the rules of warfare.'

'There *are* no rules, Ralph.'

'So I am discovering.'

'And do not take it as a personal affront.'

'But I do, Gervase. I will have some stern questions for that stinking old badger when my men catch her.'

'If they do so, that is.'

'What chance does she have against six armed men?'

'She has the advantage over them so far.'

'Temporarily.'

'She knows the forest, they do not.'

'They will find her,' said Ralph confidently. 'Or they will

answer to me. Apprehend the old woman and she may lead us to the archer herself.'

'The trail will not end there, Ralph.'

'No, it will go all the way across the Welsh border.'

They plunged off into the forest to help with the search. Gytha and Beollan followed to add two more pairs of eyes but it was all to no avail. Though they scoured the area on foot and on horseback for over an hour, there was absolutely no trace of the old woman. Somehow, she had managed to escape their clutches. It was baffling. After a last sweep over a wider area, they eventually conceded defeat.

'Where *is* she?' said Ralph through gritted teeth.

'Heaven knows!' sighed Gervase.

'The woman is a witch. She has put a spell on us.'

'No, Ralph. She has simply outflanked us again.'

'This makes my blood boil!'

'We noticed.'

'She has to be somewhere in the forest.'

'It is too full of hiding places. My guess is that she has gone to ground and is lying low until we leave.'

'Our journey was a total waste of time.'

'I disagree,' said Gervase. 'We have gathered valuable intelligence. We have learned how the archer eluded capture by Earl Hugh's men and we identified her accomplice. We also discovered something about Welsh women.'

'Yes,' said Ralph. 'Do not trust them for one second.'

'We must report this to Earl Hugh.'

'Not yet, Gervase. Let us pursue our own inquiries first. I do not relish the idea of explaining how we came to let an old woman delude the whole pack of us. He would roast us with his scorn. Wait until we have some good news to report,' he decided. 'Then he might actually show some gratitude.'

Canon Hubert was on the verge of apoplexy. His eyes widened dangerously, his breathing became laboured and his cheeks reddened until they shone like apples in the sunlight. He refused to accept what he had just been told.

'Is this some sort of cruel jest?' he asked.

'No jest, I do assure you,' said Frodo.

'Then Bishop Robert is in earnest?'

'He is, Canon Hubert, and he has my full support.'

'For a policy of calculated madness?'

'We believe that it is a wise course of action.'

'Where is the wisdom in such patent idiocy?'

Archdeacon Frodo smiled benignly. He could understand Hubert's feelings, because he had shared them himself until recently, but his opinion had slowly been changed by the pressure of events. The two men were in the cathedral vestry and their voices were suitably low and reverential. Hubert's expression, however, was one of frank horror.

'Did you seriously recommend this course of action to the earl?' he said in a hoarse whisper. 'Knowing what you know of Archdeacon Idwal?'

'Yes.'

'I am staggered.'

Frodo beamed. 'Let the idea lie around in your mind for a while and you may come eventually to appreciate its true worth.'

'It *has* no true worth.'

'We contend that it does.'

'On what possible grounds?'

'The archdeacon's special qualifications.'

'And what are they?'

'He is a Welsh churchman of some distinction and can talk to Gruffydd ap Cynan in their own language. Idwal is very much aware of the situation here and will do anything to prevent bloodshed in the city.'

'Then why does he not quit Chester?' murmured Hubert.

'We need him to speak on our behalf.'

'That is like asking Satan to speak on behalf of the Archangel Gabriel. It is an unnatural request. Idwal will turn it down summarily.'

'On the contrary, he was a willing volunteer.'

Hubert gaped. 'You *asked* him?'

'No, he came to us with the idea,' explained Frodo. 'At first, we were very uneasy about the notion and I know that Bishop Robert still has lingering reservations, but the archdeacon does offer an option that is not found elsewhere. Gruffydd ap Cynan will talk openly to Idwal. He will respect the archdeacon, listen to him, respond to his advice.'

'The only advice that Idwal will give him is that Wales must overrun England,' said Hubert with muted disdain. 'I find it incomprehensible that you could put your trust in a man whose special qualifications are no more than a gift for spreading discord, falsifying the history of Christianity in these islands and subduing his detractors with a mixture of aggression and crushing boredom.'

'Try to discern the man's virtues, Canon Hubert.'

'He has none.'

'Then how has he risen to a position of such eminence?' Frodo gave a complacent smirk. 'Only a man with remarkable qualities becomes an archdeacon.'

'That may be true of England or Normandy – but *Wales*!'

'I have a higher opinion than you of the Welsh Church.'

'That would not be difficult.'

'I have met Bishop Wilfrid of St David's on more than one occasion and found him a man of real perception. He would not appoint an archdeacon lightly. Idwal has his faults – and we all know what they are – but the time has come to look beyond them to his true self.'

'He is a Welsh patriot. That says all.'

'And a devout Christian. Nobody can dispute that.'

'I would.'

'What do you have against him, Canon Hubert?'

'The searing memory of his depredations in Herefordshire when we visited that county. His antics are burned into my mind for ever.'

'Yet he helped to forestall open warfare.'

'Is that what he told you?'

'It is what others have confirmed, apparently. Your own colleagues, for instance. According to Brother Gerold, whose word I trust implicitly, Master Bret is more than ready to acknowledge Idwal's contribution on that earlier occasion. Bishop Robert and I believe that he may be able to exert the same influence over Gruffydd ap Cynan.'

'What use is that? The man is imprisoned.'

'He remains a symbol for the people of Gwynedd,' argued the other. 'Even behind bars, his word carries immense weight. An order from their leader would compel the Welsh to cease hostilities at once.'

'Idwal is more likely to condone such hostilities.'

'And see his countrymen crushed once more by Earl Hugh?' He shook his head. 'No, Canon Hubert. He may be a patriot but he is also a realist. Barons from other parts of the county have been arriving at the castle all day with reinforcements. Earl Hugh is a mighty soldier in the field. Welsh blood will be spilled in vast quantities if he rides out with his army. Our contentious archdeacon knows that only too well.'

'I still do not trust him.'

'Overcome your prejudices.'

'What is to stop him conniving with the Prince of Gwynedd behind our backs?'

'The presence of an observer.'

'Observer?'

'Gervase Bret,' said Frodo. 'He speaks enough Welsh to understand what passes between the two men. Surely, you would put your faith in your young colleague?'

'I would.'

'Archdeacon Idwal and Gruffydd ap Cynan will not be able to conspire together while they are under such close scrutiny. Will this not content you, Canon Hubert?'

'No.'

'Would you rather risk the possibility of attack?'

'Certainly not.'

'Then why oppose the one way out of this dilemma?'

Hubert pondered. His breathing was normal and his face was no longer apoplectic. Archdeacon Frodo's plausible tongue was a powerful weapon. It had even managed to weaken some of the canon's objections to what he at first saw as a ludicrous suggestion. Gervase Bret's presence in the scheme cast a whole new light on it.

'What did Earl Hugh say to the idea?' he wondered.

'His mind is set on conflict.'

'So the intercession of Idwal will not take place?'

'Not as things stand,' said Frodo honestly, 'but we will continue to work on the earl. And on Brother Gerold. The chaplain has his master's ear. If anyone can bring Earl Hugh around to our viewpoint, then he can.'

'And in the meantime?'

'We do what the Church has always done in emergencies.'

'Watch and pray?'

'Yes, Canon Hubert,' said Frodo. 'Watch closely and pray hard. God will surely hear our entreaties. Indeed, He may already have done so. Bishop Robert and I discussed the situation at great length. We begin to think that, in His mercy, the Almighty sent us Archdeacon Idwal as the saviour of the hour. His presence here at this time is so crucial that it can only be providential.'

Apoplexy again threatened to engulf Canon Hubert.

The long journey back did nothing to soften Ralph Delchard's sense of grievance. When they entered the city again, he was still berating himself and his men for letting an old woman elude them so adroitly. Annoyance at one member of the Welsh nation spilled over into a general antipathy. In such a jaundiced mood, Ralph was ready to condemn anyone with even a remote connection with Wales. When he rode in through the castle gates with Gervase Bret and their escort, he was therefore less than overjoyed to be ambushed by a man who typified the whole country.

Archdeacon Idwal swooped on him like a giant bat.

'I am glad to see you, my lord!' he cried, as if he were the castellan himself and not merely an unwanted guest. 'We must talk as a matter of urgency.'

167

Ralph was brusque. 'As a matter of even greater urgency, we must not talk. Stand aside, Idwal.'

'But I wish to see you.'

'I have been seen. Farewell.'

Without another word, Ralph swung his horse towards the stables and moved swiftly away, leaving Idwal talking to himself. The escort followed their master but Gervase Bret dismounted to apologise to the stricken Welshman.

'You will have to excuse his rudeness,' he said.

'Can such behaviour merit an excuse, Gervase?'

'It has been a trying day.'

'Civility costs nothing,' said Idwal, wrapping his cloak around himself with dignity. 'When I offer the hand of friendship, I do not expect to be spurned so.'

'Pay no attention to it, Archdeacon Idwal.'

'His dear wife would not treat me with such indifference. Golde remembers how I helped to bring the two of them together in Hereford. She is duly grateful.' He shrugged off his irritation and stepped in to embrace Gervase. 'But you may carry my message as easily as the lord Ralph. And it will be all the more appropriate coming from you, Gervase, since you are directly involved in the business.'

'What business?'

'Our proposed visit to Gruffydd ap Cynan.'

'Ours?'

'You will be there to make sure we are hatching no dread plot against the Earl.'

'Nevertheless, Earl Hugh will not let you near his prisoner.'

'Work on him, Gervase.'

'I will try.'

'Convince him that I may be able to avert war.'

'Earl Hugh may not want it averted.'

'The rest of the city does,' said Idwal with a dramatic sweep of his hand. 'So does the Church. The cathedral is outside the city wall. That makes it very vulnerable.'

'Would a God-fearing people like the Welsh really torch a beautiful cathedral?'

'They would destroy anything they encountered, Gervase, making no distinctions at all. Such are the fortunes of war. That is why this fire must be extinguished before it gets out of control and burns all of us.'

He explained what he believed he could achieve through a conversation with Gruffydd ap Cynan and Gervase was impressed, promising to add his support to the plea already made to Earl Hugh by Bishop Robert and Archdeacon Frodo. What he could not do was to hold out any hope of success. He had seen enough of the earl to know that he was very much his own man, prone to make impulsive decisions from which nobody could move him.

Having secured Gervase's help on one matter, Idwal sought his assistance on another. He glanced across at the chapel.

'Brother Gerold tells me that you are regular in your devotions,' he recalled.

'I try to be.'

'It is to your credit,' said Idwal. 'I dare swear that the lord Ralph has yet to see the inside of the chapel.'

'He is somewhat preoccupied. His wife has joined him.'

'Then he should be on his knees to thank God for bringing her safely to Chester. These are perilous times in which to travel abroad.' He lowered his voice. 'What is your opinion of the chapel?'

'It is much like any other I have seen in a castle.'

'More ornate than most?'

'Probably.'

'More comfortable? More capacious?'

'Both, Archdeacon Idwal.'

'Earl Hugh has obviously spent money on his chapel.'

'He has spiritual leanings.'

'Does he?' said Idwal, raising a mocking eyebrow. 'Do you mean that he says grace before he boards his latest mistress? Virtue consists in abstaining from vice, not in atoning for it by building churches.'

'Brother Gerold has put that argument to him.'

'Not strongly enough.'

169

'Gerold is making headway. Slowly, perhaps, but there has been progress. He is endeavouring to lead Earl Hugh along a less sinful path through life. That will take time.'

'An eternity!'

'Nobody is better fitted for the task.'

'True,' conceded the other. 'Gerold has many of the attributes of a saint. It is a pity that he is not Welsh. But to return to the chapel. It is supremely well endowed.'

'Earl Hugh is a wealthy man.'

'And generous with that wealth, I am pleased to record.'

'Gerold will endorse that.'

'Did he show you round the chapel?'

'Yes,' said Gervase. 'I am always interested to see what spiritual provision there is for a garrison. Chaplains usually bring a touch of humanity to a bleak community of soldiers.'

'If only this community *were* bleak!' complained Idwal, eyes rolling in disapproval. 'But the earl's generosity is not, alas, confined to the chapel. He appears to keep open house here. Drinking, gourmandising, hunting, hawking and whoring. Those seem to be the staple pastimes of Chester Castle. Strange conduct for a man who claims to be a personal friend of Anselm of Bec.'

'Earl Hugh has important military duties as well.'

'As he has just been reminded.'

'Very forcibly.'

Idwal angled himself so that he could see the chapel out of the corner of his eye. He flashed a disarming grin.

'What did Gerold show you in the chapel?' he said.

'Everything.'

'He took you into the vestry?'

'Of course.'

'And what did you see there, Gervase?'

'Exactly what I expected to see.'

'A reliquary, for instance?'

'Yes,' said Gervase. 'It stood on a stout table.'

'And did Brother Gerold reveal its contents to you?' asked

the other, excitement making his voice tremble slightly. 'Did he open the reliquary?'

'No, Archeacon Idwal. We were already late for the banquet.'

'But he gave you to understand that something of great value was locked away inside it?'

'Why else have a reliquary?'

'Precisely!'

'Brother Gerold invited me to view its contents another time. I will certainly avail myself of that invitation.'

'Then we must talk further on the subject.' Idwal gave a short, high laugh then composed his features into a frown of concentration, but Gervase could see the sparkle in the Welshman's eyes. What did it portend? Border warfare was threatening, movement to and from the city was severely restricted, panic was settling in everywhere. On top of that, Idwal had just been snubbed by Ralph Delchard. Yet the man was exuding delight. Behind the serious frown, Gervase sensed that the archdeacon was chuckling quietly to himself.

In the circumstances, it was a small miracle.

By the time she finally reached the cottage, the old woman was staggering from fatigue. Her face was drawn, her body slack, and her clothes were covered with dirt. Raked by thorns, both hands had rivulets of dried blood on them. She was so exhausted that she had no strength even to speak at first.

Surprised and alarmed to see her, Eiluned took her by the arms and lowered her gently to the floor before fetching a cup of water to hold to her parched lips. The old woman swallowed the liquid eagerly and nodded her thanks. Eiluned's home was an abandoned hovel in the north-west part of the forest. It was falling to pieces but its vestigial roof offered a fair amount of shelter and the two surviving walls gave her good protection from the wind. It made the old woman's own home seem almost palatial but Eiluned had no complaints about her accommodation. It was essentially temporary.

While her visitor recovered, Eiluned scouted the area to

make sure that she had not been followed to the refuge. When she was certain that the old woman had come alone, she went back to kneel beside her and cradle her head in her lap. Dabbing a rag into the pail of water, she used it to mop the still perspiring brow.

'What happened?' she asked.

'They came looking,' said the old woman.

'Who did?'

'Soldiers.'

'What did they want?'

'To know about you.'

Eiluned stiffened. 'Is this true?'

'Yes. They asked me who was weaving a basket with me the day of the stag hunt.'

'What did you tell them?'

'As little as possible.'

'Good.'

'One of them spoke Welsh. He questioned me closely.'

'How did you get away?'

'By a ruse,' said the old woman with a tired smile. 'I told them you had left the bow and arrow in my cottage and I went to fetch it. While they were talking outside, I slipped out by a little door at the rear then hid in the forest until they called off the search.'

'Where did you hide?'

'Under some brambles.'

'It must have been very painful.'

'I could not allow them to catch me, Eiluned. I would put up with anything rather than let that happen.' She looked up with a pathetic need for approval. 'Did I do right?'

'Yes.'

'You are sure?'

'We are proud of you.'

'They knew too much, Eiluned.'

'But *how*? That is what I cannot understand.' The younger woman shook her head in anxiety. 'We took such pains to avoid detection. What put them on to me?'

172

'A lucky guess?'

'No, it was more than that. If they came all the way out from Chester to interrogate you, they must have had strong suspicions. Thank goodness you had the wit to escape.'

'I could not let you down, Eiluned.'

'You are a heroine.'

'No,' insisted the other, 'you are the real heroine. You rid us of that ogre, Raoul Lambert. I lived on his property and I know what a pig he could be to people like me. You rescued us from him. I'll never forget that. I owe you a big debt.'

'It was more than repaid today.'

'I had to get to you, Eiluned.'

'And you did.'

'Warn her – that's what I kept telling myself. You must get to her today and warn her.' The old woman went off into a fit of coughing and Eiluned poured fresh water for her. 'I am sorry,' said the other, after meekly sipping from the cup. 'I am too old to walk such distances now.'

'You got here. That is all that matters.'

'Yes.' She looked up. 'Will you take care of me, Eiluned?'

'Take care?'

'How can I go back to my own home?'

'I had not thought of that.'

'They drove me out. If I try to return, they will catch me and punish me cruelly. My body could not stand that.'

'It will not have to, I promise.'

The old woman squeezed her arm. 'I knew that I could rely on you, Eiluned. You are so like my daughter. She would have looked after me if she had lived, but . . . it was not to be. But you will save me, won't you? I'll be no trouble to you.'

'Just rest,' soothed Eiluned, stroking her hair with gentle fingers. 'Have no fears for the future. Just rest. If they found you, then they must have worked out that I was the assassin. No matter. We will not be here long enough for them to find us. In a couple of days, it will all be over and we can go across the border to Wales again. To live in freedom among our own people. Would you like that?'

The old woman's eyes were now shut and she seemed to be dozing peacefully, but her head felt strangely heavier in Eiluned's lap. Bending over her, she saw that her guest had quietly expired. The flight from her home had pushed her beyond the limits of endurance. However, there was one tiny consolation. As Eiluned gently laid the head down, she saw that there was a contented smile on the woman's face.

After one last important service to her native country, she had died happy.

Chapter Fourteen

'Do you feel better now?' asked Golde as he rolled off her.

'No, my love.'

'You dare to say that!' She gave him a sharp but affectionate dig in the ribs.

'That hurt!' complained Ralph.

'It was meant to after such an insult.'

'I was only jesting.'

'Well, your jest was in poor taste,' she said, delivering another jab to his body. 'You were in a terrible state when we came up to our apartment. Tense, moody and not fit to share a bed with anyone, especially with a tender and loving wife.'

'Is that what you are?' he teased. The third punch took his breath away. 'I asked for that,' he conceded.

'It is no more than you deserve, Ralph Delchard.'

'I know, my love.'

'When I give myself to you, I expect some appreciation.'

'That is what you had, Golde. Have you so soon forgotten?'

'I am talking about now – not then.'

'Ah!' he sighed. 'Afterwards and not during.'

'Preferably both.'

She rolled him over so that he lay face down then sat astride his naked body, massaging his neck and shoulders with practised hands. Ralph soon purred with pleasure. Golde had learned that this was always the best moment for an intimate conversation. Her husband was responsive and off guard.

'Let us start again,' she suggested. 'Do you feel better?'

'Infinitely better.'

'Has all that tension gone?'

'More or less.'

'And will you promise to stop telling me about what happened in the Forest of Delamere today?'

'Is that what I have been doing?'

'Unceasingly.'

'It must have been excruciating for you.'

'We have had more interesting exchanges.'

'This is the kind that I enjoy.'

'Why do you think I brought you to bed?' she said. 'If we had stayed at the table any longer, you would have talked my ears off. And all because some clever old woman managed to hide from you in the forest.'

'There was more to it than that, my love. You see—'

'Enough!' she ordered, slapping his buttock hard. 'I do not wish to hear another word about her. There is no room for anyone else in this bed. It belongs to you and me.'

'It does, my love.'

'Remember that.'

Golde's massage took all of the stiffness out of his shoulders and banished the memory of his setback in the forest. One woman might have escaped him but the one he loved was there to welcome him and to soothe his troubled mind. An hour alone with Golde was the perfect antidote.

When he felt completely relaxed, he changed places with her so that he could stroke her back, shoulders and arms. His strong hands could be surprisingly delicate. It was Golde's turn to murmur with delight.

'What did you do all day?' he wondered.

'I spent most of it with the Lady Ermintrude.'

'How did you find her?'

'Friendly and honest,' said Golde. 'One part of me admires that woman very much. She is so gracious and dignified. Another part of me pities her.'

'Why?'

'Her marriage is a constant ordeal.'

'What about yours?'

'An endless joy.'

He bent forward to kiss her between the shoulder blades. 'Do they ever sleep together?' he mused.

'I could hardly ask her such a question as that.'

'What did your instinct tell you?'

'That she is a long-suffering wife who has learned to live with her disappointments. Earl Hugh and she have little in common. Now that she has provided him with children, they have no need to share a bed.'

'Is that the only reason for making love?'

'Yes,' she said with a smile. 'Procreation.'

'Can it not be a pleasure in itself?'

'Of course not, Ralph.'

'Then I have been deluded all these years.'

'It is expressly against the teaching of the Scriptures. Man and wife have a duty to bring forth children. Pleasure has no part whatsoever in it.'

'You should have told me that before we came to bed.'

'Would it have made the slightest difference?'

'No.'

They shared a laugh and he kissed the back of her neck. Golde luxuriated in his touch for a few minutes before she spoke again. Her voice was now dreamy, her thoughts floating.

'The Lady Ermintrude made some strange comments.'

'I thought that there was no room for anyone else in this bed. If I am to sacrifice my old woman, you must throw out our hostess.'

'But this might interest you.'

'I already have someone to do that, Golde.'

'It concerns this threatened uprising.'

Ralph's curiosity took over. 'Oh?'

'But I will not spoil a beautiful moment like this.'

'Please,' he urged. 'Just tell me what she said.'

'In the morning.'

'Now, Golde. This might be important.'

'They were only casual remarks as I left her apartment.'

'It must have been more than that for you to draw my

177

attention to it.' He tickled her under the arms and made her squeal a protest. 'Tell me or I will do that again.'

'Very well,' she agreed. 'The Lady Ermintrude said some things which made me think that she almost wished a battle was looming because it would take her husband away from the castle for a while. Earl Hugh is a soldier at heart and always will be.'

'How odd!'

'Is it so odd?'

'I know of no other woman who welcomes a battle.'

'You are not married to Earl Hugh,' said Golde tartly. 'If I put myself in her position, I have some sympathy with her point of view. I, too, would prefer to be the wife of someone in combat rather than to be tied to a roving lecher who betrayed his marital vows as if they were wholly meaningless.'

'Does Ermintrude think that there *will* be war?'

'She is certain of it.'

'Then she gets that certainty from Earl Hugh. That is alarming. He is set on armed conflict.'

'I knew that you would be interested.'

'Yes, my love.'

But something else caught his attention at that point and it made him prick up his ears. Ralph thought that he heard a noise outside the door of the apartment. Easing himself off Golde, he put a finger to his lips to warn her to be silent and crept across to the candle in the window recess.

One hand on the bolt, he stood close to the door and listened intently. Then, without warning, he pulled back the bolt, flung open the door and used the candle to illumine the narrow passageway outside. Ralph could see nobody but he was in time to hear the departing footsteps of the person who had been eavesdropping on them. He was furious.

Precious moments alone with his wife had been shared with a spy. How long had he been there and whom did he serve? They were disturbing thoughts and not even Golde's comforting arms could drive them completely away.

*   *   *

Gervase Bret was up at dawn to attend the service in the chapel. He was surprised to find it reasonably full and was startled to see Hugh d'Avranches and his wife kneeling side by side in prayer. It was an incongruous sight and Gervase could not decide if the earl had come to the chapel to seek a blessing from above on his military expedition or absolution for his numerous sins. Ermintrude's presence suggested that her husband was in penitent mood, but he left the chapel so abruptly at the end of the service that Gervase had to revise his opinion. Earl Hugh was ready for battle.

Brother Gerold was glad that his friend lingered for a few words after the service. He came gliding down the nave towards Gervase with a smile of greeting. The two of them stepped out into the little porch.

'It was pleasing to see you there, Gervase.'

'Did you have any doubts that I would come?'

'None at all.'

'What about Earl Hugh?'

'He came of his own volition.'

'For what purpose, though?'

'Only he and God know that.'

Gervase looked across the bailey at the soldiers who were being marshalled outside their quarters. Their numbers had been substantially swelled by the arrival of newcomers from estates all over Cheshire. It was an intimidating prospect for someone so wedded to the notion of peace as Gervase.

'Earl Hugh's mind is made up, then?'

'I fear so, Gervase.'

'Is there no way to dissuade him from riding out at the head of an army?'

'None that I have been able to find. And I have tried.'

'I am sure, Brother Gerold.'

'In fairness to Earl Hugh, he did at least consider the plea from Bishop Robert and Archdeacon Frodo. They elected you to accompany that eccentric churchman from Wales down to the dungeons.'

'So I have been told.'

'Whether you and Archdeacon Idwal could achieve anything by talking with the prisoner, I do not know, but I certainly feel that it is worth a try. Your presence will make all the difference, Gervase.'

'In what way?'

'It will convince Earl Hugh that nothing underhand is taking place down there.' Gerold gave a shrug of regret. 'I was overly pessimistic when Idwal first raised the possibility of a visit to Gruffydd ap Cynan, and I am sorry that I was so dismissive. Fortunately, Idwal is not easily shaken off and he has continued to press for the opportunity to speak with his countryman.'

'I would be happy to escort him.'

'Earl Hugh took that into account.'

'What decision has he reached?'

'It has not yet been confided in me.'

'Please use what influence you have on our behalf.'

'I will, Gervase.'

Brother Gerold was about to go back into the chapel when Gervase remembered something. He put a detaining hand on the other's arm.

'One moment, Brother Gerold.'

'Yes?'

'On an earlier visit to the chapel, you conducted me round it and took me into the vestry.'

'I recall it well. Nobody else has ever shown such interest in our chapel and its contents. Is there something I omitted to show you?'

'The contents of the reliquary.'

'Ah, yes. Of course.'

'What treasures does it contain?'

'Nothing of outstanding value,' replied the other. 'We have a flask of holy water from Jerusalem and another that was blessed by the pontiff in Rome. For the rest, it is a case of minor relics of minor saints. Nothing that would really excite the interest of Archdeacon Idwal.'

'Idwal?'

'I presume that you are asking on his behalf?'

180

'Well . . .'

'Do not feel embarrassed about it, Gervase,' said the other with a grin. 'He has already questioned me in person about the reliquary but seemed unwilling to take my word for what it contained. Assure him that we have neither the toenail of St Dyfrig, the hair of St Deiniol nor the bones of St David here. Only relics of Saxon saints are interred in the reliquary.'

'I will inform him of that.'

'Give him some advice at the same time.'

'What is it?'

'In the event of war – and the signs are ominous – it might be sensible of Idwal to leave the city. Earl Hugh will work up a hatred against all Welshmen, even those in holy orders. Idwal will be safer on the other side of the border.'

'He is not a man who considers personal safety.'

'He must. Earl Hugh can be vengeful.'

'Make one last effort to halt this war, Brother Gerold.'

'I wish that I could but my counsel no longer carries the weight it used to. Events have taken on their own momentum. The murder of Raoul Lambert was provocation enough but the killing of the earl's messenger was another clear sign that the Welsh are spoiling for a fight.'

'Why?'

'Ask them.'

'Their prince is held hostage. They will put his life in danger. Why should they do that?'

'Ask them,' repeated Gerold. 'Only they have the answer. Blessed are the peacemakers, Gervase. If you wish to join that exclusive brotherhood, you should not be here in Chester Castle. The place for you to coax and persuade is in Wales itself.'

Robert of Rhuddlan carried out an inspection shortly after first light. Walking along the ramparts of the castle, he checked that the guards were alert and well positioned and scanned

181

the horizon from every point of vantage. At his side was the captain of his guard, a grizzled veteran with a livid battle scar down one cheek.

'Any incidents during the night?' asked Robert.

'Yes and no, my lord,' said his companion. 'There were some minor occurrences but nothing of any real significance. Fires were lit in a circle around the castle but they were a long way off and soon burned themselves out. Someone approached the castle in the dark but with no intent to gain entry.'

'What, then, was his purpose?'

'To leave an effigy of Earl Hugh outside the main gate.'

'An effigy?'

'Yes, my lord. An obscene one.'

'I wish to see it.'

'Do not show it to the earl himself,' advised the other. 'It ridicules his manhood.'

'What else happened in the night?'

'A few stray arrows were fired into the castle.'

'Was anyone hurt?'

'No, my lord. Nor was that the intention. The Welsh are playing games with us. They are keeping us guessing. None of these incidents amount to much in themselves but, taken together, they form a pattern. We are being taunted.'

'They are trying to draw us out of the castle.'

'That would be folly without reinforcements.'

'I know,' said Robert, 'but those reinforcements may not come for some time. I sent men enough to bear the message to Chester. It must surely have got through.'

'I hope so, my lord.'

'Why has Earl Hugh not dispatched a reply?'

'I'm sure that he has.'

'Then why has it not reached us?'

'Perhaps it has gone astray.'

'How could that happen?'

Robert of Rhuddlan saw the faint anxiety in his eye. When such an experienced soldier was uneasy, then the situation was indeed bad. The castle was well built and its garrison was drilled regularly in defensive tactics, but even a stout fortress like Rhuddlan could not hold out indefinitely. More men and supplies were urgently needed but they could only come from Chester. The road had to be kept open.

Robert stared out over the battlements in the direction of the border. Messengers were sent regularly to and fro without any problem. Communication with Chester was so straightforward that it was taken for granted. Worrying changes seemed to have taken place and they were all the more alarming because Robert did not know exactly what they were. After years of feeling very secure, he now realised how vulnerable he might be if the castle were cut off.

Chester suddenly seemed an impossible distance away.

'Send more messengers!' he declared.

'How many, my lord?'

'A dozen at least.'

'Is it wise to lose so many soldiers?' wondered the captain. 'They may be needed here.'

'We must know why Earl Hugh's reply has been delayed,' said Robert. 'A lone rider, even two, would be at risk. A dozen will be able to defend themselves against attack.'

'What are their orders?'

'I will deliver them myself.'

'They will be ready instantly, my lord.'

The captain barked a gruff command and men came running from their quarters. Horses were quickly saddled, weapons collected and orders given by Robert of Rhuddlan. Twelve soldiers in helm and hauberk went out in a column along the twisting road. Warned of danger, they proceeded with caution and remained vigilant.

An hour away from Rhuddlan, they began to relax. Nothing even vaguely suspicious had been seen. The only thing that troubled them was the light drizzle which had started to fall. They surged on with growing confidence. A few miles farther on, that confidence was brutally shattered. The road curved around a hill and their destriers kept up a steady canter until the route straightened and gave them a clear view of what lay ahead.

A narrow pass cut through the dark mountains but trees had been felled to block it. Boulders had been rolled against the timber to seal off the road completely. The troop came to a halt while they considered what to do. To reach Chester, they would now have to make a detour that would add several miles and great inconvenience to the journey, but that option, too, was suddenly removed. As they swung their horses round to retrace their steps, they saw with horror that a large Welsh raiding party had descended the hill to cut off their retreat.

They were trapped.

At the insistence of Hugh d'Avranches, Earl of Chester, the funeral of Raoul Lambert was held in the cathedral church of St John with no less a personage than Robert de Limesey himself officiating. To outsiders like Ralph Delchard and Gervase Bret, it seemed strange that someone who was not of high baronial rank should be accorded such an honour, but nobody else in the congregation found the situation unusual. Raoul Lambert had been a popular figure among men for whom hunting was a daily pleasure and his murder had sent tremors through the whole county. They came in large numbers to see him laid to rest in his grave.

The somnolent mood in which Earl Hugh had begun the day in the chapel had now deepened into a black gloom. With his wife beside him, he sat at the front of the congregation to have an uninterrupted view of the wooden coffin which bore the body of his friend. William Malbank, Richard Vernon, Hamo of Mascy, Gilbert Venables, Ranulph Mainwaring, Reginald Balliol, Bigot of Loges and Hugo of Delamere were in close attendance. The burial of Earl Hugh himself could not have been surrounded with more ceremonial.

Robert de Limesey rose to the occasion magnificently. His reedy voice echoed down the nave and he delivered such a moving encomium that several tears had to be wiped away. Judged by the praise heaped upon him, Raoul Lambert had been a remarkable man, loyal, upright, caring, devout and free from any blemish. His skills as a huntsman were legendary. Cheshire, it was emphasised, was suffering a huge loss.

Ralph and Gervase were not caught up in the general emotion. When Mass was sung and the coffin taken out to be lowered into its grave, they lurked on the fringes and took a more objective view of it all.

'This huntsman sounds like a paragon,' noted Ralph.

'That is not the picture of him which we have,' said Gervase. 'Read between the lines of our documents and Raoul Lambert emerges as a rapacious landowner who treats his sub-tenants with a disdain bordering on cruelty.'

'Who, then, was Bishop Robert talking about?'

'Someone close to Earl Hugh and thus above reproach.'

'But why, Gervase?'

'We can only guess.'

'What was the nature of the friendship between earl and huntsman that makes for such a grand funeral? And why does a bishop describe the dead man in such glowing terms?'

'Diplomacy.'

Ralph was about to rid himself of a few cynical remarks about the episcopacy when he became aware of a pungent smell. At first he thought it was emanating from the corpse, but the coffin had been sweetened with herbs to counter the stench of death. What now assaulted his nostrils was the powerful stink of Idwal's lambskin cloak, a garment that looked more ragged by the day and which acquired new and more terrible odours by the hour.

The Welshman stepped in between the two men, his voice, for once, low and gentle, his manner uncharacteristically subdued.

'A funeral is a humbling experience for us all,' he said.

'There was no humility here,' observed Ralph. 'This man went into his grave with pomp worthy of a leading baron. I do not look to have such a service when I pass away.'

'You misunderstand me, my lord,' said Idwal. 'What is humbling is the reminder that all flesh must perish. The wealthiest in the land, no less than the poorest, go to their Maker at the end of their days.'

'Raoul Lambert went before his time,' said Gervase.

'Sadly, he did. But we may profit from that.'

Gervase was surprised. 'In what way, Archdeacon Idwal?'

'His body lies here beside the cathedral.'

'So?'

'Outside the city walls,' added Idwal. 'Bishop Robert and Archdeacon Frodo implored Earl Hugh not to get drawn into a war because their cathedral might be attacked. So might the grave of Raoul Lambert. Earl Hugh was deaf to their entreaties but the notion that the corpse of his dear friend might be abused by a marauding army may make him think again. That is why I am here.'

'I do not understand,' said Gervase.

'This is our last opportunity.'

'For what?'

'Swaying the earl to our purpose. Look,' said Idwal with a nod in Hugh's direction, 'others are already trying to take advantage of the moment.'

The funeral was over and the congregation was slowly dispersing. Earl Hugh remained beside the grave with Robert de Limesey, Archdeacon Frodo and Brother Gerold around him. All four seemed to be engaged in a silent conference.

'They are willing him to let me speak to Gruffydd ap Cynan,' said Idwal. 'I will bide my time until Earl Hugh is about to leave, then I will add my own plea.'

'That might not be appropriate,' suggested Gervase.

'It would be disastrous,' said Ralph. 'The very sight of a Welshman would make him reach for his sword. Keep well away from him, Idwal. And, for God's sake, do not stand upwind of him in that revolting cloak of yours.'

'Leave the persuasion to others,' agreed Gervase.

Idwal was offended. 'My intercession could be crucial.'

'It would be!' sighed Ralph.

'Does he not want this war averted?'

'At this precise moment, no. He is too full of anger over the murder of Raoul Lambert. Revenge is at the forefront of his mind.' Ralph put a hand on the archdeacon's shoulder. 'Do not let him see you here, Idwal. He will take it as a personal insult. Withdraw while you may.'

'It might be politic,' said Gervase. 'What persuasion can be applied will come best from Bishop Robert and the others.'

'But I am the only man who can talk with Gruffydd.'

'If and when permission is granted. And it will not be if Earl Hugh is aware of your presence here.'

Idwal protested but they eventually convinced him that a tactical retreat was in the best interests of everyone. When the Welshman slipped away and the fierce aroma from his cloak gradually lost its intensity, Ralph and Gervase turned back to watch the figures beside the grave.

An animated conversation was now taking place. Bishop Robert and Archdeacon Frodo were presenting their case with renewed vigour. Earl Hugh seemed to be resisting their arguments and they soon withdrew into the cathedral. Brother Gerold now took over, talking to his master in a more confiding way and indicating the open grave as he spoke. Earl Hugh became reflective. Instead of arguing back, he was now simply listening.

Viewing it all from a distance, Ralph and Gervase were given some insight into the subtle power which the chaplain exercised over the earl. The funeral was an emotional event and even a man as flint-hard as Hugh d'Avranches was moved. Brother Gerold took him by the arm to lead him away from the grave and continued to pour words of advice into his ears. Hugh's face was grim and it was difficult to see what effect the chaplain's plea was having on him.

Suddenly, it was all over. Earl Hugh muttered something to Gerold then strode off to join the other mourners. As he swept past Ralph and Gervase, his eyes were dark and menacing.

'The appeal has been rejected,' said Ralph.

'I fear that it has, Ralph.'

'He is like a hawk in the sky. Eager for a kill.'

'That is what frightens me.'

Brother Gerold came across the grass towards them. 'I did not expect to see you here,' he said.

'We wished to pay our respects,' explained Ralph.

'Yes,' said Gervase, 'and to hear Bishop Robert give his paean of praise. We learned much about Raoul Lambert.'

'So did we all,' said Gerold quietly. 'But I am glad to find you, Gervase. It will save me the trouble of searching for you at the castle. Our wish has been granted.'

'Has it?'

'Earl Hugh has agreed that we may at least try to solve this crisis by diplomatic means.'

Ralph was astounded. 'He has authorised a meeting between Archdeacon Idwal and the prisoner?'

'Yes, my lord.'

'What is my role?' said Gervase.

'To observe and record what passes between them.'

'Watch them,' counselled Ralph. 'They will be slippery.'

'I have a lot of respect for Idwal,' said Gervase. 'For all his deficiencies, he has great integrity and is as committed to preserving the peace between the two nations as anyone. No,' he continued, reflecting on what lay ahead, 'the Archdeacon of St David's is not the problem here. The unknown quantity is Gruffydd ap Cynan, Prince of Gwynedd.'

Chapter Fifteen

Returning from the cathedral, Ralph Delchard met his wife on the stairs in the keep. He was just in time to snatch a few words with Golde.

'Are you deserting me, my love?' he complained.

'Only for a short while.'

'Where are you going?'

'To sit with the Lady Ermintrude.'

'She was at the funeral.'

'That is why she asked me to visit her,' said Golde. 'She is bound to be upset by the experience. Company can sometimes help to alleviate grief.'

'Your company can alleviate anything,' he said, stealing a kiss. 'Be off to do your good deed for the day. No, wait,' he added as a thought surfaced, 'you may be able to help us.'

'How?'

'By probing our hostess about Raoul Lambert.'

'What do you wish to know about him, Ralph?'

'Why he and Earl Hugh were such close friends,' said her husband. 'And why a huntsman merited a funeral service in a cathedral.'

'The Lady Ermintrude may not be able to provide the answers,' warned Golde. 'She and the earl lead largely separate lives. He only tells her what he wishes her to know.'

'It will not hurt to ask.'

'If the moment arises.'

'Oh, it will, Golde. You'll make certain of that.'

A second kiss sent her trotting up the stairs.

Golde was soon admitted to Ermintrude's chamber by a gentlewoman who immediately left the two of them alone. The atmosphere was sombre. Ermintrude was seated in a chair, gazing wistfully out of the window as if playing with fond memories of lost joys. Golde went quietly across to her.

'I intrude upon your sadness, my lady,' she said. 'Would you prefer me to go away again and return when you feel more ready for company?'

Ermintrude looked up at her with surprise. 'I did not hear you come in, Golde.'

'You sent for me, my lady.'

'There is nobody I would rather see at this moment.'

'Thank you.'

'Sit down. Please. Beside me.'

Golde moved the stool close enough to her to be able to touch her if the need arose. As she settled down, she took a closer look at Ermintrude and saw no signs of real grief. If the funeral had been a harrowing event for her, the older woman had made an astonishing recovery.

Ermintrude gave a sad smile and supplied an explanation. 'I went to the funeral out of a sense of duty, Golde.'

'I see.'

'My husband requested it.'

'Then you had no choice.'

'I grieve over the death of any man – especially one who is felled by an assassin – but I will not pretend to have known Raoul Lambert well enough to mourn his passing.'

'It is better to be honest about these things.'

'I wore the correct face at the funeral,' said the other with slight asperity. 'Hugh can ask no more of me.'

'He is blessed in his wife.'

'My husband may think otherwise.'

'Then he is seriously at fault.'

Ermintrude reached out to squeeze her arm in gratitude. 'In the time that we have been here,' she said, 'there have been far too many funerals. I have lost count of them. And if, as seems likely, war is to break out once again, there will be many more. We will be the losers, Golde.'

'We?'

'Wives, mothers, daughters, lovers. When our menfolk take up arms, many will be doomed to die. All that we can do is sit here impotently and suffer the consequences.' She looked deep into Golde's eyes. 'Did you tell your husband about our earlier conversation?'

'Which one, my lady? We have had several.'

'When we talked about his being a born soldier.'

'Oh, that,' said Golde. 'No, I did not.'

'Were you afraid to raise the subject?'

'I suppose I was.'

'What would he have said?'

'Exactly what you predicted, my lady. If there is to be a battle, Ralph would feel compelled to be involved in it. That is why I have been praying that hostilities may somehow be prevented.' She shrugged her shoulders. 'It now seems like a forlorn hope.'

'You will get used to those, Golde.'

'Forlorn hopes?'

'They are an inextricable part of marriage.'

'I have not found that with Ralph,' said Golde loyally.

'Was it different with your first husband?'

She lowered her head. 'Yes, my lady.'

'That means he was chosen for you.'

'By my father.'

'Did you protest against the match?'

'Loudly. But in vain.'

'What did your father say?'

'That I could not hope for a better husband. I had to accept his hand and be grateful.' Golde's face crumpled at the memory. 'I never expected to marry a brewer, my lady. Before the Conquest, my father was a thegn with holdings all over the county. He had wealth and influence. When I was born, I was destined to marry a member of the nobility.'

'And you did.'

'Only by complete chance.'

'That sometimes contrives better than we ourselves. Well,' said Ermintrude without irony, 'I am sure that the Norman aristocracy does not arouse the same pride in your breast as the Saxon nobility but I, for one, am grateful that you have come into the former. How else would I have met you?'

'You would not have done so, my lady. Unless you were seized with a passion to ride to Hereford in search of beer.'

Ermintrude gave a polite laugh. 'I am never seized by passions, Golde. And that one sounds the most unlikely of all. Let us just be thankful that our paths did cross. Though I could wish they had done so at a less complicated time.'

'So do I.'

'I fear for him,' said Ermintrude softly. 'Though I am no longer a true wife to him, I fear for my husband's life.'

'Earl Hugh is in no immediate danger, surely?'

'That depends on the arrow.'

'What arrow?'

'The one which killed Raoul Lambert in the forest. Was it really intended for him or was it aimed at Hugh? My husband is convinced that he was the target.'

'Then he will not be caught off guard again.'

'No,' said Ermintrude, 'but there is the battle itself.'

'The battle?'

'My husband is inclined to be reckless in the field. That can prove fatal. Anything might happen to him.'

'Not according to Ralph.'

'Go on.'

'He was very impressed with the quality and discipline of Earl Hugh's men. They amount to a formidable army. Ralph does not believe the Welsh would have much chance against them in open combat.'

'There are other ways of fighting, Golde.'

'Other ways?'

'Raoul Lambert was not killed in open combat.'

'That is true.'

'The Welsh are crafty.'

'That is what Ralph always says of them.' Golde recalled the favour which her husband had asked of her. 'My lady,' she said.

'Yes?'

'What sort of man was Raoul Lambert?'

'I am not the best person to tell you.'

'From what you have heard, was he honest and God-fearing?'

'He was a rare huntsman, I know that,' said Ermintrude, fishing in a sea of vague memories. 'I cannot speak for his honesty but I would question his devotion. Nobody who takes part in the revelry which Raoul Lambert enjoyed here can claim to be wholly devout. Like so many of my husband's friends, he was wedded to excess.'

'You know more about him than you think.'

'He was pleasant enough when I spoke to him.'

'Yet he was not a pleasant man,' speculated Golde. 'That is what your tone would seem to suggest.'

'He was a deep man.'

'In what sense?'

'Raoul Lambert kept a great deal hidden.'

'But not from your husband.'

'Oh, no,' conceded the other. 'Hugh had the very highest opinion of him. He entrusted things to Raoul which he would confide in nobody else.'

'What sorts of things?'

'I have no idea, Golde.'

'Did your husband give you no indication at all?'

'None,' said Ermintrude briskly. 'And now that you have put to me the questions that Ralph asked you to put, perhaps we can talk about something more seemly. Raoul Lambert is dead and he should be allowed to rest in peace.' She gave an understanding smile. 'I do not blame you, Golde. You are a faithful wife and did as your husband requested. But no more of it, please. I have suffered the pangs of such fidelity.'

Golde was cowed. 'I am deeply sorry, my lady.'

'There is no need.'

193

'Would you like me to withdraw?'

'No, Golde,' said the other. 'I wish you to cheer me up by telling me how to brew beer. Perhaps it is not too late for me to master the art for myself.'

Gruffydd ap Cynan, Prince of Gwynedd, tempered his anger with discretion. Wanting to vent his spleen again upon the door of his cell, he knew that such violence would only result in his being fettered and that was an indignity he wished to avoid at all costs. What annoyed him most was the abrupt loss of his privileges. Instead of being allowed out daily for exercise in the bailey, he was kept permanently in his dungeon. In place of food of good quality, he was now fed on scraps. And fresh straw was no longer brought into his tiny domain on a regular basis to combat the fetid atmosphere.

Once an important prisoner of state, he was now treated like a common criminal and it rankled. When he heard feet approaching along the passageway, he rushed to put his face to the grille in the door to shout a protest but it died in the back of his throat. Antagonising the guards would only worsen his plight. He backed away to the wall and glowered.

A key was inserted into the lock and the door creaked open to admit one of the guards. The man clearly disapproved of the duty which he had been given.

'You have visitors,' he grunted.

Not understanding, Gruffydd darted forward involuntarily.

'Get back, you Welsh rogue!' said the guard, pushing him in the chest. 'If it was left to me, you would be allowed to see nobody. I would simply lock you in here and throw the key away. Now be quiet and do as you are told.'

The Welshman resisted the urge to spring at him.

'Are you ready?' called a voice from the passageway.

'Bring them in!' ordered the guard before pointing an admonitory finger at the prisoner. 'Behave yourself, do you hear? Or the visitors will be hauled straight out again.'

Gruffydd watched sullenly from his position against the wall but his resentment fell away when Idwal came into the cell and

194

greeted him in Welsh. It was the first time in months that he had heard his own language spoken. Gervase Bret followed the archdeacon in and coughed as the stench hit him. The door was locked on all three of them.

'Who are you?' asked Gruffydd warily, not certain whether they were friends or interrogators. 'What do you want?'

'To talk to you, my lord,' said Idwal.

'What about?'

'Peace.'

Idwal introduced himself then explained why Gervase was there with him. Gruffydd took time to be convinced of their sincerity but his reservations gradually faded. If nothing else, he could use them as a means of learning about what was happening in the outside world. Questions burst out of him.

'One at the time, my lord,' said Idwal, holding up a restraining palm. 'We will tell you everything you wish to know. But we must speak more slowly. Gervase Bret will not understand either of us if we gabble and it is important that he hears every word that we say.'

'I accept that, Archdeacon Idwal.'

'Then what is your first question?'

Gruffydd ap Cynan had it ready for them. He reminded himself that he was still a Prince of Gwynedd and no amount of degradation could alter that fact. Straightening his back, he lifted his chin with pride. His voice was accusatory.

'Why are they treating me with such disrespect?'

Robert of Rhuddlan spent the whole morning on the battlements. An eerie silence had settled on the castle as if it was waiting for some terrible blow to fall. The captain of the guard was as conscious of it as Robert. Looking out at the road to the east, he ran a ruminative hand across his chin.

'I do not like it, my lord,' he said.

'No more do I. This quiet is unsettling.'

'There is nothing to be seen but I am certain that they are out there somewhere. Watching and waiting.'

'I, too, feel their eyes upon us.'

'How can we fight an invisible enemy?'

'It is impossible.'

Robert forced himself to leave the ramparts in order to ease the discomfort he was feeling inside. It was bad for the morale of his men to see their commander subject to any fear or doubt. His soldiers needed to draw confidence from him and they would not do that if he patrolled the battlements with such anxiety. Preparing his garrison to resist any attack was a more immediate priority.

But he had no time to put it into effect.

'My lord!' called a guard on the rampart.

'Yes?'

'Someone is approaching.'

'Soldiers?'

'No, my lord. A waggon.'

Robert went quickly back up the wooden steps with the captain of the guard at his heels. They joined the man who had raised the alarm and saw why he had done so. A waggon was heading towards them along the road from the border. It was being driven with such speed that it was swerving crazily from side to side. A whip was being used to coax even more effort out of the carthorses.

As it got closer, they could see that it was being driven by a man in the armour of a Welsh warrior. Standing up and brandishing his whip, he seemed to be relishing his work and they soon began to catch the sound of his triumphant song on the wind. Robert of Rhuddlan was baffled. Was the lone warrior intending to attack the castle on his own?

When it got within half a mile, the waggon suddenly described a semicircle and came to a juddering halt, enabling the watching party to see what the vehicle was carrying. A group of men were trussed up in the rear of the waggon. Robert noted that there were twelve helms and he shuddered.

The driver jumped nimbly into the back of the vehicle and hurled his cargo roughly out, one man at a time. Bound hand and foot, unable to resist the rude treatment, the soldiers groaned in pain as they hit the solid earth and rolled over.

The driver worked fast and his entire load was soon squirming in agony on the ground. Still singing at the top of his voice, the driver leaped back on to the driver's seat and whipped the horses into action. The waggon rattled off in the direction from which it came.

Robert of Rhuddlan descended the steps again and mounted a horse to lead a troop of men out to the stricken soldiers. When they reached them, they saw that their iron helms were the only things they had been allowed to keep. The twelve men who had been dispatched to Chester had been sent back stark naked. Their bodies were covered with bruises and lacerations.

Robert was bewildered. Why had their lives been spared when the men could so easily have been killed by their captors? What game were the Welsh playing this time?

Gervase Bret was both impressed and unsettled by Gruffydd ap Cynan. The man had a presence and authority which was enhanced in the confined space and, after ridding himself of bitter recriminations, he showed great composure. At the same time, there was a deviousness about him which made Gervase watch him very closely. More than once, when he felt that he was deliberately being misled, Gervase asked for clarification of the words that had been spoken by the Prince of Gwynedd.

Archdeacon Idwal was in his element. Honoured with what he saw as a key role in the negotiations between two nations, he behaved with scrupulous fairness. Though his heart was clearly on one side of the border, he strove to be as detached and objective as possible.

'This war must be stopped,' he insisted. 'Otherwise, my lord, countless lives will be needlessly lost.'

'What can I do?' asked Gruffydd.

'That is what we have come to discuss.'

'I have no power to alter the course of events.'

'You can hardly condone it, my lord.'

'Why not?'

'Because it puts your own life in question.'

'I would gladly sacrifice it for my country.'

197

'Bold words,' said Idwal approvingly, 'but you would not be helping the people of Gwynedd by surrendering your own life. You are their prince. They look to you for leadership.'

'It is difficult to lead anyone from a castle dungeon.'

'Messages can be sent. Signed by you.'

'They would be suspect, Archdeacon Idwal. My people would think that they had been extracted from me by force.'

'Not if I delivered them myself.'

'Well, no,' he agreed thoughtfully, warming to Idwal. 'That might indeed make a difference.'

'Besides,' said Idwal with a smile of admiration, 'you are renowned for your bravery. Nobody could compel you to write something against your will.'

'That is true.'

'Your followers realise that, my lord. They would recognise your true voice. A letter from you would have the power of an edict.'

'Not necessarily.'

'What do you mean?'

Gruffydd did not answer and Gervase once again had a feeling that he was dissembling slightly. He kept the prince under even closer scrutiny when Idwal took up his argument again. A new thought dawned on Gervase. The hesitation and evasiveness of Gruffydd ap Cynan might not arise from a natural craftiness at all. The man was in a quiet panic. Events were moving too far and too fast. Things over which he patently had no control were being done in his name and throwing his own life into jeopardy.

It was time for Gervase himself to join the conversation.

'Do you have any rivals, my lord?' he asked.

'Rivals?'

'People who would take advantage of your imprisonment to advance their own claims to the throne.'

Gruffydd was insulted. 'My position is unchallenged.'

'Are you certain?'

'Nobody would dare to supplant me!'

'How can you know that when you are locked down here?'

'I am the Prince of Gwynedd.'

'In that case,' said Gervase, 'you must approve of all the action that has been taken for your people have, in a sense, only been carrying out your orders. Is that not so?'

'I will not discuss my policy with a Norman.'

'I come from Breton and Saxon stock, my lord.'

'You are not Welsh,' said the other dismissively.

'No,' said Gervase, 'but if I were, I would swear my fealty to my prince and look to him for leadership. Earl Hugh holds you hostage in order to subdue Gwynedd yet it is now massing for battle. Why? Your people are either obeying some plan devised by you or acting on their own accord. If you are not leading them, my lord, who is?'

Gruffydd was momentarily perplexed. Idwal stepped in.

'You can hardly expect him to divulge secret matters of state, Gervase,' he scolded. 'We are here to sue for peace, not to interrogate the Prince of Gwynedd for information which the most arduous torture would not extract. In common with other Welsh princes, Gryffydd ap Cynan rules by right and title. His court is constantly on the move around his domain. Unlike your king, he is a visible monarch.'

'Not while I am buried down here!' protested Gruffydd.

'I am glad that you mention other Welsh princes,' said Gervase as a new idea occurred to him. 'Could it be the case that one of them is trying to seize power in Gwynedd?'

'No!' shouted Gruffydd.

'Cadwgan ap Bleddyn of Powys, for example?'

'He would never dare!'

'How could you stop him, my lord?'

'This is irrelevant,' said Idwal sternly. 'May I remind you that you are supposed to observe, Gervase, and not to examine? I am trying to work towards a peaceful outcome of the present hostilities but I cannot do so if you keep interrupting us.'

'I am sorry, Archdeacon Idwal,' said Gervase deferentially, before turning to Gruffydd. 'And I apologise for any offence I may inadvertently have caused. Ignore my wild guesses. They have no place in this discussion.'

199

'No place at all,' stressed Idwal.

'Cadwgan would never supplant me!' said Gruffydd, deeply hurt by the notion. 'While I live, I rule in Gwynedd.'

Idwal smiled. 'Then let us do all we can to protect that life, my lord. Peace will not only safeguard your own position, it will put Earl Hugh in a more generous frame of mind. You will be rewarded with privileges.'

'My freedom is the only privilege I seek.'

'That, too, will come in time.'

'It will,' vowed the other.

A look passed between them but Gervase was unable to translate it. For the first time since they had been in the dungeon, he began to suspect that Idwal might not be as impartial a negotiator as he pretended. Gervase was stung. He hated the thought that his affection for Idwal had blinded him to the man's deeper purpose. Scrutinising the little archdeacon now, he found himself wondering if Idwal really was an honest mediator with a commitment to peace or an artful manipulator who was holding one conversation with Gruffydd while simultaneously passing messages to him by other means.

Idwal tried to move the prisoner towards a decision. 'Will you help us, my lord?' he cooed.

'Us?'

'The doves of peace.'

Gruffydd smiled for the first time. 'You are an unlikely dove, archdeacon.'

'I speak for the Church and it abhors warfare.'

'Yet it condones holy crusades.'

'That is not what we have here, my lord.'

'I believe that it is,' argued Gruffydd. 'A crusade for freedom from Norman overlordship. Surely you should be giving your blessing to that instead of acting as the lackey of the Earl of Chester?'

'I am nobody's lackey!' asserted Idwal indignantly.

'Then what are you doing here?'

'Searching for peace.'

'What use is peace without freedom?'

'What use is freedom without peace?' countered Idwal. 'A nation constantly at war is doomed to misery and hardship.'

'Until they throw off the yoke.'

'We all pray for that deliverance, my lord, but most of us would prefer to live quiet and useful lives in the meantime. And we cannot do that if we turn Wales into a battlefield once more.' He lowered his voice. 'Freedom can be achieved by other methods than force of arms.'

Another glance passed between them and Gervase was again puzzled by its meaning. There was a long silence. The two men seemed to be at once weighing each other up and haggling over the terms of some private contract.

'I ask again,' said Idwal at length. 'Will you help us?'

Gruffydd erupted. 'I will not help Hugh the Gross! That fat pig deserves to be put on a spit and roasted throughout eternity. He has been the scourge of my people. I will never help Earl Hugh.'

'Help your own people through him,' urged Idwal. 'Stop bloodshed, save lives, ensure a future. I am not here at Earl Hugh's bidding, as Gervase will testify. He refused to let me near you at first. I come in spite of him, my lord.'

'That is true,' corroborated Gervase.

'The earl is a soldier. He relishes battle.'

'He is an animal!' said Gruffydd contemptuously.

'Do you want to let him loose on your people once again?'

Gruffydd held back his reply and turned away to ponder. His expression was blank but Gervase sensed that his mind was in turmoil. The Prince of Gwynedd was being asked to make a crucial decision, based on incomplete information, about a situation that was not of his own making. He was lost in meditation for some time and Gervase wondered if his hesitation was prompted by the distant fear that, even if he did urge his followers to sue for peace, they might not obey him. Policy in Gwynedd was now being hatched by someone else.

Idwal's patience gave way to muted irritation. 'Well?' he pressed. 'Time is fast running out.'

Gruffydd turned to face him. 'How do I know that you are telling me the truth?'

The archdeacon was appalled. 'Would I lie to you?'

'Probably.'

'I come in good faith, my lord.'

'On whose authority?'

'The forces of reason.'

'Earl Hugh is a force of reason?' sneered the other.

'We persuaded him to let me come here, my lord. I am grateful to him for that concession. Your choice is simple. You can either send word to your people and intercede before warfare breaks out again. Or,' he added, raising his voice for emphasis, 'you can stay down here like a rat in a trap while your people are being butchered. Yes, there will be losses on this side of the border as well, I know that. It will be a Pyrrhic victory. But your army will lose. Your men are fine warriors but they are greatly outnumbered and they lack their prince to lead them in battle. Do you want them to suffer another ignominious defeat?'

Gruffydd looked from one man to the other. 'What guarantees will I have?' he asked.

'None,' said Gervase honestly.

'Then what do I stand to gain?'

'Look at it the other way, my lord,' suggested Idwal.

'Other way?'

'If you do not help us, what do you stand to *lose*?'

There was another long, considered pause.

'Very well,' decided Gruffydd, fighting off doubts.

'You will send a message?' said Idwal hopefully.

'Bring me pen and paper.'

Chapter Sixteen

Canon Hubert despised inactivity. It was wholly alien to his temperament. Behind the surface bluster was a diligent man with a probing mind and the tenacity of a terrier. After long hours spent poring over documents, he consulted with Brother Simon then took him to the castle in search of Ralph Delchard. Simon was mortified at the thought of visiting the abode of the egregious Hugh the Gross and he went through the main gates with the reluctant step of someone expecting to find a Bacchanalian orgy taking place in the courtyard. He was not reassured to see that the castle was instead alive with armed soldiers preparing for battle.

'This is a fearful sight, Canon Hubert,' he moaned.

'War is always hideous, Brother Simon.'

'Let us withdraw to the sanctuary of the cathedral.'

'Not until we have spoken with the lord Ralph.'

'Why do we have to come here?' said Simon, almost jumping out of his skin as four horsemen rode by within inches of him. 'Could we not send word for the lord Ralph to wait upon us?'

'Our findings brook no delay.'

'They are largely suppositions.'

'Grounded in fact.'

'But what relevance do they have?'

'That is what we must find out,' said Hubert, dodging a pile of horse dung as he led the way towards the keep. 'We may be in possession of valuable intelligence. The lord Ralph must hear what it is.'

Simon trudged after him. 'Will there be a battle?' he said,

nervously eyeing the show of military might. 'Are the Welsh going to invade the city?'

'I hope not.'

'I am afeared, Canon Hubert.'

'Call your faith to your aid.'

'I travelled to Cheshire to act as the scribe to royal commissioners, not to be hacked to death in a Welsh rebellion.'

'That will not happen,' Hubert assured him. 'Whoever else is the target for Welsh hostility, Brother Simon, it will not be you. They have other objectives.'

When they reached the keep, they did not have to go in search of Ralph Delchard. He was coming out of the hall with William Malbank and two other barons. There was an air of quiet satisfaction about them. Seeing his visitors, Ralph broke away from his companions.

'What has brought you to the castle?' he wondered.

'We need to speak with you, my lord,' said Hubert. 'On a matter of some significance.'

'Then let us seek some privacy. Follow me.'

Ralph led them up to his apartment and locked the door once they were inside the chamber. Simon recoiled from the sight of a bed in which carnal passion had certainly taken place and he averted his gaze at once.

Before Hubert could speak, Ralph told him the news.

'I have just come from a meeting with Earl Hugh,' he said. 'Wisdom has prevailed. Archdeacon Idwal has persuaded the Prince of Gwynedd to intercede on the side of peace. Writing materials have been sent for so that he can send word to his people.'

'These are wondrous tidings!' exclaimed Simon.

Hubert was unconvinced. 'They might be if they were not intertwined with the name of Idwal. How can we be sure that he is not in league with Gruffydd ap Cynan?'

'We can be certain that he is,' said Ralph, 'in the sense that they are both Welshmen and thus bonded together at a deep level. But there has been no skulduggery by Idwal. He has done what he promised to do. Gervase was there as a witness.'

'I thank God for this act of deliverance!' said Simon.

'I reserve my judgement,' said Hubert.

'We must all do that,' agreed Ralph. 'Gruffydd has consented to send word to his people but we have no guarantee that it will reach them in time to stop hostilities. Once a war is set in motion, it will swiftly get beyond the control of any one man. But you know this well enough,' he said. 'And you did not come here to talk about the technicalities of battle.'

'No, my lord,' said Hubert, taking his cue. 'Our interest is in what we believe may be one of its causes. The murder of Raoul Lambert.'

'Lambert?'

'We have studied his career more closely, my lord.'

'Then I hope that you have divined more than I have managed,' said Ralph with a rueful smile. 'Gervase and I attended his funeral today in order to learn something of the man but we came away more confused than ever.'

'He covered his tracks very well,' said Simon.

'Indeed,' said Hubert, delivering a sentence he had rehearsed on his way to the castle. 'Raoul Lambert was a huntsman who is himself supremely difficult to hunt.'

'Yet you picked up his trail, Canon Hubert.'

'Only with great perseverance, Brother Simon.'

'What did you discover?' asked Ralph.

'A great deal, my lord,' said Hubert, dipping a hand into his scrip to take out the scroll on which he had recorded his findings. 'I have no wish to speak ill of the dead but I am compelled to say that Raoul Lambert was not, in my opinion, the upright man of common report.'

'Then what was he?' said Ralph.

'A grasping landlord. A liar, a thief, a bully, a dissembler, a petty tyrant and – if my guess is correct – a man who is guilty of even greater crimes.'

'Bishop Robert made no mention of these aspects of his character in his funeral oration.'

'He may be unaware of them, my lord.'

'Or constrained by the presence of Lambert's friends.'

'That, too.'

'Tell me about the grasping landlord.'

Hubert referred to his scroll. 'That alone would take me all day if I furnished the complete details. Suffice it to say that Raoul Lambert is involved in far more of the property disputes which we came to settle than appeared at first glance. He not only increased his own holdings by illegal seizure, he seems to have helped others to do likewise.'

'Why did the first commissioners not arraign him?'

'Because he was too elusive and plausible.'

'And vouched for by Earl Hugh himself,' said Simon.

'That is the critical factor,' continued Hubert. 'The indulgence shown by the earl towards his huntsman. It is quite striking. Earl Hugh could not have rewarded him more lavishly if Raoul Lambert had been his own son.'

Ralph grinned. 'From what I hear, Lambert is about the only man in Cheshire who is not one of Hugh's bastards. The earl has scattered his affections far and wide.'

Simon quailed. 'It is an abomination!'

'It is human nature,' said Ralph.

'If I may resume,' said Hubert, commanding their attention by holding up his scroll. 'When I examined the full list of Lambert's holdings, I noticed that they had certain features in common. They came into his possession at regular intervals, usually no more than a year apart.'

'What did you deduce from that?' asked Ralph.

'That they were less like random gifts than a sort of annual wage. I acquired the strong impression that Lambert was being paid for services rendered.'

'Have you identified what those services were?'

'I will come to that in a moment, my lord,' said Hubert, determined to proceed at his own pace. 'Let me comment further upon the holdings first. All those on this side of the border were formerly in the hands of three particular barons. One was an absentee landlord and his property appears to have been seized without his knowledge. When our predecessors came to Cheshire to compile their survey, he was not here to attest his claim to the estate and it remained by default in the hands of Raoul Lambert.'

'What of the other two men from whom land was taken?'

'Both died, my lord.'

'Before or after their property was seized?'

'Before.'

'That was convenient.'

'It is the manner of their deaths which alerted my suspicions,' said Hubert, tapping his scroll. 'Coincidence can only stretch so far.'

'What do you mean?'

'Both men were killed in hunting accidents.'

'Ah!'

'On each occasion, Raoul Lambert was in the party.'

'Are you sure?'

'I took the trouble to speak with the town reeve again.'

'Canon Hubert has been admirably thorough,' said Simon. 'He has gone to great pains, my lord.'

Hubert struck a pose. 'One cannot marshal an argument without facts and they have been extremely difficult to confirm in this particular case. Several of the people I questioned were evasive or untruthful. Fortunately, the town reeve is a man of some integrity.'

'What did he tell you about those accidents?' said Ralph, anxious to hear more.

'One man broke his neck when thrown from his horse.'

'And the other?'

'Struck down by a wayward arrow.'

'Who first found the dead bodies?'

'Raoul Lambert.'

'Was he alone at the time?'

'So it seems.'

Ralph let out a low murmur. 'How accidental were these so-called accidents?' he wondered.

'We have no means of knowing, my lord,' admitted Hubert, 'but one is bound to entertain suspicions. Do not forget what happened in Lambert's berewics on the other side of the Welsh border. The two men who held the land before him protested violently when it was taken from them. One was drowned in the River Gowy and the other vanished from sight.'

'What is your conclusion?'

'The obvious one.'

'Lambert killed them deliberately?'

'At the very least,' ventured Hubert, 'he was somehow involved in their deaths. And that is supported by some of the other facts I was able to unearth by patient research.'

'Let me hear them.'

Canon Hubert unfolded his scroll and read its contents with a reverence which he normally reserved for Holy Writ. Ralph was enthralled by the picture of Raoul Lambert which began to emerge, completely at variance, as it was, with the description of the deceased that was given at the funeral. Hubert had been particularly assiduous in tracking down the heirs of the landholders whose deaths had removed large obstacles from the path of the huntsman.

When the recital of facts and figures came to an end, Hubert poked the scroll back into his scrip and awaited congratulation. Ralph was more than willing to offer it.

'Well done, Hubert!' he said effusively. 'I applaud your persistence and your assiduity. You have not only uncovered the truth about Raoul Lambert, you have provided a motive for his assassin.'

'A motive, my lord?'

'Revenge.'

'He has many enemies.'

'I am surprised that he still has any friends,' commented Ralph. 'He is such a dangerous character with whom to consort. Three men died when Lambert appropriated their land. Two Norman barons and a Welshman. Each had a son who would have expected to inherit his father's holdings. I know how I would feel in their position.'

'Lambert was killed by a Welsh arrow.'

'Then we can hazard a guess who employed the archer.'

'My choice would be the son of Owen ap Hywel,' elected

Hubert. 'According to the town reeve, he was as vociferous as his father in threatening Lambert. Yes, it has to be him.'

'What of the man who simply disappeared?'

'Mansel of Denbigh? He was without male issue, my lord.'

'He must have some sort of family.'

'Yes,' piped Brother Simon. 'He has a daughter.'

Ralph Delchard felt a thud in the pit of his stomach. 'A daughter, you say?'

Eiluned drew back the bowstring until it caressed her cheek then took careful aim. When the arrow was released, it flew through the air until it embedded itself in the trunk of a tree a hundred yards away. A young man in peasant garb stepped out from behind the trunk and waved to her in approval. After pulling six arrows out of the tree, he took them back to her.

Grinning in appreciation, he spoke in Welsh. 'You never miss the target, Eiluned.'

'Only because I practise regularly,' she said. 'My father insisted on that. There was nothing he loathed so much as a wasted arrow. A miss was a stigma on the archer.'

'He taught you well.'

'I have put his teaching to good use, Dafydd.'

'You are our secret weapon.'

They strolled back to the deserted cottage to gather up Eiluned's few belongings. She glanced around the ruins.

'I am not sorry to leave this place.'

'It has been poor habitation for you.'

'It was somewhere to lay my head. That is all.'

'When this is over,' he said, kissing her softly on the cheek, 'you may lay it on a pillow beside my head. We deserve each other, Eiluned.'

'Our work is not yet done.'

'It soon will be.'

He put an arm round her shoulders to guide her away but she broke from him gently and walked off into the trees. Dafydd followed her. Sturdy but lithe, he had long black hair and a shaggy beard through which white teeth gleamed like eggs in a bird's nest. He knew where she was going and he shared her sadness.

Eiluned paused beside a mound of fresh earth and offered up a silent prayer. Dafydd came to stand beside her. He had helped to bury the old woman who had been such a good friend to Eiluned. Lacking a priest, they had conducted their own service. As she stared down at the grave, her eyes were moist.

'She saved my life,' she murmured.

'And gave her own to warn you.'

'Yes,' said Eiluned. 'She so wanted to be buried under Welsh soil but it was not to be. She will have to lie in an unmarked grave here in the Forest of Delamere.' A wry smile brushed her lips. 'There was one consolation.'

'What was that?'

'She lived long enough to see Raoul Lambert die.'

'That must have given her great satisfaction,' he observed. 'If her cottage was on his land, she must have been one of his many victims.'

'She was, Dafydd. It drew us together.'

He put a comforting arm round her and she nestled into his shoulder. They stood in silence over the grave until they heard a sound behind them. Both reacted with speed, spinning round and moving apart. Dafydd pulled a long dagger from its sheath and Eiluned had an arrow from its quiver in a flash, but neither weapon was needed. The bird who had caused the noise now flapped its wings and took to the air. It was a white dove.

'A symbol of peace,' noted Dafydd with light sarcasm.

'There has been little enough of that in this forest,' she said. 'It is a place of death and darkness. No wonder Raoul Lambert was at home here.' She put the arrow away. 'Are the others ready, Dafydd?'

'They will be arriving shortly.'

'Then we must not keep them waiting.'

'The horses are tethered nearby.'

'Lead the way.'

After a last sorrowful glance at the old woman's grave, Eiluned followed him into the trees until they reached the spot where the horses were concealed behind thick foliage. They were soon riding due west on their way out of the Delamere Forest. The white dove trailed them for a few miles then lost them in heavy woodland.

Ralph Delchard could never bring himself to like Canon Hubert any more than the latter could ever choose him as a soulmate, but their long conversation about Raoul Lambert had moved them closer together than they had ever been before. There was a new respect for his colleague on Ralph's part and a growing realisation by Hubert of how much his personal safety depended on the soldier who led the commissioners. Critical of his shortcomings in the past, the canon was now more willing to acknowledge his virtues. If conflict lay ahead, it was men like Ralph Delchard who would protect him. The cathedral church was an inspiring place of sanctuary but it would prove a poor fortress against a concerted attack.

Hubert's mind was suddenly concentrated on his survival. 'Should we move to the castle, my lord?' he asked.

'Yes,' said Ralph. 'In the interests of security.'

'No!' wailed Brother Simon.

'This is the safest place in Chester.'

'It may protect our bodies, my lord, but think of the spiritual damage it may inflict. This is a haven of sin and fornication. My soul shrinks at the very notion of being immured in such a den of vice.'

'It might be an education for you,' teased Ralph.

'Heaven forfend!'

'We will move to the castle,' decreed Hubert, riding over the protests of his companion. 'Our presence here might help to cleanse the atmosphere. I know that you have severe qualms, Brother Simon, but I hold that a castle which has a chaplain of such quality in its midst cannot be the fount of wickedness that we might fear. We will lend our strength to that of Brother Gerold.'

'Must we desert Bishop Robert and Archdeacon Frodo?'

'They will be scurrying in here themselves before too long,' prophesied Ralph with a chuckle. 'If there is to be a Welsh uprising, that is, and it is very much in the balance.'

Simon wrung his hands. 'But you told us that the Prince of Gwynedd is to intercede on the side of peace.'

'Indeed, I did. And I pray that he may succeed in exerting some control over his people. But there is no guarantee of that,' said Ralph. 'The Welsh are a capricious race.'

'None more so than Idwal!' groaned Hubert.

'Give him his due, Hubert. He has worked hard to stave off war and may yet turn out to be our saviour.'

'That would be too great a burden to bear!'

'Would you rather be embroiled in a war?'

'No, my lord.'

'Then give thanks where thanks are due,' said Ralph tolerantly. 'Idwal worships the same God as we do, albeit in a different language. If he would only take off that dead sheep that he wears, I might even grow to like him.'

'But he reviles the English Church.'

'Why, so do I on occasion, Hubert. The English Church seems to come through unscathed from both our aspersions.' He became brisk. 'But you must excuse me. I have much to do and you must seek some accommodation in the castle.'

'No!' cried Simon.

'Yes!' declared Hubert.

'Argue about it elsewhere,' suggested Ralph.

Turning on his heel, he unlocked the door and held it open for them to leave. A telltale sound alerted him. Somebody was descending the stairs at speed. Ralph was enraged to discover that the eavesdropper had been outside his door again.

'God's tits!' he howled.

While Canon Hubert grimaced in disapproval and Brother Simon put his hands protectively over his ears, Ralph went charging down the stairs in pursuit, swearing aloud as he did so and pulling out his sword to brandish it in the air. But his mad descent bore no fruit. When he reached the bottom of the steps, there was nobody in sight.

His anger surged until his temples were pounding. 'Where *are* you?' he bellowed.

A door opened behind him and Brother Gerold stepped out. 'What is the trouble, my lord?' he said innocently.

Idwal, Archdeacon of St David's, flung his cloak back over his shoulders and pulled himself up to his full height. A sense of pride coursed through him. He had persuaded Gruffydd ap Cynan to advocate peace and now stood over him while he committed his promise to paper. Gruffydd was allowed out into the dingy passageway to sit at the small wooden table used by the guards. Fresh candles were lit to illumine what might turn out to be a vital document. Idwal grinned with delight as he watched the stylus scratching its way over the parchment. The fact that the missive was in Welsh added a lustre to it.

Gervase waited in the background until the prisoner had finished writing. When he had first read through it himself, Idwal passed the document to Gervase so that he could study its contents. The message was short, simple and quite unequivocal. The Prince of Gwynedd exhorted his followers to cease forthwith any preparations for war that they had been making. There were only two words that Gervase did not recognise but he was satisfied when Idwal translated them for him and added his own thanks to the prisoner.

Gruffydd ap Cynan rose to his feet and turned resignedly towards his cell. Gervase put a hand on his shoulder. 'You are to be allowed some exercise, my lord.'

'Am I?' said the other, his spirits lifting.

'I told you that Earl Hugh would be grateful,' Idwal reminded him. 'Enjoy the fresh air again, my lord. We will show your letter to the earl, then I will carry it in person across the border.'

Farewells were exchanged, then Gervase led the way out of the dungeons and up to the hall. The Earl of Chester was waiting for them and they were admitted at once. Hugh was seated at the head of the table with a few of his barons in attendance. Idwal scuttled across to him with an air of self-importance and placed

213

the document on the table with great ceremony, as if delivering the Ten Commandments.

'Here it is, my lord,' he said solemnly.

'What does it say?'

'Let me translate it for you.'

'No,' said Hugh sharply. 'I do not trust you. Gervase must translate it for me. Slowly. Word for word.'

'Yes, my lord,' agreed Gervase.

'But I helped to draft it,' boasted Idwal.

'Then you have already exceeded your orders.'

'Gruffydd ap Cynan needed much persuasion, my lord.'

'Your work is done. Stand aside.' His nose wrinkled in disgust. 'What is that dreadful stink?'

Gervase stepped in to ease Idwal gently away and to lessen the impact of his malodorous cloak on Hugh the Gross. Standing beside the earl, he took him methodically through the document, using a finger to indicate each word as he translated it. Idwal was peeved that Hugh was not more impressed with the phrasing of the missive.

'That last sentence was my suggestion, my lord.'

'I do not need to know that,' said Hugh.

'Will you authorise me to deliver it?'

'You?'

'It will give the letter credence.'

'I have messengers enough at my disposal.'

'But they will suspect a forgery, if I am not there to assure them of the document's authenticity. I gave my word to Gruffydd ap Cynan that I would bear it in person.'

'You had no right to do so.'

'Nevertheless, my lord,' said Gervase, cutting in to ease the growing friction, 'I do believe that Archdeacon Idwal should be allowed to deliver this message. Only he can convince Gruffydd's people that they must heed the orders of their prince. Dispatch him at once, my lord. I will go with him, if you wish, with as many of your men as you choose to send with us. But I beg of you to take speedy action here. Time is of the essence.'

Earl Hugh picked up the document and looked at it with misgivings. Prepared for a battle, he felt cheated by the prospect of peace, especially as it might be instigated by a prisoner in his dungeons and not by any negotiation on his own part. He wrestled with his ambivalence for some minutes. Idwal could contain himself no longer.

'Delay could cost lives, my lord,' he claimed.

'Be silent!'

'That message must be sent at once.'

'I make the decisions here,' growled Hugh, 'and I do not need your interference. A close friend of mine was laid in his grave today, a fine man cut down by some cowardly Welsh archer. Should I not avenge the death of Raoul Lambert instead of trying to make peace with his killers?'

'No, my lord.'

'One person shot that arrow,' said Gervase reasonably, 'and not the entire population of Gwynedd.'

Hugh turned on him. 'Who slew my messenger?' he demanded. 'Who gathered a raiding party outside Rhuddlan Castle? Who is threatening to attack this city? We are up against far more than one man here, Gervase.'

'Deliver that message from Gruffydd ap Cynan,' said Idwal, 'and you may be up against nobody at all. You fought hard to impose peace on North Wales, my lord. Will you throw it away so recklessly?'

'I told you to be quiet!' snarled Hugh.

'But I have been your mediator.'

'*Enough!*'

The force of his yell quelled even the ebullient Idwal. Hugh rose from the table and stalked off down the hall with the letter still in his hand. Gervase tried to catch the archdeacon's eye and signal him into discretion. Having gone to such trouble to obtain the co-operation of Gruffydd ap Cynan, it would be galling to see it spurned now. Idwal bristled with disgust but held his tongue.

Earl Hugh struggled with his conscience. Though his instinct was for military action, he was keenly aware of the possible

215

consequences and knew that he was bound to suffer losses. Even without their prince to lead them, the Welsh army would be formidable. The city of Chester would not thank him if some of its menfolk fell in an unnecessary conflict.

On the other hand, Raoul Lambert's murder inflamed him yet and he still believed that the assassin's arrow was really intended for his own heart. Such audacity, he felt, should not go unpunished. He glanced through the window and saw Gruffydd ap Cynan being escorted round the perimeter of the bailey by four guards and the vision swayed him. Why had he taken the man hostage if not to preserve peace? What power the prisoner still had over his people should be used to enforce a truce. Precipitate action would serve nobody.

Turning to face the others, he held out the letter. 'So be it,' he said. 'See it delivered.'

'Praise be to God!' exclaimed Idwal.

The archdeacon moved forward but Gervase held him back with a hand on his arm, indicating that he himself would receive the document from the earl. Before he could do so, however, there was a banging on the door and it swung open to reveal a breathless soldier in full armour. Covered with dust and perspiration, the man had clearly been riding hard.

Hugh immediately beckoned him over and withdrew to a corner to hear his tidings. His rage soon ignited again. When he swung round once more, his face was purple with fury. Instead of handing the letter to Gervase, he tore it into a dozen pieces and threw them in the air.

'My lord!' cried Idwal in despair. 'You have just destroyed our one hope of peace.'

'The Welsh army has already done that,' retorted Hugh. 'They have blocked the road to Rhuddlan and are gathering for attack. We will be ready for them.' He glanced out of the window again. 'Suspend all privileges for Gruffydd ap Cynan. Throw him back into the dungeon where he belongs!'

Chapter Seventeen

The news hit Golde with the force of a blow. Flinging herself into his arms, she clung tightly to her husband and looked up beseechingly into his face.

'Do not get involved, Ralph,' she implored.

'I may have to, my love.'

'This is not your battle.'

'Every able-bodied soldier will be needed.'

'But that phase of your life is over now,' she cried. 'You have said so many times. You came here as a commissioner on royal business, not as a soldier.'

'Nothing is more important than protecting the border, Golde,' he said. 'That, too, is royal business. You know it as well as anyone. You lived in Hereford all those years and saw the damage that the Welsh can do when they launch an attack. How can I stand aside when we are threatened by a marauding army?'

'You are too old to fight.'

'Thank you!'

'It is true, Ralph.'

'I still have strength enough to lift a sword,' he said with a grin, 'and energy enough for other exertions, as you can bear witness. Do not consign me to the mortuary just yet. I have a few more years in me before I expire from old age.'

'Will nothing stop you?'

'No, my love.'

'Not even my entreaty?'

'If I am called by Earl Hugh, I must go.'

'Why?'

'It is a question of duty.'

'You owe none to the Earl of Chester.'

'He is our host. I have a natural obligation.'

'To lay down your life because he has become embroiled in a war against the Welsh?' She clung even tighter. 'I'll not let you go, Ralph. I'll keep you back by force.'

'And shame me in front of the others? No, Golde.'

'I don't want to lose you.'

'Nor will you,' he said, holding her by the shoulders and gazing into her anxious face. 'I was born and bred to fight, my love. I have come through a dozen battles with no more than a scratch. Why should this one be any different?'

'Your luck is bound to run out one day.'

'Luck!' He gave a mirthless laugh. 'There is no luck in surviving a battle, Golde. It takes strength, skill and guts. I know that you fear for your husband but there is no need to insult him as well.'

'I am sorry.'

'Pride is at stake here, my love.'

'I know.'

'And my oath of loyalty to King William. What would he think of me if I skulked here in the castle while Earl Hugh was leading his army in the field? He would never forgive me. More to the point, I would never forgive myself.'

Golde sighed and pulled away. 'She was right.'

'Who was?'

'The Lady Ermintrude.'

'What did she say?'

'That you could not resist a call to arms.'

'It depends on who does the calling.'

'I do, Ralph,' she said with passion. 'I call you to stay with your wife. You have nothing to prove to me. I saw your bravery in York, in Canterbury and in Oxford. I know that you are a fine soldier. But the time has come to retire.'

'I do not recognise the word.'

'The Lady Ermintrude warned me of that as well.'

'Then you should have listened to her.'

'I thought that I knew you better, Ralph.'

'Well, I am sorry to disappoint you, Golde,' he said with a shrug. 'Try to stop seeing this as a betrayal of you. If I do get involved in the fighting – and it is by no means certain at this stage – but if I do, I will be helping to protect you and everyone else in this city. What would happen if every husband laid down his arms and stayed at home with a frightened wife? It is not possible, my love. It is not just.' He spread his arms. 'It is not manly.'

She nodded in agreement and heaved a sigh of regret.

They were in their chamber at the castle. Golde had been talking with Ermintrude when she heard the agitation down in the courtyard and saw the soldiers being hastily assembled to receive their orders. Rushing back to her own apartment, she found Ralph torn between sadness and excitement, distressed by the apparent collapse of the peace initiative set up by Archdeacon Idwal yet almost exhilarated by the opportunity to take his part in the coming conflict.

For her benefit, he tried to play down the dangers he might face and to hide the inner thrill that he was experiencing.

'It may be over in a matter of days, my love.'

'An hour of fighting would be too long.'

'I may not see any action at all.'

'I will pray that you do not, Ralph.'

'Marry a soldier and there is always a faint risk.'

'So I have learned,' she said, pursing her lips and breathing heavily through her nose. 'But what brought about this change? I thought they were trying to find a peaceful solution to the conflict.'

'They were, my love.'

'What happened?'

'Idwal and Gervase went down to the dungeons to bargain with Gruffydd ap Cynan,' he explained. 'They actually got him to send word to his people to refrain from any further action. Gervase tells me that he and Idwal were on the point of leaving to deliver the message.'

219

'What prevented them?'

'News of other developments.'

'What are they?'

'Does it matter?' he said, not wishing to be drawn into a full discussion. 'The simple fact is that the Welsh do not seem to want peace. Hence, the call to arms. That is all I know at this stage. Earl Hugh is a skilled commander who has beaten Welsh armies time and again. He will do so again.'

'And sustain losses.'

'Probably.'

Golde tried to master her anxiety. She forced a smile. 'What must you think of me?' she said. 'Behaving like a young bride whose husband is about to go off to war. I should have more confidence in you. And more control over myself.'

'It is good to show your concern.'

'The Lady Ermintrude prefers to mask it.'

'That is why I am married to you and not to her.'

'I feel that I have let you down.'

'Far from it, Golde,' he said, taking her in his arms again. 'You are bound to worry. So am I, if I am honest. But we must bow to the inevitable. When duty calls, I must go.'

'Yes, Ralph,' she whispered.

'I've fought the Welsh before and lived to tell the tale.'

'I'll remember that.'

'Good.'

He placed a kiss on her forehead then pushed her gently aside while he darted across to the door, flinging it open and stepping through it. There was nobody there. Golde was alarmed. She came out to join him.

'What is the matter?' she said.

'I thought he would be here again.'

'Who?'

'The eavesdropper.'

'Are you sure that he exists?'

'I'm certain of it, my love,' he affirmed. 'He was out here listening to us the other night. And he was back again today.'

'When?'

'When I was in here with Hubert and Simon.'
'Why should anyone want to eavesdrop on you?'
Ralph took her back into the chamber and closed the door.
'That is what I'll ask him when I catch the villain.'

Security which was already tight was now markedly increased. Movement to and from Chester was even further restricted. City gates were barred and guards doubled on the walls. Those who had brought their goods to sell in the market found that they were unable to return to their homes. Boats which sailed up the River Dee were turned back before they reached the port. A city which had been preparing for the possibility of conflict now knew that it was unavoidable. The clatter of destriers' hooves rang through the streets. Anvils sang in the armourers' workshops. Tactics were discussed.

The last vessel to be allowed into port before the new restrictions were imposed was a small boat which was loaded with pelts. Two guards watched the crew unload their cargo.

'Where are you from?' demanded one of the guards.
'Ireland,' said the captain of the vessel.
'Have you traded here before?'
'No, but we heard that we would get a good price.'
'How many in your crew?'
'What you see. Three men. Four of us in all.'
'How long did you plan to stay?'
'A day or so,' said the other. 'No more.'
'Think again.'
'Why?'
'Orders,' said the guard with a grim chuckle. 'Nobody is to sail in or out of Chester until further notice. You may be here for a week. A month even.'
'But we must get back to Ireland.'
'Not until we are ready to let you go.'
'And when will that be?'
'You will be told.'
'We have families!' protested the captain.
'They will have to wait.'

221

'You can't keep us here against our will.'

'Nobody leaves.'

'But we are expected back.'

'Nobody.'

Having made his point, the guard sauntered off with his colleague to question the captain of a vessel which was unloading its catch of fish. The Irishman continued to voice his complaints and his crew did the same. All four of them were standing on deck, bemoaning their fate, when a fifth man crept out from the tarpaulin under which he had been hiding and slipped quietly ashore. Having seen him safely off the vessel, captain and crew stopped their protestations at once and resumed their work.

The fifth man, meanwhile, lost himself in a maze of streets, zigzagging through the city with a confidence born of close acquaintance with it. When he came to a house on the eastern side, he made sure that he was not being followed then rapped on the door. It opened immediately and he darted inside.

Eiluned and Dafydd embraced the newcomer in turn.

'We knew that you would come,' she said.

'Nothing would have stopped me.'

'What if they had turned your boat away?' asked Dafydd.

'I would have swum here,' said the newcomer. 'When I make a promise, I honour it. Whatever the obstacles.'

Gervase Bret was seething with frustration. Having been involved in the negotiations with Gruffydd ap Cynan, he was proud to feel that he might, in some small way, have helped to bring peace to the region and it was dispiriting to watch his hopes so cruelly swept aside. The consequences were quite unimaginable. Open warfare might keep him and the other commissioners trapped in the county for some time and his immediate thought was of Alys, pining for him in Winchester and fretting when he did not return.

Gervase also worried about Ralph Delchard. Unable to fulfil his commitments at the shire hall, his friend would not sit idly on his hands while a battle was going on nearby. Ralph would be certain to join in and Golde would be equally certain to suffer the agonies common to all soldiers' wives. Gervase would share those agonies with her. Ralph was very dear to him and he could wish him elsewhere than in the middle of a quarrel in which he had no legitimate part.

Frustrated by the turn of events, he was not blind to the suffering of others. Archdeacon Idwal, he realised, would be even more devastated, having laboured so hard to bring his countryman round to the notion of peace. Time spent with him in the dungeon had increased Gervase's admiration for Idwal but it was tinged with suspicion. Notwithstanding the letter which the archdeacon had wrested from the Prince of Gwynedd, his behaviour in the dungeon had left Gervase with the vague feeling that he had been subtly duped.

The only way to allay that feeling was to confront Idwal himself and Gervase resolved to do just that. While the rest of the city was in a state of turbulence, he used his status as a royal commissioner to gain the right to leave the city by a postern gate and he strode off towards the cathedral. The first person he met there was Frodo, coming out of the main door. The archdeacon was very surprised to see him.

'What are you doing here?' he said.

'Searching for Archdeacon Idwal.'

'You would be far safer in the city,' advised the other. 'Bishop Robert has withdrawn to his palace and taken most of the holy brothers with him.'

'What about you?'

'My place is here, Gervase. At the cathedral.'

'It will offer you scant protection from attack.'

'I will worry about that when the time comes,' said Frodo with a brave smile. 'But I have a bounden duty to be here and you do not. Even Canon Hubert and Brother Simon have fled. You should do likewise.'

'Only when I have seen the archdeacon.'

'He is not in a talkative vein.'

'He is here, then?'

'Oh, yes!' sighed Frodo. 'Idwal is here. Throbbing with

223

remorse. He does not have to speak for us to be aware of his presence. His silence is just as deafening as his voice.'

'He feels betrayed.'

'So do we all.'

Frodo shook his head disconsolately and padded off.

Gervase soon found Idwal. The archdeacon was kneeling at the altar rail and staring up at the crucifix. Instead of being in an attitude of submission, he was still frothing at what he felt was a great betrayal and he mixed prayer with accusation. Gervase waited at the rear of the nave until his friend finally rose to leave.

The Welshman's eye kindled when it fell on Gervase. 'Fresh news?' he said hopefully, hurrying down the aisle.

'Alas, no.'

'No change of heart by Earl Hugh?'

'He is adamant.'

'War would lead to catastrophe.'

'There is nothing to stop it, Archdeacon Idwal.'

The Welshman's face crumpled into despondency. 'They are idiots, Gervase!' he declared. 'They had peace in the palms of their hands and they threw it away. Fools!' He remembered where they were. 'Come outside,' he urged. 'My words are unfit to be heard in the house of God.'

Gervase followed him out through the main door. 'I came to commiserate with you,' he explained.

'That was a kind thought.'

'You tried so hard to bring peace about.'

'I did no more than my Christian duty,' said Idwal, 'but I did it to remarkable effect. Just think, Gervase. Two armies ready to close with each other and we stood between them.'

'Unsuccessfully.'

'It need not have been so.'

'No,' agreed Gervase. 'If you had been allowed to visit the prisoner a day earlier, the situation might have been quite different. As it was, we were too late.'

'Thanks to some impulsive Welshman,' said Idwal sadly. 'That is what hurts me most. Peace was wrecked on the other

224

side of the border by people who stood to gain from it. I am an impulsive man myself but there are times when one must check those impulses. They have ruined everything.'

'And sent their leader back to the dungeon.'

'Gruffydd will be lucky if that is where he stays. Earl Hugh will not scruple to kill a hostage if he is pushed. He needs little enough excuse.'

'Why are they doing it, Archdeacon Idwal?'

'Who?'

'The people who are making decisions over the border. Surely they know that they will imperil their prince's life?'

'Yes, Gervase.'

'Is that their intention?'

'I begin to fear that it is.'

There was a long pause. Gervase felt unable to break the silence and Idwal used it to study his companion, cocking his head to one side and peering intently at him.

'You have another reason, Gervase,' he said at length.

'For what?'

'Seeking me out. I see it in your face.'

'I merely wished to share my feelings of disappointment.'

'And suspicion.'

'No,' lied Gervase.

'Your eyes betray you, my young friend. You question my honesty. I sensed it when we were in that dungeon together. You felt that I was scheming with Gruffydd.'

'It did cross my mind,' admitted the other.

'And so it should have. Trust nobody. Not even me.'

'Why not?'

'Because I am first and foremost a Welshman,' said Idwal. 'That means that I view the world through different eyes. In any border dispute, I will always side with my countrymen. I only interceded here in the hope of saving them from a defeat which will surely come.'

'What are you telling me?'

'That you were wise to suspect me but that your suspicion was unfounded. I was not trying to pass some secret message

225

to Gruffydd. You saw the difficulty I had bringing him round to reason. That was not dissembling.'

'I know.'

'How?'

'Instinct.'

'It is very sound.'

Idwal punched him on the arm and let out his celebrated cackle. Just as the archdeacon seemed to be recovering his buoyancy, Gervase hit him with a blunt question.

'What exactly are you doing here?' he asked.

'Doing here?'

'In Chester.'

'I have told you. Forging links.'

'That requires the hand of friendship,' said Gervase, 'yet you seem to go out of your way to antagonise people. Bishop Robert does not feel any links have been forged, nor does Archdeacon Frodo.'

'Give me time. I will wear them down.'

'You are here for another purpose and it has nothing to do with diplomacy. Why did Bishop Wilfrid send you here?'

'On a mission of good will.'

'I find that hard to believe.'

'Why else should I be here?'

Gervase studied him levelly. Idwal's smile slowly wilted under his gaze and he saw that he had met his match. Gervase was unrelenting. Fond as he was of the Welshman, he was not going to let him squirm out of answering his question.

'Tell me,' he invited. 'What is the *real* reason?'

'What do you think it is, Gervase?'

'You are after something.'

'Am I?'

'Something which you feel may be locked away here,' said Gervase, indicating the cathedral, 'or in the vestry of the chapel, perhaps. Something which has made you probe Archdeacon Frodo, Brother Gerold and even me. What is it?'

'Nothing of consequence.'

'You came all the way from St David's for nothing of

226

consequence? No man would subject himself to such a journey unless there was something important at the end of it.'

Idwal beamed. 'There was. The pleasure of meeting you and Ralph again,' he said. 'Not to mention Canon Hubert and that walking skeleton of a scribe.' The gaze was turned upon him again with even greater intensity this time. 'You are a shrewd young man, Gervase Bret.'

'And immune to flattery,' cautioned the other.

'Then I will insult your intelligence no longer.'

'Thank you, archdeacon.'

'First, however, I must swear you to secrecy.'

'Why?'

'You will understand in time,' Idwal assured him. 'Do I have your word that you will divulge nothing of what I am about to confide in you? Give me your promise or the bargain is void.'

'Very well,' decided Gervase. 'You have it.'

'Then I can let you know the truth, my friend.'

'What brought you to Chester?'

Idwal stepped in close to speak with conspiratorial glee. 'St Teilo!'

Rhuddlan Castle began to feel more isolated than ever. The road to the east was blocked and those that led in other directions were also cut off. Human obstacles were used in the latter cases. As Robert of Rhuddlan looked out over the battlements, he could see bands of warriors encamped at strategic points on every route. Effectively, the castle was surrounded, with no means of summoning help from Chester.

The captain of the guard was at his side again.

'What are they doing?' asked Robert.

'Biding their time, my lord,' said the other.

'For what?'

'Attack.'

'They have no ladders, no siege engines.'

'But they have archers in abundance. We can see their bows. They can rain down arrows on us whenever they choose.'

'And when will that be?'

'Who knows, my lord?'

Robert was mystified. Twelve of his best men had been captured then inexplicably released. The castle looked out on a show of force that stayed just out of range of any weaponry. Guards patrolled the battlements day and night but their nerves were becoming frayed by the interminable wait for action that was being denied them. Robert felt disadvantaged. He wondered how long it would be before his uncle came from Chester to relieve the situation.

That situation was transformed in an instant. The bands of armed men on all sides mounted their horses and, at a signal from some unseen commander, began to ride towards the castle. Robert of Rhuddlan raised the alarm himself and the captain supplemented his yell with a stream of orders. The whole garrison swarmed up the stairs to the battlements to repel the first assault, weapons at the ready, baskets of stones in waiting to be tipped on to anyone who reached the walls. Days of delay at last seemed to be over.

But the attack never came. As soon as they had kicked their horses into a gallop, the various bands veered away from the castle and took up different vantage points from which they could watch and intimidate. The cavalry charge had been feigned. There was no intention to engage in fighting. They had merely wished to scare their enemy.

Robert of Rhuddlan was more confused than ever. He rounded on the captain of the guard in sheer annoyance. 'What are they up to *now*?' he hissed.

Idwal was incredulous. 'You have never heard of St Teilo?'

'Only vaguely,' confessed Gervase.

'You should be ashamed of your ignorance.'

'Educate me.'

'I will,' said Idwal. 'St Teilo was a monk and bishop whose work was centred on Llandeilo Fawr. He lived at the same time as St Dyfrig and was indeed a pupil of his for a while. He also studied under Paul Aurelian.'

'A learned man, then?'

'You will not find a Welsh saint who is not.'

'What connection does he have with Chester?' asked Gervase.

'Did he visit here, preach here, die here?'

'No,' said the other. 'When plague struck his native country, St Teilo went to Brittany to work for seven years, staying with no less a man than Samson of Dol.'

'Now, there is a name I do recognise.'

'Then you will know its worth, Gervase.'

'I do.'

'When he left Brittany, St Teilo made his way back to Llandeilo and eventually died there. It was then that the miracle occurred.'

'Miracle?'

'The bones of a saint are treasured relics. Llandeilo naturally wanted to keep his body but Llandaff and Penally also laid claim to it. The dispute, I understand, was fierce.'

'How was it resolved, Archdeacon Idwal?'

'Miraculously,' said the other, palms uplifted to heaven. 'The single body multiplied into three so that each of the claimants could have their own St Teilo. I have seen his remains at Llandaff, Penally and Llandeilo.'

'That does not explain what brought you here.'

Idwal looked around to make sure that they were alone. 'I came for his Gospel, Gervase.'

'His what?'

'The Gospel of St Teilo. It is a priceless document, containing the earliest known sentences in the Welsh language. When he died, it was left in the keeping of Llandeilo church.'

'How, then, did it reach Chester?'

'It was stolen, Gervase.'

'By whom?'

'Saxon monks who wanted relics for their own foundations. Welsh churches were regularly pillaged. The Gospel was taken, along with hundreds of other valuable relics.' He tapped his chest. 'Bishop Wilfrid set me to find it to return it to its rightful place. I have traced it as far as Chester.'

'From where?'

'Lichfield.'

Gervase was surprised. 'Bishop Robert has it?'

'I believe so,' said Idwal, 'though I have yet to lay eyes on it. But I know that it is here somewhere. When the bishops had their seat in Lichfield at the cathedral church of St Chad, they had the gall to refer to St Teilo's Gospel as that of St Chad. Sacrilege!'

'What do you intend to do?'

'Restore it to Wales once again.'

'You hope to *steal* it?' said Gervase in horror.

'It is not an act of theft.'

'Then what is it?'

'Legitimate restitution.' Idwal beamed. 'Just think, my friend. St Teilo's Gospel can return home at last. I am so glad to share the wonderful news with you. It makes such a difference to me.'

'In what way?'

'I am no longer working alone. I have an accomplice.'

'Who is that?'

'You, Gervase.'

Chapter Eighteen

The three men heaved hard and Hugh d'Avranches was levered up into the saddle of his destrier. He was in full armour with his sword belt strapped on and a lance in one hand. He rode the length of the bailey to inspect the ranks of knights who were drawn up in readiness. Some had little stomach for yet another battle against the Welsh but none dared refused his summons. The Earl of Chester did not nurse grudges. He took punitive action instead.

William Malbank waited with his own bevy of knights, sad that the efforts to find a peace had broken down but resigned to the fact that the day of the hawks had come. As he watched the massive figure of the earl ride past him, he writhed at the thought of his mistress being crushed beneath such a huge, urgent body. A foolish wager had consigned the woman to untold pain and humiliation.

Hugh's horse trotted back to the head of his men and he gave the signal for the gates to be opened. Before he could leave, however, he was accosted by an indignant Ralph Delchard.

'Let me ride with you, my lord!' he protested.

'Not today.'

'My place is beside you.'

'No, Ralph,' said the earl. 'It is here with your wife and your colleagues. You did not come to Chester to fight our neighbours. It would be unfair to draw you into our quarrel. Stay here in the safety of the castle until we return with rebellion quashed.'

'I want my share of the action.'

'We have men enough to serve our purpose.'

'How many of them have my experience?'

'Very few, I grant you. Yet we are still a strong enough force to quell this revolt. In their latest reports, our intelligencers say that the enemy is gathering on the border but in numbers greatly inferior to our own.' He gave a macabre chuckle. 'It may be a short engagement but I promise that it will be a bloody one.'

'Let me see for myself.'

'There is no need.'

'My pride urges me to go.'

'Your offer is welcomed but refused.'

'Why, my lord?'

'Because I say so,' came the peremptory reply.

Earl Hugh wasted no more words in argument. With a wave of his hand, he set off through the gates with the long column trailing behind him. There was a sense of power about his army that was quite breathtaking. As it thundered out into the street, everyone who saw it predicted its success. The Welsh were valorous but they had none of the discipline and tactical expertise of Norman soldiery.

Feeling rejected, Ralph turned away in disgust. Then he caught sight of Golde, standing in the window of their chamber in the keep and gazing down with such gratitude that his heart softened. There would be other chances to fight. Ralph tried to put his disappointment aside and headed for the keep.

Golde was waiting for him in the apartment.

'You decided not to go,' she said with delight.

'Hugh would not have me.'

'My prayers have been answered.'

'And mine were denied,' he sighed.

They waited inside the house until the army went past. It was a long wait as hundreds of hooves pummelled their way along the narrow street. When the three of them finally emerged, the last of the horses was just going through the city gate. The young man stood between Eiluned and Dafydd. Taller than both, he had the same swarthy skin and cast of feature. The others took their lead from him.

'How long must we wait, Sion?' asked Dafydd.

'A couple of hours at least.'

'That long?'

'Yes,' confirmed the other. 'We stick to the plan.'

'I am ready now,' said Dafydd. 'What about you, Eiluned?'

'There is no hurry,' said Sion. 'Eiluned will walk the streets to make sure that all is well. A woman will attract less attention than two men.'

'What do we do?'

'Wait patiently, Dafydd.'

'If you say so.'

'I do,' insisted Sion. 'I have not come all this way to bungle the attempt. Months of planning have gone into it. I came out of exile in Ireland to take my part. We must not fail. That would be a disaster.'

'You will not find me wanting,' said Dafydd.

'Nor me,' added Eiluned.

'I know. You have both done well so far. We are very grateful.' Sion grinned. 'Now it is my turn. I was born in Chester. I lived here for years until they sent me into exile. The city owes me a favour. I am here to collect it.'

Gervase Bret argued long and hard with Archdeacon Idwal about the morality of stealing the Gospel of St Teilo. Whatever action the Welshman took, Gervase wanted no part of it, though he promised that he would not break any confidences. Leaving Idwal at the cathedral, he made his way back to the city and was about to enter the postern gate when Canon Hubert came bustling through it. Gervase could see that he was agitated.

'What is the matter?' asked Gervase.

'Brother Simon has let us down for once.'

'That is unlike him.'

'I know,' said Hubert, 'and I have chastised him roundly.'

'What is his fault?'

'Carelessness. When he heard about the imminent battle, he flew into such a panic that he could not get back into the city soon enough, even though it meant being in the castle with Earl Hugh. In his haste, he left a satchel of documents behind.'

'That is indeed a bad mistake. Those documents are highly important and must not fall into the wrong hands.'

'I made that point very clearly to Brother Simon.'

'Let me fetch the satchel,' volunteered Gervase.

'No,' insisted the other. 'It is our responsibility. I will get it myself, Gervase. You may be better employed soothing the lord Ralph.'

'Why?'

'Earl Hugh refused to let him ride out with the army.'

'How has he taken it?'

'He is mortified.'

Gervase understood why. He waved Hubert off then went in through the postern gate and walked towards the castle. The streets were largely deserted. Fear kept most people indoors. Even the yapping dogs seemed to have fled. Gervase was rather surprised, therefore, when he saw a young woman strolling idly past the castle and throwing it a casual glance. She seemed oddly out of place. He watched her until she turned a corner and vanished, wondering why she was wearing a voluminous cloak on such a warm day.

After the third feigned attack by the raiding parties, Robert of Rhuddlan began to lose his patience. He ordered a troop of his own men to saddle up so that they could issue forth and intercept one of the bands when next they rode past the castle. If he could inflict losses on the enemy, they might be forced into a direct fight. He was still giving orders outside the stables when the captain of the guard summoned him to the rampart. Robert went quickly up the steps.

'What is happening?' he said.

'I do not know, my lord.'

'Are they playing more tricks on us?'

'Not this time, I think,' said the captain. 'It seems as if they are joining into one large force.'

'They mean to attack at last,' decided Robert.

234

'Do not be so sure, my lord.'
'Why?'
'Look!'

When the bands of warriors came together, they faced the castle in a long line and waved their weapons aloft. After jeering derisively, they swung their horses around and rode off to the west. Robert felt cheated of his confrontation with them. Once again, they had comprehensively deceived him.

'They never intended to fight us,' he said.
'Why, then, did they come here, my lord?'
'To keep us penned in here.'
'For what purpose?'
'I wish I knew.'

Danger was over but mystery remained. Robert of Rhuddlan would have much to report to his uncle when Earl Hugh finally reached him. What troubled him most was the feeling that he had been the victim of a cruel hoax.

His opportunity came at last and he seized it eagerly. When Idwal of St David's saw that the cathedral was completely empty, he hurried off to his tiny chamber to collect the object which he had left there. Back within a matter of minutes, he let himself quickly into the vestry and lowered the latch softly behind him.

The oak chest stood in a corner, stout enough to deter most people but posing an irresistible challenge to Idwal. Putting down the object on the floor, he took a long-bladed knife from beneath his cloak and probed the lock with its point. It was slow work, calling for skill and patience. Idwal evinced both in the gloom of the vestry and was suitably rewarded in time by the sound of the lock clicking open.

'At last!' he said to himself.

Lifting the lid, he gazed into the chest and saw exactly what he had hoped to find. The Gospel of St Teilo, an illuminated manuscript which bore a picture of the saint himself, seated on his episcopal throne. Idwal's heart lifted and he reached out to pick up the unique relic but a noise from the cathedral checked him. He crept to the door and inched it open until he could peer into the nave.

Canon Hubert was coming down the aisle towards him with a satchel over his shoulder. Idwal's first reaction was one of desperation but his agile brain soon framed itself to the emergency. Closing the door, he went back to the oak chest. Hubert, meanwhile, having genuflected in front of the altar, made his way to the vestry. He tapped lightly on the door then opened it to enter the chamber.

A startled Idwal stepped back guiltily from the box. 'Hubert!' he exclaimed.

'What are you doing here?'

'I was just . . . looking round.'

'Who opened that chest?' asked Hubert, suspicion flooding.

'I found it like this.'

'Archdeacon Frodo would never have left it in that state. It contains the cathedral's relics, including a copy of the Gospel of St Chad.'

'St Teilo.'

'St Chad of Lichfield.'

'St Teilo,' corrected Idwal, taking the Gospel out from beneath his cloak. 'A Welsh saint from Llandeilo Fawr.'

'What are you doing with it?'

'Restoring it to its rightful place in Wales. It was taken from there centuries ago by a Saxon monk, hunting for relics. I am taking it home.'

Hubert blenched. 'You are *stealing* it?'

'Merely repossessing it, Hubert.'

'It amounts to the same thing.'

'Not to me,' said Idwal pedantically. 'Theft is a crime and I would never sink to that. Reclaiming stolen goods is a matter of honour. That is all that I am doing.'

'I will report you to Archdeacon Frodo.'

'Why? He will not miss the Gospel.'

'He is bound to,' said Hubert. 'The moment that he opens the chest, he will see that it has gone.'

'But it has not,' explained Idwal, reaching into the chest to take out a copy of the Gospel identical to the one he already held. 'You see? Though I take one relic, I replace it with another. The one I have brought is a clever forgery. If I exchange it for the genuine Gospel, nobody will know the difference.'

'I will,' boomed Hubert. 'And I will not condone such a heinous offence. Put the relic back before you damage it.'

'But it belongs in Llandeilo,' pleaded Idwal.

'It is the property of this cathedral and I'll not stand by and watch it being stolen. Put it back!'

He stood over Idwal until the archdeacon consented to replace the Gospel which he had just lifted out of the chest. Hubert closed the lid firmly and the lock clicked into place.

'Thank heaven I came,' said Hubert, preening himself. 'I was searching for Archdeacon Frodo but I found you here instead, trying to steal the most precious relic that the cathedral possesses. This is a heinous crime.'

'I was acting with the best of intentions.'

'You should be reported to your bishop for this outrage.'

'He will have a full account of what happened here.'

'I trust that he will take the appropriate action. Really, Archdeacon Idwal,' clucked Hubert sanctimoniously, 'I am surprised at you. I have accused you of many things but I never thought that you would stoop to bare-faced theft.'

Idwal was penitent. 'I am sorry.'

'You should be thoroughly ashamed.'

'I am, Hubert. I persuaded myself that what I was doing was justified. Especially as I was taking one Gospel and replacing it with another that was almost identical.' He held up the copy in his hand. 'Will you forgive me, Canon Hubert?'

'Only God can do that.'

'Will you tell Bishop Robert about this?'

'I must. It is my duty.'

'Yes,' said Idwal sadly. 'I see that. You are right. It is as well that I am leaving Chester today. My face no longer fits and I have caused enough trouble.'

'That is certainly true.'

Idwal gazed longingly at the chest then ran a covetous hand

237

along its surface. Hubert clicked his tongue and the archdeacon backed away at once.

'I leave you in peace,' he said.

'I will not pretend to grieve at this parting.'

'Nor would I expect you to, Hubert. Give my regards to Brother Simon and . . . do not think too harshly of me.'

Idwal went swiftly through the door and closed it behind him. Canon Hubert basked in his own righteousness for a few minutes then went to the chest to stroke it. He had the satisfaction of knowing that he had just prevented a dreadful crime from being committed and dispatched the troublesome Welshman out of the city at the same time. They were achievements of which he felt inordinately proud.

An hour later, Archdeacon Idwal was riding happily out of the city with the genuine Gospel of St Teilo packed away in his satchel. Having switched them before Hubert came into the vestry, he was able to take exactly what he had come for and to leave the replica in the oak chest. Nobody at the cathedral would ever know that their Gospel was a fake and that Hubert's proud claims were really the boasts of a gullible man who had been thoroughly tricked.

Idwal's cackle of delight sent his horse into a gallop.

Ralph Delchard had overcome his disappointment at being left behind at the castle. He was beginning to think that his presence there was fortuitous. Gervase Bret agreed.

'I believe that it is part of an elaborate plot.'

'What is, Gervase?'

'The way that Earl Hugh has been lured out of Chester.'

'But the Welsh are massing on the border.'

'Are they?'

'So it is reported.'

'That is how they wish it to seem,' argued Gervase, 'in order to cause a distraction. Study the pattern of events. A favourite hawk is killed. What better way to enrage Earl Hugh? His close friend is murdered to keep that rage bubbling. His messenger is killed on the way to Rhuddlan to give the impression that an army is on the march.'

'It may well be, Gervase.'

'I wonder.'

'Why has the road to Rhuddlan been blocked?'

'To convince Earl Hugh that a rebellion is stirring on the other side of the border. Am I making sense, Ralph?'

'Too much sense,' said the other. 'You are thinking like a soldier for once. It is what I should have been doing instead of feeling sorry for myself at being left behind. Creating a diversion is one of the arts of war. The Welsh appear to have created a number of them.'

'To what end, though?'

Their eyes locked and they realised the answer to the question simultaneously. Ralph leaped up from his chair and reached for his sword. Gervase opened the door of the chamber and led the way down from the keep.

'What will we do, Ralph?'

'Dispatch messengers after Hugh. Urge him to turn back. They have only been gone a couple of hours. Fast horses will soon start to gain on them.'

'Suppose he refuses?'

'He is not stupid. He will see the wisdom of our advice.'

'And meanwhile?'

'Meanwhile,' said Ralph, delighted at the prospect of action, 'we must hope that we get there in time.'

The first arrow pierced the guard's throat and sent him gurgling to the ground. Dafydd hurried forward to drag the body out of sight. The second arrow picked off another man with uncanny accuracy. Once again, it was left to Dafydd to haul the corpse away. Eiluned stepped back into the doorway as she fitted another arrow to her bow. Two of the obstacles had been removed without any difficulty. She awaited further orders from Sion.

From his position in the upper room of a house, he had a good view of the castle. When a third guard emerged from the postern gate, Sion gave the signal and Eiluned's arrow claimed yet another victim. Dafydd was on hand to pull the man behind a stone trough. He looked up at the house and saw the wave from Sion. It was time to move in.

All three of them were soon crouched outside the postern gate. Sion used the hilt of his dagger to pound the studded oak. A bolt was drawn, a key put in a lock and the heavy door swung back far enough for them to slip through. Once inside, they paused to take stock of their surroundings.

The plan had worked. Earl Hugh and his army had departed, leaving only a minimal garrison at the castle. What guards remained were patrolling the walls and looking outwards. They did not see the figures emerging from the shadows by the postern gate. Sion went first with Dafydd close behind him, both carrying daggers in their hands. Eiluned was several yards behind them, ready to provide cover, keeping low as she ran and scanning the bailey with sharp eyes. The three of them reached the entrance to the dungeons unchallenged.

Leaving their archer on sentry duty, Sion and Dafydd opened the door and slowly descended the steps. Only one guard was in the passageway and he was knocked senseless with a blow from Sion's mailed fist. Hooked on the man's belt was a large iron key ring. While Dafydd grabbed the keys, Sion ran to the cell where he knew their prince was kept. Peering through the grille, he saw Gruffydd ap Cynan fast asleep in the straw.

'My lord!' he called. 'Wake up, my lord!'

'Surely, they have not killed him?' said Dafydd, trying the different keys in the lock. 'My lord! We've come for you!'

The figure turned lazily in the straw and they were reassured. Dafydd eventually found the right key and the door was opened. They dashed in to kneel beside the Prince of Gwynedd. Sion shook him by the arm.

'Wake up, my lord!' he urged.

Ralph Delchard obeyed at once, opening his eyes and launching himself upwards with such force that he knocked Sion off his feet. A punch to the stomach took all the wind out of Dafydd's lungs and bent him double. Ralph chopped down hard on the back of his neck and sent him reeling.

Sion had now recovered enough to realise that they had been outwitted. Hurling himself at Ralph, he got a grip on his throat and started to apply pressure but he reckoned without his victim's strength. With a loud grunt, Ralph lifted him bodily and hauled him against the wall, cracking open his head and spraying blood everywhere.

He looked down in disappointment at the two groaning figures in the straw. 'I was hoping for more fight out of you than that,' he mocked. 'Why give up so easily?'

Before they could recover, the two men were overpowered by the guards who rushed in from the adjoining cell where they had been hiding. Sion and Dafydd were pinioned within seconds. Their attempt at liberating the Prince of Gwynedd was over.

Crouching beside the entrance to the dungeons, Eiluned wondered what was causing the delay. A voice behind her made her swing round, an arrow already fitted into her bowstring.

Gervase Bret was watching her with keen interest.

'I was hoping that we would meet,' he said in Welsh.

'Who are you?'

'An admirer of your skill. I have never heard of anyone shooting arrows with such precision. The one that killed Raoul Lambert was even better than that which brought Earl Hugh's hawk down out of the air.'

'I have an arrow for you as well,' she warned, pulling back the bowstring. 'Stand back.'

'You cannot kill us all,' he said easily.

She stole a glance around her and saw that she was now ringed by archers. There was no escape. Bow still ready, she fell back on cold defiance.

'I am proud of what I did,' she boasted. 'Raoul Lambert deserved to die. It was my duty to cut him down.'

'Why?'

'He abducted my father. We never saw him alive again.'

'Are you sure that Raoul Lambert was responsible?'

'Quite sure,' she said. 'There were others. Many others. That is what he did. Killed to order. Why else would Earl

Hugh have so much time for him? Raoul Lambert was his executioner.'

Gervase walked slowly towards her then made a sudden grab for her bow but she was too quick. Eluding his hand, she ran up the steps to the battlements and stood with her back to them. Guards closed in from both sides and Gervase went up the steps after her. He tried to reason with her.

'Give yourself up,' he advised. 'You have no chance.'

'I'll never surrender.'

'You won't get out of here alive.'

'I won't need to.'

She discharged her last arrow high into the air and Gervase looked up to follow its flight. When he turned back to Eiluned, she had disappeared from sight, having flung herself violently from the battlements to avoid arrest. Gervase looked down to see the broken body on the ground below, oozing blood and twisted into an unnatural shape.

Ralph joined him to gaze down at the hideous sight.

'Two captured and one dead,' he said. 'One more left.'

'Who is that?' asked Gervase.

'Their confederate. They must have had somebody inside the castle to tell them exactly where Gruffydd was being kept and how best they could gain entry. It was the same man who sent them word about the hunting parties, and was always listening outside my door to see what he could pick up. I set four guards to watch the postern gate and arrest him as soon as he had let the conspirators in.'

'Who is he, Ralph?'

'See for yourself.'

There was a shriek of protest as Durand was dragged across the bailey and taken down into the dungeons. The dwarf unleashed a torrent of abuse at Ralph but the latter only smiled benignly.

'I had guessed his identity even before he gave us the proof of his treachery just now. It was Golde who put me on to him,' said Ralph airily. 'She told me that I should never trust a man who allows bad beer to be served.'

Epilogue

A single week effected the most profound changes in Chester. Restored to the shire hall, the commissioners sat in judgement on a stream of cases and managed to put right some glaring anomalies missed by their predecessors. Land formerly in the possession of Raoul Lambert was either returned to its original holders or their heirs, or distributed between other tenants with claims against him.

Ralph Delchard was at his most effective, Gervase Bret was a penetrating examiner of evasive witnesses, Canon Hubert was pleased that the Church was able to recover so much land which had been seized unjustly from it and Brother Simon was happy to be engaged in the work which had brought him to Chester in the first place. The four of them worked well as a team and they left the city in no doubt that the King's writ ran as far as Cheshire.

After losing Raoul Lambert and being duped so effectively by the Welsh, Earl Hugh was strangely subdued and Brother Gerold's influence over him gradually increased again. The conscience which had smitten him intermittently in the past no longer seemed quite so incompatible with his behaviour. Though the banquets continued unabated and the hunting expeditions resumed, the earl nevertheless seemed to have mellowed slightly. He was even observed talking to his wife on one occasion.

Eiluned was given a Christian burial by Gerold but her accomplices were imprisoned in the dungeons along with Durand and the man they had tried to rescue. At Ralph's suggestion, Gruffydd ap Cynan was treated with the respect

243

due to his position and allowed regular exercise and edible food. The Prince of Gwynedd still languished in captivity but there was a definite improvement in his lot.

At the end of another satisfying day, the commissioners were entitled to congratulate themselves. Canon Hubert led the way.

'We were in supreme form today,' he boasted.

'You always are,' said Brother Simon.

'Thank you.'

'Hubert is right,' said Ralph. 'It was our most productive session so far. The more cases we study, the more clearly does Lambert's villainy emerge. He stole land from everyone.'

'With the help of a certain friend in an exalted position,' reminded Gervase discreetly. 'That is how he got away with it.'

'Property was his payment,' said Ralph.

'Yes, Eiluned was right about him. He was the earl's executioner. Whenever someone had to be removed to satisfy a whim or pay off a grudge, Raoul Lambert was called in. He knew the earl better than anyone.'

'That is why he had to be bribed into silence.'

'Yes, Ralph.'

'And why Hugh was so shocked by his death. He leaned so heavily on Lambert when he was alive. A man like that could not easily be replaced.'

Brother Simon stifled a yawn then shocked them all. 'I miss Archdeacon Idwal,' he admitted.

'Saints preserve us!' exclaimed Hubert.

'That is like saying you miss a disfiguring disease,' said Ralph. 'Idwal was a menace.'

'There was no real harm in him,' said Simon.

'That is where you are wrong,' chimed in Hubert. 'I was on hand to prevent him from committing a serious crime that would have left the cathedral without its most treasured relic. As it is, the Gospel of St Chad has been rescued and Idwal has gone home to Wales with his tail between his legs.'

Simon was wistful. 'I still miss him.'

'Why?' demanded Hubert.

'He enlivened the city.'

'Wildfire would do that.'

'And cause less damage,' added Ralph.

'I agree with Brother Simon,' said Gervase. 'Idwal brightened up our day. As long as you did not stand downwind of him, he could be a charming companion. And he did persuade Gruffydd ap Cynon to urge peace on his followers.'

'The Welsh are a bizarre race,' opined Hubert. 'None more so than Idwal. What kind of man imagines that he can get away with a crime against a cathedral? I simply would not condone it.'

The four men packed up their satchels and made for the door. Hubert remembered an invitation he had been asked to pass on.

'One moment, my lord.'

'Yes, Hubert?'

'You and your dear wife are cordially invited to dine at the bishop's palace tomorrow, if you are free.'

'We should be delighted to, Hubert,' said Ralph with gratitude. 'When the festivities are over.'

'Festivities?'

'Golde and I have to go down to the river first.'

'Why?'

'To see punishment being meted out.'

'To whom?' asked Simon.

'The brewer who supplied that disgusting beer to the castle. Golde reported him in order to save others from the fate that she suffered. He was ordered to pay a fine of four shillings.'

Gervase baulked. 'As much as that?'

'The brewer took the same view and refused to pay.'

'What will happen to him?'

'He has been sentenced to the cucking stool.'

'Serves him right,' said Hubert.

Simon was more sympathetic. 'You mean that he will be strapped in and ducked under the water?'

'Yes,' said Ralph, 'and I hope that he swallows a mouthful every time he goes under.'

'Why, my lord?'

'Because then he will know what his beer tastes like!'

Brother Simon emitted his first laugh of the year.